SEXUAL HEELING

'I imagine,' Mary said, 'you were wondering how you are to enforce discipline, without canes?'

'Yes, I was.'

'Our enforcers often do. Would you like to see your instruments?'

She nodded. 'Um, please.'

Mary lifted out a smaller version of the case already open on the desk.

'Open it, my dear.'

Doing so, she picked out one of the feathers inside and turned it, her mouth bending down with mock uncertainty.

'And now you're wondering what exactly you *do* with it, aren't you, my dear?'

She nodded, putting the feather back into its slot.

'Come, my dear. Bring the feather case with you. We have some girls in need of . . . *discipline*.'

By the same author:

DISCIPLINED SKIN
BEAST
PALE PLEASURES
SIX OF THE BEST
VAMP
PRIZE OF PAIN

SEXUAL HEELING

Wendy Swanscombe

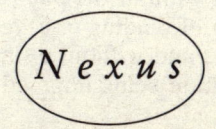

This book is a work of fiction.
In real life, make sure you practise safe, sane and
consensual sex.

First published in 2004 by
Nexus
Thames Wharf Studios
Rainville Road
London W6 9HA

www.nexus-books.co.uk

Typeset by TW Typesetting, Plymouth, Devon

Printed and bound by Clays Ltd, St Ives PLC

ISBN 0 352 33921 7

You'll notice that we have introduced a set of symbols onto our book jackets, so that you can tell at a glance what fetishes each of our brand new novels contains. Here's the key – enjoy!

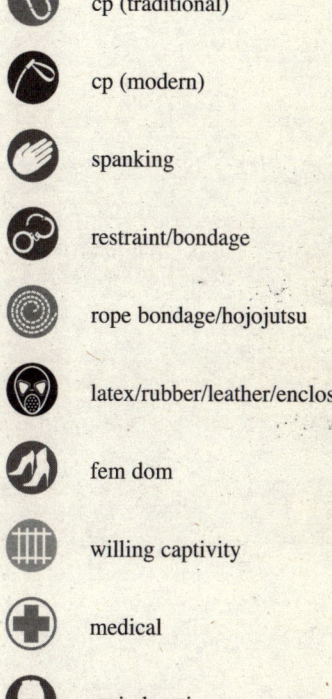

cp (traditional)

cp (modern)

spanking

restraint/bondage

rope bondage/hojojutsu

latex/rubber/leather/enclosure

fem dom

willing captivity

medical

period setting

uniforms

sex rituals

Contents

The tray was freighted with the most exquisite and shapely *pantoufles*, sufficient to make Cluny a place of naught. There were shoes of grey and black and brown suede, of white silk and rose satin, and velvet and sarcenet; there were some of sea-green sewn with cherry blossoms, some of red with willow branches, and some of grey with bright-winged birds. There were heels of silver, of ivory and of gilt; there were buckles of very precious stones set in most strange and esoteric devices; there were ribands tied and twisted into cunning forms; there were buttons so beautiful that the buttonholes might have no pleasure till they closed upon them; there were soles of delicate leathers scented with *maréchale*, and linings of soft stuffs scented with the juice of July flowers. But Venus, finding none of them to her mind, called for a discarded pair of blood-red *maroquine*, diapered with pearls. They looked very distinguished over her white silk stockings. As the tray was being carried away, the capricious Florizel snatched as usual a slipper from it, and fitted the foot over his penis, and made the necessary movements. That was Florizel's little caprice.

> Aubrey Beardsley, *The* Story of Venus and Tannhäuser,
> or, Under the Hill (1907), *Chapter II,*
> *'Of the manner in which Venus was*
> *coiffed and prepared for supper'.*

A martyr, steadfast in faith, who stood fast as a conqueror amidst the racks and burning plates, was ordered by him to be smeared with honey and to be made to lie under a blazing sun with his hands tied behind his back, so that he who had already surmounted the heat of the frying pan might be vanquished by the stings of flies. Another who was in the bloom of youth was taken by his command to some delightful pleasure gardens, and there amid white lilies and blushing roses, close by a gently murmuring stream, while overhead the soft whisper of the wind played among the leaves of the trees, was laid upon a deep luxurious feather bed, bound with fetters of sweet garlands to prevent his escape. When all had withdrawn from him a harlot of great beauty drew near and began with voluptuous embrace to throw her arms round his neck and, wicked even to relate, to handle his person, so that when once the lusts of the flesh were roused, she might accomplish her licentious purpose. What to do, and whither to turn, the soldier of Christ knew not. Unconquered by tortures he was being overcome by pleasure. At last with an inspiration from heaven he bit off the end of his tongue and spat it in her face as she kissed him. Thus the sensations of lust were subdued by the intense pain which followed.

Saint Jerome, The Life of Paulus,
the First Hermit *(374–379).*

Paphiopedilum (*Paphos,* city of Cyprus sacred to Aphrodite, + *pedilum,* slipper) A genus (qv) of orchid (qv) found growing wild only in Asia (qv) and on some islands of the Pacific (qv). The labellum (qv) is shaped like the toe of a woman's shoe or slipper; hence the popular names of 'lady's slipper orchid' and 'Venus slipper orchid'. Almost all the roughly fifty species are terrestrial (qv) in habit, but a few are epiphytic or lithophytic (qqv).

Miranda Faversham,
The Universal Dictionary of Flowers (1976).

Song of Solomon 7:1 How beautiful are thy feet with shoes, O prince's daughter! the joints of thy thighs *are* like jewels, the work of the hands of a cunning workman.

1

Lady's Slipper

'You have brought your canes?'

'Yes,' she said. She lifted the long, flat, rectangular case from beside her chair and laid it on the desk, turning it so that her interviewer could see what was inside, then clicked the steel catches open and swung the lid up. The canes glistened in their slots in the green velvet, each with its name in flowing silver script on its palm-polished handle: the thin, flexible *Vespa*; the sturdier, noded *Crabro*; the rubber-spined *Malleus Natium*; the ridged *Lacrimae Rerum*; and the five thick sections of the *Decimator*.

'Ah,' said her interviewer. 'I had heard so much about them. It's strangely moving to see them . . . in the flesh, as it were. I can scarcely believe that they are so old. They were used by the nuns, I believe?'

'Yes,' she said. 'The Sisters of Perpetual Succour. On novices and servant-girls.'

Her interviewer nodded.

'Vespa, I know, means "wasp",' she said, 'but what about the others?'

She smiled, and began to name the others one by one, tapping each with an affectionate fingertip.

'This is the Hornet . . . this is the Bum-Hammer . . . this is the, um, well, it means "Tears of Things", literally . . . and this is what it says on the label. The *Decimator*.'

'Ten at a stroke?'

'Yes.'

'Might I see it extended?'

'Certainly.'

She began to lift out the sections of the *Decimator* and screw them together, her wrists shaking faintly as the cane extended and its weight grew. When the cane was fully assembled, sprouting over the desk like a giant fishing rod, the interviewer nodded.

'Most impressive,' she said. 'But I am afraid you will have to forgive me, Ms Jackson. I asked to see the canes out of idle curiosity – alas, no more than that. You will have no need of them should you decide to accept my offer and take up a post here at Orchid Paradise.'

'Then . . .?'

The tip of the *Decimator* wobbled with her emotion and the interviewer's severe face lit with a smile.

'Yes, Ms Jackson. I made my decision while I was reading your application, with its excellent references. The interview has merely confirmed it.'

'Then thank you, Ms Phalaenopsis,' she said. 'I accept the offer gladly.'

The interviewer's smile became warmer.

'Please, call me Mary,' she said. 'We managers adopt these foolish names for the public's sake, and we do not encourage members of staff to use them. Will you join me in a celebratory glass of wine?'

'I would be delighted. Mary.'

As the interviewer pushed her chair back and walked to a cabinet along one wall, the interviewee started to disassemble the *Decimator* and put its sections away one by one, wondering what the older woman had meant when she said there would be no need for canes. Then how would she enforce discipline? Ms Phalaenopsis – Mary – turned away from the cabinet carrying two small glasses of clear golden wine. She handed one to the interviewee and sat down in her chair, raising her own glass with a flourish.

'*Bonne santé*,' she said.

They sipped almost simultaneously.

'How do you find it?'

She licked her lips and took another sip, rolling the wine on her tongue, then allowing it to trickle down her throat. She nodded appreciatively. 'Delicious.'

'But perhaps a little sweet?'

'Just a little.'

'Yes. It's one of our experimental early vintages. An orchid wine we intend to start marketing in the new year.'

She had been about to take another sip of the wine; now she lifted the glass away from her lips with surprise, lifting it to the light.

'You are surprised that it is an orchid wine?'

'Yes. And delighted.'

It seemed to be the right answer; Mary nodded and smiled, taking another sip of her own wine.

'I imagine,' she said, 'you were wondering how you are to enforce discipline, without canes?'

'Yes, I was.'

'Our enforcers often do. Would you like to see your instruments?'

Her glass was at her lips again. She nodded. 'Um, please.'

Mary laid her glass on the desk, tugged a drawer open, and lifted out a smaller version of the case already open on the desk. The younger woman swung the case of canes shut and pushed it aside and Mary slid the smaller case across the desk to her.

'Open it, my dear.'

It had steel catches too; she flicked them open and swung the lid up, and frowned with puzzlement. The slots inside were filled with . . . feathers. She looked up across the desk.

'Take one out, my dear.'

She picked one of the feathers up and turned it, her mouth bending down with mock uncertainty.

3

'And now you're wondering what exactly you *do* with it, aren't you, my dear?'

She nodded.

'Drink up and I'll show you.'

She put the feather back into its slot and picked up her glass. Her head was starting to sing a little and she felt herself smile foolishly as she lifted the glass to her lips and drained it. There was a double *cluck* as they laid their drained glasses to the desk simultaneously.

'Come, my dear. No. Bring the feather case with you. We have some girls in need of . . . *discipline*.'

The interviewer smiled foolishly too, and the newly hired enforcer felt her nipples peak momentarily, hardening at the thought of discipline, softening at the thought of what she had to discipline with. Feathers. She closed the case, picked it up, and followed the older woman out of the room and down a cream-walled, cream-carpeted corridor. Glass cases of orchids were set into the walls, framed like paintings, and the interviewer paused in front of one of them, tapping the glass with an unpainted fingernail.

'My favourite, my dear,' she said. '*Paphiopedilum hirsutissimum*. It looks quite genuine, doesn't it?'

She walked on, and the enforcer paused at the case. A glistening orchid spread purple wings to her, thrusting forward between them what looked like the toe of a green-and-chocolate shoe beneath an arrow-head fan. Not real? She had to trot to catch up: the interviewer was nearly at the end of the corridor, tapping a code into a keypad by a closed door. As she reached the interviewer, the door swung inward.

'Come, my dear. Your *disciplinandae* await.'

She followed her through the door into warm, moist air, full of floral scents and the sound of trickling water: a small greenhouse, with orchids in many colours trailing down from large, oddly shaped hanging baskets.

'Here, my dear,' the interviewer said, walking forward and taking hold of a cord dangling from one of the baskets. 'She refused her vitamin shots twice last week.'

She? The enforcer shook her head, trying to focus properly as the interviewer tugged on the cord and the basket began to descend. She walked forward a little unsteadily. What sort of basket was it? It seemed, a little stomach-turningly, to be a marble container shaped like an eighteen- or nineteen-year-old girl lying on her back with her knees drawn up over her stomach and orchids sprouting from every available cleft or orifice on her body: from her gaping mouth, her ears, and her nostrils; between her breasts and on her nipples; from her vagina and anus; from the fold of conjoined calf and thigh and in her belly-button; between the fingers of the two hands held flat in mid-air; and between the toes of her bare, pink-soled feet. The basket reached breast-height and the interviewer stopped tugging on the cord. The enforcer noticed an odd smell of sweat and saw that the smooth marble skin of the basket was sheened with moisture, little drops of it seeming to cluster on tiny hairs in the skin. And then her eyes, attracted by a flicker of movement, jumped to the sculpted marble face and she nearly dropped the case of feathers she was carrying. The eyes had moved, had *blinked*.

'It's . . . she's *real*,' she said.

'But of course, my dear. Orchid Paradise does not grow orchids in any other way. They may appear to be growing conventionally in our public showrooms, but our public showrooms are precisely that: for the public.'

Now she saw that the girl was bound: thin copper bands encircled her thighs and stomach, breasts and neck, wrists and ankles, locking her into place for the orchids to be grown on her body as she hung on thin wires from the ceiling. She looked up left and right and saw that the hanging baskets were all living women, all bound with copper in the same way, all sprouting vividly coloured orchids from their clefts and orifices.

'Don't you like it, my dear?' the interviewer asked.

'No,' she said. 'It's . . . it's disturbing.'

'Is it? You'll soon get used to it, my dear. You don't think we're being in the slightest bit *cruel*, do you? You do? But my dear, if you could see the *queues* we have on girl-recruitment days. Orchid-bed is a much sought-after position, believe me.'

She looked at the eyes of the hanging basket in front of them again, flickering in the pale face.

'What's she doing?' she asked.

'Reading, my dear. Lean forward and have a look for yourself, if you don't believe me.'

She leant forward and looked more closely at a sheet of coloured light that seemed to be hanging in front of the girl's face. There were, yes, there were words hanging in the air, back to front from her point of view, so she managed to read only a sentence and a half before the woman blinked again and the page was replaced by a new one. *I would not accost him yet. He descended the one step, and advanced slowly and gropingly towards the grass-plat. Where was his daring str–*

She leant back, looking at the interviewer.

'*Jane Eyre?*' she said.

'Yes. Holographic projection, controlled by her eyelids and adjusted to the height of the orchid-bed. This is . . . yes. It's young Anastasia. She's an English student. Victorian women's literature, I think. Something like that. Most of them are studying English. It's an ideal opportunity for them, a month of solid reading.'

The girl blinked again and the page was replaced by a new one.

'How fast is she reading?'

'Three hundred words a minute. It's part of the package.'

'Package?'

'Hypnosis. Why do you think she's taking no notice of us? She thinks she's snug in a Swiss hotel-room, reading by an open fire, or lying in a hammock on Mauritius, or something like that. I'd have to check her file.'

'But how do they eat?'

'They don't. They're fed by tube. See her nose?'

She looked more carefully and saw that a thin plastic tube curved up from behind the girl's neck over her cheek and into one of her nostrils. She nodded.

'That's how they eat,' the interviewer said. 'The orchids absorb all their wastes, and some of the girls aren't here just to put some solid reading in. Martha, there, for example.'

She nodded upwards at one of the other hanging baskets, a peach-bottomed girl whose orifices and clefts trailed yellow and purple orchids.

'And Jasmine.'

She nodded upwards at another peach-bottomed girl, this one trailing orange, pink, and white orchids.

'They're delighted to lose some weight on their month's stay, though we use their "Before" photos when we send the orchids out, of course.'

' " 'Before' photos"?'

'Yes. Most of our girls are growing for clients, and some prefer ... *zwaftig* orchid-beds. But Anastasia conforms more to their usual tastes. She's a pretty little thing, isn't she?'

She looked back at the girl hanging in front of them, eyes flickering as she raced her way through *Jane Eyre*.

'Yes. She is.'

'Caneable?'

'I'm sorry?'

'Is she caneable, my dear?'

'Ah.'

She swallowed, imagining the girl bent before her, small firm bottom raised to meet the threat of *Vespa* or *Crabro*, then nodded.

'Yes. Very.'

'Then how about . . . plumable?'

'Plumable?'

'She's been a very naughty girl. Refused her vitamin shots twice as I said. Said she was still sleepy when she was dehypped in the morning. So she has to be punished, doesn't she?'

'Yes,' she said, more confidently, her professional instincts beginning to guide her. But what on earth did "pluming" mean?

'So plume her, my dear.'

She realised what the interviewer meant. Plume. Feather. The case of feathers. She squatted on her heels, lifting the case onto her knees and opening it.

'I recommend . . . a falcon primary,' the interviewer said. 'Very stiff and strong. You can choose something subtler when you've had more practice.'

Which one was the falcon primary? She guessed, and lifted a feather up.

'Excellent, my dear. Now, plume her. Plume her thoroughly. I'll just dehyp her. Bring her out of hypnosis, that is.'

The interviewer stepped closer to the girl's body and bent to say something into her ear. The enforcer closed the case, slipped it off her knees, and stood up, still wondering what to do. Was she being tested? Plume her. Punish her with the feather. But how . . .? Ah, she saw. The girl's feet, the girl's bare feet, the girl's bare tender feet, their soft pink soles raised and supremely vulnerable beneath the ten, orchid-separated little toes, twitching as the girl came out of hypnosis. She raised the feather and brought its tip forward to the girl's left foot, just brushing the sole. The foot jerked, trying to withdraw from the irritation, but the girl couldn't move. The interviewer had moved back round from the girl's head.

'That's it,' she said. 'Plume her. Mercilessly.'

She glanced up at the girl's face, seeing the eyes widened and glaring at her tormentrix, the taut lips writhing round the mouthful of orchid as the girl tried to express her indignation. The enforcer's nipples stirred and she felt her pussy throb and begin to melt with the familiar old pleasure. She lifted the feather back to the sole and stroked the tip down it, sweeping it a little from side to side. The girl's body rocked in its copper bands, and the enforcer's pussy throbbed again, beginning to leak its first sticky tears of pleasure. She swung the feather to the opposite sole and stroked that too, running the feather tip from just below the toes to the heel, and the girl's body rocked again, the toes of the foot clenching and separating.

'Try a whisker now too,' the interviewer said. 'I recommend tiger, to begin with.'

Whisker? What did she mean? But when she opened the case again she saw the whiskers sitting in their narrower grooves underneath the feathers. Which one was tiger? One of the long ones? She slipped one of the whiskers out and the interviewer popped her lips.

'Well, lion's good too. See how it goes.'

She raised the feather and the whisker and set to work simultaneously on both soles, sometimes crossing her hands so that she could work with the whisker on the sole she had just been working on with the feather, and with the feather on the sole she had just been working on with the whisker. The whisker was good for pricking the sole, not just tickling it, and she was discovering how to use more of the feather than just the tip. The girl's body was almost penduluming now, she was struggling so violently against the assault on her feet, and patches of her skin had started to flush and dapple, pink and crimson beneath rolling beads of sweat.

'Excellent,' the interviewer said; 'excellent. I knew you wouldn't let me down.'

She was sweating herself, becoming more and more aroused as she worked at the soles, so small, so delicate compared to the broader, firmer expanses of buttock on which she had plied her trade before. Caning was sculpture, a three-dimensional art requiring strength of wrist and of will; tickling was painting, painting in miniature on two small canvases, a two-dimensional art requiring steadiness of wrist and subtlety of mind. She painted busily, now working on one sole with both whisker and feather, now working on the other, now working on both, and she saw the skin of the girl's inner thighs, glistening with sweat beneath the orchids trailing from her pussy, begin to twitch and corrugate.

'No,' said the interviewer. 'Careful. Don't bring her off. It can damage the roots of the orchids and bruise their vaginas. Soothe her now. Calm her.'

She began to tickle more gently, no longer using the stiff lion's whisker so cruelly on the pink skin of the sole, working on the underside of the toes too, one by one, moving the feather and whisker more and more slowly, less and less strenuously. Droplets of sweat were beginning to click to the floor beneath the hanging girl, but she was calming, her inner thigh-skin smoothing, shaken less and less often by tremors of pleasure.

'And . . . enough,' said the interviewer. The enforcer released a long sigh, her shoulders and wrists aching as though she had just caned her way through half-a-brothel's worth of miscreants, and laid the feather and whisker back into their grooves in the case.

'Ms Jackson, I believe you're a natural. Shall we get to work on Imogen now?'

She stepped back to the hanging basket's head and bent again to whisper in her ear, and the enforcer watched the girl's face smooth and clear, losing its look of frustration as the girl fell back into hypnosis and her eyes searched for the holographic page hanging in front of her face.

'There,' the interviewer said. 'Back to Jane.'

She tugged the dangling cord twice, and the girl's body was suddenly rising on its wires, moving back to the higher air and the uninterrupted hours of high-speed reading.

'Do they not get cramp?' she asked the interviewer as she followed her to another dangling cord. 'And what about muscle-wasting?'

'No,' said the interviewer, taking hold of the cord and tugging on it. Another girl began to descend to them. 'We run a gentle electric current through them twice a day, and that takes care of all that. Gets the muscles working. I don't know the details, but you can ask our company physio if you're really interested.'

The girl had reached breast-height and the interviewer stopped tugging on the cord.

'That's why they're bound with copper, you see,' she said. 'Now, this is Imogen, and she's been refusing her vitamin shots too. Says they make her bottom sore, if you please, and we've been using a pain-free no-sting hypodermic since Orchid Paradise first started using organic orchid-beds.'

'Falcon primary and lion's whisker again?' she asked, watching the interviewer bend to the girl's ear. The interviewer paused, pursing her lips.

'As you please, my dear, but feel free to experiment.'

She bent to the ear and whispered, and Imogen's toes twitched and trembled as she started to come out of hypnosis. The enforcer realised that she had barely looked at her face, and she no longer regretted the spray of orchids falling from her anus and obscuring the curves of her buttocks. The soles of her feet were almost completely bare, and that mattered much more. She squatted again, resting the case on her knees, opening it and choosing another feather and another whisker.

'And after lunch,' said the interviewer, 'I will have another little job for you, with the feathers. It may leave them a little . . . sticky.'

She set to work on the new pair of soles, wondering what the older woman meant. After lunch, she found out.

'Do you like her?'

She appraised the girl sitting quietly in the interviewer's office, apparently unaware that she was being watched over a monitor. Dark hair, pale skin, slender shoulders, small breasts, aged . . . twenty? Maybe 22, 23?

'Yes, I like her.'

'And what would you like to do to her? Cane her? Watch. She should be getting out of her seat any time now. I always . . . adjust the prints before my secretary shows them into the room. So I can see them move.'

She looked at the monitor again. The girl was looking behind her now, at one of the orchid prints on the wall; then, frowning a little, she got out of her seat and walked to the print, lifting her hands to either side of the frame, adjusting it minutely. The interviewer touched a button and the picture on the monitor changed, now showing the girl's bottom bouncing slightly in her dark dress. The enforcer pictured it bare, bare and bent before her, two white mounds of cream for the golden tongue in her hand.

She blinked and looked away from the monitor at the interviewer.

'Yes. I would.'

'More than you would like to plume her?'

The enforcer looked back at the monitor. The girl seemed to have adjusted the print to her satisfaction; now she was walking round the office, stopping in front of the other prints, bending her head first one way, then the other. The enforcer watched her sensible shoes rise and fall as she walked, imagining the pale, slender, pink-soled feet within them.

She looked away from the monitor again.

'No. Less.'

'Then you shall plume her, my dear. She is an unwitting candidate to replace one of our current orchid-beds, whose orchids have not flourished as we expected. We have to test her pH and require a sample of each of her body fluids and secretions. Saliva, sweat, urine, ear-wax, nasal and rectal mucus. And pussy-juice. Do you think you can make her sweat?'

'Yes. Easily.'

'And pussy-milk her?'

She looked back at the monitor, imagining the girl's black-capped vulva, its narrow lips pursed on the warm, faintly musky slot of her vagina.

She looked away from the monitor again.

'Yes,' she said.

'Then let's do it. When I ask her about her health, watch for my signal, then come and fetch your feathers. And this.'

She tapped the neat loop of white rope sitting beside the monitor. The enforcer nodded, then followed the interviewer from the monitor-room, surprised to find that the door opened straight into the office where the girl was waiting. The girl turned from the orchid print she was examining, blushing a little as the two older women came into the room.

'Good afternoon, my dear,' the interviewer said, advancing on her, one strong hand extended. 'It's Caroline, isn't it?'

'Yes.'

Her voice was very quiet. Scottish?

'Then sit down, my dear, and we'll get under way. My name is Ms Phalaenopsis. And this is Ms Jackson. You won't mind her sitting in on things, for the first fifteen minutes?'

'Um, no. I don't mind.'

Yes, Scottish. But it was obvious she did mind. She sat down again, folding her skirt under her carefully, and the enforcer sat down in one of the other chairs, watching her out of the corner of her eye. The interviewer sat down too behind her desk, opened a drawer, and pulled a file out. She laid it on the desk and opened it.

'This is your application form for the post of secretary, Caroline. We'll just run through it, then go on to the interview proper. Now, you say . . .'

The enforcer stopped listening, looking at the orchid prints herself. They were all *Paphiopedilum* species, she realised. Lady's slipper, with a shoe-shaped labellum between wings or sails of yellow or white or red or purple. Like the orchids she had seen sprouting from Anastasia and Imogen and Leah, in the greenhouse. Was that all Orchid Paradise grew? Lady's slippers? A phrase in the interviewer's slow, measured voice struck her and she started paying attention.

'. . . general health, my dear? Good?'

The girl nodded.

'Yes, Ms Phalaenopsis,' she said. 'I would say it is excellent.'

'What about your feet, my dear?'

'My feet, Ms Phalaenopsis?'

'Yes. It's something we pay particular attention to at Orchid Paradise, because of the amount of walking between departments our secretaries have to do.'

'They're fine, Ms Phalaenopsis.'

'No athlete's foot? Bunions? Ingrown toe-nails? Problems with . . . odour?'

'No, Ms Phalaenopsis. Not a thing. I never thought . . .'

'Could I see them, please?'

The girl frowned.

'Ah'm . . . ah'm sorry, Ms Phalaenopsis,' she said, and the enforcer noted with interest that her accent had suddenly strengthened. 'Ah don't understand.'

'Your feet, Caroline. Could I see them?'

14

The enforcer tensed, waiting for her signal. The girl was frowning now, shaking her head faintly.

'You want to see mah feet, Ms Phalaenopsis?'

'That's it. Just to see for myself that they are trouble-free. Not that I don't doubt your word, my dear, no, not in the slightest, but the proof is in the prodding, as they say.'

'They do?'

The interviewer frowned herself, looking stern.

'Come, come, Caroline. Do you want the job or don't you?'

The girl paused and then nodded, blinking.

'Then take your shoes and stockings off and let me see your feet. It won't take a moment.'

The girl swallowed, still looking uncertain, then pushed her chair back and bent to start taking her shoes off. Now the interviewer looked away from her and nodded, and the enforcer got up and went to fetch her feather case and the loop of rope. When she was in the dimly lit monitor room, she stopped to watch the images glowing on the screen. The girl had taken one of her shoes off and was tugging down her stocking, and she waited, watching the thin black sheath being peeled away. Ah, there it was: her foot, her slender, shapely foot, perfect as an orchid. She turned quickly from the monitor, picked up her feather case and the loop of rope, and went back into the office to watch the second shoe being taken off and the second stocking being peeled from the second foot.

When she was back in the office, pushing the door shut behind her, her nostrils flared. Was there a new fragrance on the air? A *soupçon* of powder and sweat, trickling from the pale foot now resting on the carpet as the girl slipped out of her second shoe and began to tug her stocking down? She crossed the room and sat in her chair, resting the feather-case on her lap, the loop of rope on the feather-case, exchanging a glance with the

15

interviewer before both of them turned their hungry gazes to the unsuspecting would-be secretary. Ah, there, again, the pale perfection of a foot was emerging from the dark sheath of a stocking. The interviewer leaned forward over her desk, trying to see the girl's feet, the tip of a thick tongue stroking between her lips.

'Perhaps, my dear, if you just put them on the desk, so I can have a closer look.'

The girl's mouth opened, then closed. She swallowed and stole a glance at the enforcer, who smiled reassuringly at her, and then looked back at the interviewer, who was sliding another drawer open. She paused as she saw the girl's hesitation.

'Come, come, my dear. Feet up on the desk. We are all women together, I hope, and feet are nothing to be ashamed of.'

The girl swallowed again and, blushing, tried to lift her feet on to the interviewer's desk. Her skirt slid up her thighs and she blushed harder, then lowered her feet to the carpet and pushed her chair backwards before trying again, holding her skirt down on her knees. The interviewer lifted something out of the drawer and slid the drawer shut, then raised what she was holding. The enforcer snorted faintly with amusement when she saw what it was. A large magnifying glass. Now the girl's feet were on the desk, and the interviewer leaned forward with a sigh of satisfaction to examine them.

'Beautiful, my dear,' she said. 'I haven't seen such a pretty pair of feet in a very long time. Now . . .'

She laid the magnifying glass down and suddenly her hands flashed forward, seizing the girl by the ankles. The girl gasped with shock, her accent stronger than ever as she stammered, 'Ms Phalaenopsis, what . . . what are ye doin' . . .?'

'You can shut up, you little slut,' the interviewer said. 'Ms Jackson, if you would enforce the contract we spoke of earlier. The binding one.'

The girl turned her head as the enforcer picked up the loop of rope, dropped the feather case beside her seat, stood up, and advanced on her, loosening the rope as she came.

'Ms Phalaenopsis!' the girl said. 'What . . .'

She started to struggle, trying to kick her feet free of the interviewer's strong hands, but the interviewer smiled grimly and hung on. The enforcer reached the girl and quickly began to coil the rope round her body, binding her firmly into her chair, hands behind her back.

'Good,' said the interviewer above the girl's cries of protest, still firmly clutching her ankles. 'Now, put the foot-cuffs on her. They're in the second drawer on the left.'

The enforcer tested the rope, then trotted to get the foot-cuffs. Second drawer on the left . . . She slid it open, reached inside, and pulled out a pair of what looked like large hand-cuffs. Foot-cuffs.

'There's a little groove under the edge of the desk on her side,' the interviewer said, having to raise her voice again, a little breathless with the effort of holding the girl's feet in place. 'There's a projection on each of the cuffs that fits there, then she won't be able to move and you can slide her feet apart to any required angle.'

The enforcer nodded and walked back round the desk, fitting the foot-cuffs round the girl's slender, struggling ankles, then bending to force them into the groove the interviewer had mentioned. They clicked home one by one and the girl's feet were cuffed to the desk. The interviewer grunted with satisfaction as she surveyed the bare soles sitting in front of her.

'Look at them, Ms Jackson. Are they not sweet?'

The interviewer leaned forward over her desk and planted a kiss on each sole in turn. The girl wriggled and swore. Now the interviewer was sniffing the feet, then licking them, running her tongue up the sole, then

17

working it between each toe, foot by foot. When she had finished she sat back in her chair with a sigh of satisfaction, passing her tongue over her lips.

'Delicious,' she said. 'Clean girl-sole. There's no finer smell and no finer taste in the world. Her soles are like warm velvet. Just look at them, Ms Jackson. Have you ever seen two finer arguments for the existence of an all-wise, all-benevolent creator?'

Her voice broke a little as she spoke, as though she were overcome by her foot-lust, and she leaned forward again to plant more kisses on the girl's soles, and lick them again, lingeringly.

'Oh,' she said, her breath coming faster and her sturdy breasts rising and falling quickly. 'Fetch your feathers, Ms Jackson, please. I can barely restrain myself.'

She sat back in her chair, picking up the girl's application form again, snorting. The enforcer walked back to her chair, hearing the interviewer open the application form behind her and turn two pages. When she turned back to the desk with her feather case, the interviewer was looking hard at the girl, one firm forefinger stabbing at the page in front of her.

'Caroline,' she said. 'You say here that you are a "willing and conscientious worker". Is that right?'

The girl shook her head, still struggling against the foot-cuffs and the rope looped round her slender body.

'Come on,' the interviewer demanded. 'Answer me.'

'Yes, Ms Phalaenopsis. Ah am. Honestly Ah am.'

'You are, are you? Then spell "conscientious".'

The enforcer put the feather case upright on the desk and snapped the steel locks open. The girl began to stammer a reply.

'C – O – N . . . C – O – N – S – I . . .'

'No!' the interviewer shouted, slapping her open hand down on top of the application form with a crash. 'It is C – O – N – S – C – I . . . You're an ignorant little slut, aren't you? Ms Jackson, you may expose one body part for each word she misspells. She has misspelt one word, therefore you may expose . . . her left nipple. And tickle it with a feather.'

The girl cried out, struggling furiously in her chair, as the enforcer began to unbutton her blouse, feeling the buttons jerking under her fingertips to the girl's movements. She peeled the blouse open, exposing the girl's white cotton bra, and began to work a breast out of its cup, her mouth drying at the warmth and smoothness of the girl's skin, the firmness of the breast. There. The nipple was out, peeking over the top of the cup, and surely it was hardening. She took hold of it and squeezed gently, and the girl cried out again.

'Tickle it, Ms Jackson,' the interviewer said. 'Make her sweat.'

The enforcer turned back to her open feather case on the desk. She poised her hand over it, choosing, then slipped out a stiff white feather.

'Seagull primary,' said the interviewer. 'Stiff enough to withstand a North Sea gale. Very suitable.'

She turned back to the girl, and had to adjust her bra-cup again: the nipple had slipped half out of sight as she struggled against the rope. There. She began to tickle the nipple with the tip of the feather, circling it, stroking the aureole, and the interviewer hissed with excitement.

'Look how the little whore is responding.'

The nipple was swelling and lengthening, protruding at them like a little tongue as the enforcer continued to tickle and tease it. The girl moaned with frustration.

'Ah . . . ah cannae help it,' she said, tears shining in her eyes. 'Ye awld bitch.'

The interviewer gave a short laugh.

'Of course you can help it, you slut. A nipple is under perfect control of the will, and you obviously do not will it to remain . . . unresponsive. Now, let us see . . .'

19

She looked at the application form lying on her desk, turning back a page, her head turning from side to side as she scanned the text. Then she tutted sorrowfully and her forefinger stabbed out.

'Here,' she said. 'You say you studied the "Scottish Renaissance" in high school. Spell "Renaissance".'

The girl gulped, her face flushed as the enforcer continued to work at her nipple with the feather.

'R – E . . .'

She swallowed, trying to hold back a gasp of pleasure as the enforcer begin to wiggle the tip of the feather over her nipple.

'R – E – double N . . .'

'No!' The interviewer's palm crashed down on the desk. 'It is R – E – *single* N – A – I – double S – A – N – C – E. You have misspelt another word, and Ms Jackson will now expose another body part. Your right nipple.'

The girl's chest was rising and falling quickly now as she panted with the pleasure of the feather on her nipple, and she moaned when the enforcer rested the feather on the desk and began to lever down the bra-cup over her right breast.

'Is she sweating, Ms Jackson?' the interviewer asked.

'Yes, Ms Phalaenopsis.'

'Then I will test her pH shortly.'

There. Her right nipple was exposed, protruding insolently too, fed vicariously in the warm, scented darkness of the bra-cup on the pleasure of its sister. The enforcer turned back to the desk and picked up the seagull feather, then turned and began to tickle the right nipple. The girl cried out and struggled, her breast-cleft beginning to shine with sweat, and the interviewer grunted.

'She looks ready.'

The enforcer heard her slide open a drawer and put something on the desktop. She glanced over her shoulder and saw the interviewer opening a white plastic container with green lettering on the top: *pH Kit*. She looked back at the girl, hearing the lid come off with a pop behind her. The interviewer took something out of the container and then pushed her chair back and came round her desk.

'You're familiar with the concept of pH, Ms Jackson?' she said, and the enforcer, busy on the girl's right nipple again, glanced up to see her holding a small beaker in her left hand and what looked like an electronic thermometer in her right.

'Acid and alkaline?' she said. 'But that's all I can remember.'

'It's enough,' the interviewer said. 'A pH of 7 is neutral. Below that is acid, above it alkaline. Each of our orchids has its own preference, and we must match the orchid-bed to the orchid. I intend to grow an epiphytic between her breasts, so let's see what's on offer. If you'll just . . .'

The enforcer stopped tickling the girl's nipple with the feather and stepped back, and the interviewer put the tip of the pH-meter between the girl's breasts and worked it slowly up and down until there was a sharp little beep. She lifted the pH-meter and clucked with satisfaction.

'Six point three,' she said. 'Mildly acid. Should be perfect for a little *Vanda* hybrid we have recently developed. Now, while I'm at it, I'll just take her saliva and ear-wax pH too.'

She put the tip of the pH-meter into the small beaker she was holding in her left hand.

'Now, you little slut, open your mouth.'

The girl shook her head, eyes narrowing with determination as she realised she could resist by refusing to obey an order. The interviewer grunted with satisfaction.

'Hold her nostrils shut, Ms Jackson.'

The enforcer put her feather on the desk and turned back to the girl to pinch her nostrils shut.

The interviewer waited, humming to herself, and after about thirty seconds said conversationally, 'When it's in, Caroline, you can bite it as hard as you like. The plastic is quite tough enough to cope. Ah, thank you.'

The girl's mouth had come open, gasping for air, and she neatly slid the tip of the pH-meter inside, working it over the girl's gums and tongue.

'Pull your face as much as you like, my dear. It won't –'

The pH-meter beeped again and she pulled it out.

'Ah. Seven point five. Excellent again. Should be just right for a *Paphiopedilum callosum* that's selling very well at the moment. Now, her ears . . .'

She dipped the tip of the pH-meter back into the beaker, then said, 'If you could just hold her head still for me, Ms Jackson.'

The enforcer took hold of the girl's head, locking it into place between her palms as the interviewer slipped the tip of the pH-meter into the girl's left ear, waited for the beep, removed the meter, clucked with satisfaction, slipped it into the beaker again, then walked round the girl to slip it into her right ear. When it had beeped again and she had examined the result on the tiny display she said, 'Thank you, Ms Jackson. You can release her now. I had hardly hoped for such good readings. Now, that's breast-cleft, mouth, both ears. We still want front bottom and back bottom.'

It took a moment for the girl to understand what she meant; then she began to struggle and protest again, but the interviewer walked calmly back to her desk, sat down, and began to scan the application form. After a few moments she nodded and her forefinger stabbed at the page. She looked up, and her eyes were so stern and authoritative that the girl choked into silence.

' "Committed", ' the interviewer said. 'Spell it.'

'C . . .' the girl began. 'C – O – double M – I – D . . . double T – E – D.'

'Slut,' the interviewer said. She looked back at the application form, and her forefinger stabbed at the page again almost immediately.

'Your hobbies, my dear. Your leisure time. Spell . . . "leisure".'

The girl gulped. Her mouth opened, then closed.

'Well?' said the interviewer.

'L . . .' the girl quavered. 'E – E – A . . .'

She stopped as a cruel smile lit the interviewer's face.

'It's L – E – I, I'm afraid, my dear. Get her knickers down, please, Ms Jackson.'

'No!'

But the girl's hands could only clench and flutter futilely as the enforcer slid her skirt up and exposed her tight white knickers, happily breathing in the warm sweat-scented air that had collected between her thighs as she submitted to the nipple-pluming and the pH-testing. She began to roll the girl's knickers down, slowly exposing the black triangle of her pubic hair.

'Get her knickers to her ankles then swing her feet apart,' the interviewer said. The knickers were rolled into a double ring now, and the enforcer could slide them down the girl's thighs and over her knees. When they were round her knees she started to push the girl's feet apart, sliding the foot-cuffs in the groove to which they were attached, and the knickers stretched wider and wider, growing taut as her thighs swung open and the swollen, glistening lips of her pussy were exposed.

'That's enough,' said the interviewer. 'Has she . . . responded?'

The enforcer twanged the taut, stretched knickers and turned back to the girl, slipping a finger between her involuntarily splayed thighs and sliding it down her pussy lips, then up them, then lifting it away, rotating it so that light gleamed off the juice with which it was coated.

'Yes,' she said.

'It must have been the feather. Do it again. We want a good sample.'

The enforcer wiped her finger on the girl's pubic hair, savouring its warmth and softness, then turned back to the desk and picked up the seagull feather.

'Use two,' said the interviewer. 'One on her feet, one on her nipples.'

'OK.'

The enforcer selected another feather from her case.

'Excellent,' said the interviewer. 'A swan covert. Her nipples ought to respond very nicely to that.'

The enforcer turned back to the bound and helpless girl, took two deep breaths, and set to work. Her nipples, peeking provocatively over the white cups of her bra, had softened and drooped; now, as the enforcer tickled and stroked them with the swan's feather and tormented the soles of her feet with the seagull feather, they stiffened and began to protrude again, and the girl moaned and rocked in the chair.

'Is she seeping?' the interviewer asked.

The enforcer glanced between the girl's thighs.

'Yes. She's going to leave a nasty stain on that chair.'

'No matter. It will come out of her first week's wages. Try the swan's feather on her feet too.'

The enforcer followed the suggestion, beginning to tickle and stroke the girl's soft pink soles with the swan's feather. She moaned again, her head swaying on her neck, and the interviewer said, 'Tickle her clit with the seagull feather. Just the tip. Very gently.'

Still working at the girl's soles with the swan's feather, the enforcer slipped the seagull feather between her thighs and began to tickle at her clitoris with just the tip. The girl's whole body quivered, then quivered again, and her head went back, tendons standing out in her neck. Her mouth came open in a small O, gradually widening as she moaned on a rising note that broke, as the enforcer tickled her feet harder with the swan's feather and stroked the seagull feather over her clitoris, into squeals and moans of orgasm.

The enforcer lifted both feathers clear as the girl's moans subsided, glancing sardonically back at the interviewer.

'I think you've got a good sample,' she said, and the interviewer nodded, licking her lips, then picked up the pH-meter and came round her desk again. When she pushed the tip between the swollen lips of the exposed pussy, the girl moaned wonderingly, and the enforcer saw her hips trying to rock at the intruder. The interviewer waited for the beep and lifted the meter clear, shaking it to break a clear thread of pussy-juice that had started to stretch from the girl's pussy lips. She looked at the reading and clucked with satisfaction.

'Three point seven,' she said. 'I know a little *Odontoglossum* that's going to be in heaven. Now, back bottom.'

She returned to her chair and sat down, putting the tip of the pH-meter into the neutralising solution as she began to scan the application form again. Her forefinger stabbed out and she looked up.

' "Im–",' she started to say, but the girl was flopping in her chair, drooling slightly with the effects of her orgasm.

'Ms Jackson, get her to pay attention, will you? A whisker works wonders, so I always say.'

The enforcer replaced the two feathers in the case, slipped out a lion's whisker, and set to work on the girl's left foot. After a few moments the girl shook her head, her eyes clearing and focusing, and with a shiver she sat up, looking fearfully towards the interviewer, who smiled and said, ' "Immediately", Caroline. Spell it.'

'I . . . I – double M – E – D – I – A – T – E – L – Y.'

'Slut.'

The interviewer snorted and looked back at the application form, and looked up almost immediately with a triumphant little smile.

'The three words pronounced "there",' she said. 'Spell and define each.'

The girl swallowed nervously.

'T – H – E – I – R. That means . . . belongin' to them. T – H – E – R – E. That means . . . in a place a little ways away. An' T – H – E – Y – apostrophe – R – E. That –' her voice gathered confidence as she realised she had got everything right '– that means . . . it's a shortenin' of "they are".'

The interviewer nodded slowly.

'Excellent, my dear. Truly excellent. Perhaps we won't be able to examine your back bottom after all.'

She looked down at the application form, then up again, her eyes narrowing slyly. The girl's face had lightened as she was praised; now she looked apprehensive again.

'But how about . . . "pastime"?'

The girl blinked, then her lips moved silently for a few moments.

'P,' she said, 'A – S . . .'

She paused, and the enforcer could see a smile twitching in the corner of her lips.

'P,' she began again, 'A – S – T – I – M – E.'

The interviewer nodded again, looked down at the application form, then up again.

'One more, perhaps, my dear?'

The girl nodded, trying to hide the optimism in her face.

'Then how about . . . *Cattleya amethystoglossa*,' the interviewer said. The girl's face fell and her mouth opened slightly.

'Ah'm . . . ah'm sorry, Ms Phalaenopsis?'

' "*Cattleya amethystoglossa*",' the interviewer repeated. 'Spell it.'

'But . . . but that's not in mah application form!'

The girl was panting again, her exposed nipples stiffening and jerking with her emotion.

'Your application is for a job at Orchid Paradise,' the interviewer said. '*Cattleya amethystoglossa* is an orchid. Spell it.'

The girl burst into tears.

'I will take that as an admission that you cannot spell the word, my dear,' the interviewer said, picking up her pH-meter. 'Back bottom, Ms Jackson, please.'

2

Pussyfoot

'Well, doctor, it's like this.'

She paused, swallowing nervously.

'Yes, my dear?'

'I'm . . . I'm worried, doctor.'

'Hmmm? About what, my dear?'

'About . . . about whether I can still have children, doctor.'

'I see. But why, my dear?'

'Bec– because of what happened after the green star fell.'

'The green star?' he said.

'Yes, doctor. Surely you remember. The green star that fell over Daddy's training field last summer.'

'Ah,' he said. He pulled his matches from his pocket and re-lit his pipe, sucking hard at it, puffing smoke, then shook the match out, dropped it into the 44-mm shell resting on his desk, shook the box, and put it back in his pocket. When the smoke cleared he saw her looking seriously at him across the desk.

'*That's* when it happened, doctor. After the green star fell.'

'But my dear Miss Bleathington, you haven't said what *it* is, yet, have you?'

She pursed her lips, casting her eyes down, then looked up with a small smile.

'No, doctor. Perhaps if I . . . perhaps if I tell you what happened that day. The day after the star fell, I mean. The stalagtite.'

'Meteorite, my dear Miss Bleathington.'

'Yes. That. You see, it was like this. I took Necromancer out for an early morning run, and the nearer we got to the field the fresher he became. I'd never seen anything like it, even with him. He wasn't obeying the reins or anything, and when I tried to jump the gate with him – you know, the one just by the oak blasted the summer-but-last –' he nodded sagely, puffing on his pipe, barely paying attention '– he shied as though he hadn't jumped it a thousand times before and the next thing I knew I was on my back watching the clouds and trying to get my breath back.'

He nodded again, puffing on his pipe, imagining the eighteen-year-old in her tight jodhpurs, a quirt in her slender hand, hitting the dewy earth with a thump, her firm breasts quivering under her sweater.

'It was *very* lucky there was nothing beneath me when I fell, I told Mummy later, because there was an awful lot of deadwood on the ground that I've been going on at Daddy for ages to have cleared away and he finally got round to it after that because Mummy got on to him too and *anyway*,' she said, breath hissing into her mouth between her smooth lips, her breasts heaving and making him blink, '*that's* when I saw them, on the other side of the gate.'

'Saw what, my dear?'

He glanced surreptitiously up at the clock over the door. Not much fun for the doctor today, unless the little pest got her story out of the way much more quickly than now seemed likely.

'*Cobwebs*, doctor,' she said breathlessly, and he grunted.

'Did you say . . .' he began.

'Yes, doctor, I did. Cobwebs. Heaps and heaps of cobwebs all over the field on the other side of the gate.

29

Only they weren't, you see. After I'd got up and had a jolly good curse at Necro, who must've been halfway back to the stables by then, I looked over and saw them and honestly, I couldn't believe my eyes. I thought I must've banged my head because there were so many of them and they were so *large*. I remember thinking, "They must be jolly big spiders who've spun webs *that* big," so maybe I did bang my head a little, because it was a silly thing to think, wasn't it, because they couldn't really have been cobwebs *at all* and *anyway* when I walked over and had a look they weren't. Not at all.'

'Not cobwebs?'

'No, doctor. Because really they weren't moving at all, though there was quite a strong breeze blowing, and when I touched them they were sticky, which is why I said to Araminta that really they weren't like –'

She broke off as he remembered that Araminta was her best friend, a sturdy nineteen-year-old with annoyingly good health who hadn't been near his surgery since the previous winter, when he had treated her for a chesty cough over two delicious weeks. He coughed, his cock beginning to stiffen at the thought of the decongestant he had had to massage into her breasts, then dragged his mind back to the equally delicious and perhaps even firmer-breasted eighteen-year-old in front of him.

'Really they weren't like what, my dear?' he said.

'Like cobwebs, doctor,' she said, and he realised she had gone pink.

'Ah,' he said. 'Sticky, so not like cobwebs, like . . . something else.'

'Yes, doctor.'

She had gone pinker. His cock jerked to full erection in his trousers and he stopped taking surreptitious looks at the clock.

'And then what did you do, my dear?'

30

'I climbed over the gate and had a closer look, doctor.'

'And what did you find, my dear?'

'Well, that it wasn't the *whole* field that was covered with . . . with the cobwebs, doctor, just the part near the gate, round a big burnt patch on the grass, as though something had been burning there. And then . . .'

'Then what?'

'I . . . I don't remember what happened next, doctor. Not *properly*. I heard a humming sound, only it wasn't a *sound*, because I didn't so much *hear* it as *think* it. Inside my head. Does that sound silly, doctor?'

'Not at all, my dear. As you say, you think you *had* had a little bit of a whack on the head, and it's not at all unusual to hear things a little out of the ordinary in a case like that.'

'And see things too, doctor?'

'Yes, my dear. Like the, er, the cobwebs.'

'Not just the cobwebs, doctor. I saw a silver light, only I didn't so much *see* it as think it, like the humming sound. And then I don't remember anything until I was trudging back up the drive with a jolly big blister on my ankle and an even bigger one on my big toe.'

'I see,' he said, unable to resist lowering his eyes as though he could see her feet through the desk, snug in their shining black shoes and white silk socks.

'Yes, doctor. And that's how I think it happened, because the next day was the first time I noticed it.'

'Noticed what, my dear?'

'That . . . that it was, well, that she was *restless*, doctor.'

'Restless?'

'Yes, doctor.'

'Who was restless, my dear?'

'It might be easiest if I just show you, doctor.'

She stood up and loosened the broad leather belt he had noticed she had been wearing when she came in,

31

then wriggled, then wriggled again, making her breasts bounce. He raised his eyes quickly to her face when she said, 'She's moving, doctor.'

She wriggled, pursing her lips, starting to bend her body oddly to the left, wriggled again, and then suddenly clapped her hand to her left shoulder, circled the upper arm with her fingers, and started to squeeze downwards.

'I've got her, doctor. You'll see her in a second.'

He watched her, frowning with puzzlement, wondering whether she had gone mad. She had flattened the hand of the arm she was squeezing and turned it palm upwards, and was staring intently at it. Her fingers were squeezing down over her forearm now, and he caught a movement under the sleeve of her light purple cardigan, as though there were a small animal trapped there, reluctant to emerge from beneath her clothing into the light.

'There,' she said triumphantly, and leaned forward over the desk holding her left hand out to him, the fingers of her right hand firmly gripping the wrist. He rose a little in his seat (but not too much, because he didn't want her to see the bulge in his trousers) and grunted with surprise. What on earth was it? There were two pigmented furrows of flesh on her palm, no, two *pairs* of pigmented furrows of flesh on her palm, pressed close and looking exactly like . . . exactly like . . . He sat back heavily in his chair, lips moving silently for a moment round his pipe.

'But . . . but . . . but it's a *fanny*,' he said.

'Yes, doctor. It's *my* fanny.'

His knees felt stronger and he lifted himself to take another look, and nearly fell back into his seat when he saw the furrows of flesh nudge forward on her palm, sliding up over her fingers, then retreat towards her wrist.

'No you don't,' she said, tightening her grip on her wrist. 'Not till Doctor Adams has had a jolly good look at you.'

32

'It's your fanny?' he said.

'Yes, doctor. My fanny. At first she was just moving a little, but now she goes absolutely everywhere. All over my body. That's why I have to wear this big belt jolly tight, and jolly tight suspenders with my stockings too, doctor, or she might pop out on my face or something like that when I'm out in public.'

He took his pipe out of his mouth and put his thumb there instead, biting on it hard. When he took it out he could see the marks of his teeth, red grooves in the flesh of his thumb-ball.

'No, doctor,' she said. 'Honestly, you aren't dreaming, unless I'm dreaming too and then you're not really there. So if you *are* really there, I'm not dreaming, and neither are you. Do you see?'

He nodded slowly.

'I'm . . . I'm unable to fault your reasoning, my dear. Do you . . . do you mind if I touch it?'

'Her, doctor. I know it may sound jolly silly, but I've given her a name now that she can move. She's more like a pet than a proper fanny. In fact, she *is* like a pet.'

'Then do you mind if I touch . . . her?'

'No, doctor, please do. That's why I've brought her here. For you to examine her.'

He pushed his chair back and got up, no longer caring that she saw his trouser-front now, because the shock had shrivelled his erection away to nothing. He crossed the room to the little sink and washed and dried his hands, then took a jar of lubricating cream from a shelf and turned back to his desk.

'If you could just rest your hand here, my dear,' he said, sitting down again and putting the jar on the desk top. 'It may be more comfortable for you.'

'Yes, doctor.'

He slid open a drawer and took out his magnifying glass, then leaned forward over her hand. The lips of the fanny pouted up at him from the hand, firm and fleshy, fringed with her silky black maidenhair, and he recognised a mole on her left labium majus. He grunted, and gingerly reached out a finger and touched the fanny, stroking the skin where it seemed to merge with the skin of her palm. There was an odd tingling under his fingertip and he grunted and lifted the finger away.

'Did you feel it too, doctor?' she asked.

He glanced up at her.

'A tingling, my dear?'

'Yes, doctor.'

He put his finger back, touching the fanny itself now, and jerked in his seat when it shifted under his hand, sliding back towards her wrist again.

'She's very skittish today, doctor.'

'Yes. I can see she is. By the way, *what* name have you given her?'

She was silent for a moment and he looked up to see her face washed delicately with pink again.

'Philippa, doctor. Philly, for short.'

He grunted, remembering a pub limerick from his medical student days, and put his magnifying glass down so he could use both hands.

'I'm just going to slide one finger inside, my dear, so . . .'

He unscrewed the jar of lubricating cream and massaged some into the fanny-lips before gently prising them apart and starting to slide a finger inside, feeling his cock re-stiffening uncertainly in his trousers. He had often done this to her before, but never quite like this. Never like this at all. Then came his second shock: his finger continued to slide into her beyond the thickness of her hand, as though the whole vagina lay behind her vulval lips.

'Lift your hand a little, my dear,' he said.

She obeyed and he glanced underneath. Nothing but empty air, though his finger was inserted into her to the second knuckle.

'Put it back, my dear.'

She lowered it to the desk top again and he pushed the finger deeper. By now it should have been brought up short by the wooden surface of his desk, but nothing happened until his fingertip touched her cervix.

'See, doctor?' she said, her voice a little huskier than before. He looked up at her.

'There appears ... there appears to be everything there, my dear. Your whole –'

'Fanny, doctor,' she interrupted. 'Yes. Not just the lips, the sheath too. Even when it's on my face, doctor.'

He gently slid his finger out, beginning to count backwards from a hundred in sevens and feeling, to his relief, that his cock was subsiding.

'I'll tape your wrist for you, my dear, and then you don't need to worry about holding your other hand round it any more. That will keep her there while I give you a fuller examination.'

He pushed his chair back again and stood up to fetch a roll of sticking plaster and pair of scissors.

'Thank you, doctor,' she said, when he'd wound a length of it three times round her wrist and cut it loose from the roll. 'That ought to keep her in her place. Eh, Philly?'

She lifted her right hand away, wiggling the fingers, and the vulva on her palm, seeming to sense one obstruction had been removed, slid towards her wrist again. He watched it, frowning as a memory struck it. It moved just like a paramecium, that oval protozoon, sliding over her skin as though through the field of a microscope. When it reached the sticking plaster it stopped short, then nudged sideways, left and right, testing the new obstacle, sliding all the way round her wrist, then reappearing and retreating to her palm again.

'What does it feel like, my dear?' he said. 'Moving on your skin like that?'

'Like being tickled, doctor. When she's on a sensitive spot, I sometimes can't help laughing.'

'I see. Well, my dear, if you could just get your clothes off I'd like to have a look at the rest of you.'

'You mean between my legs, doctor?' she said, pushing her own chair back and standing up. 'That's just what Araminta wanted to see too.'

She walked across the room to the screen in one corner.

'Araminta has seen it too?' he said.

'Yes, doctor,' she said from behind the screen. 'I showed it to her three days after it started happening. Started happening *properly*, that is.'

Her cardigan was thrown over the top of the screen.

'When she was moving everywhere. Philly, that is. Because I didn't know whether I was going mad.'

Her belt was thrown over the top of the screen, then her skirt, then her bra and knickers, then she appeared from behind the screen still in her stockings and suspenders, holding her hands cupped over her crotch as she walked over to the examination couch.

'So I showed her to Araminta, when she was sitting on my palm,' she said, slipping onto the couch and smiling at him. 'Philly, that is. And Araminta saw her too, so I knew I wasn't going mad. But the first thing she wanted to see was between my legs. Just like you.'

As he walked over to her she lifted her hands away from her crotch and swung her thighs apart for him.

'See?'

The dark triangle of her pubic hair was still in place, but beneath it . . . nothing. Just bare, smooth skin, firm and warm beneath his fingers as he probed at it.

'See, doctor? Nothing. Because she's on my palm.'

She lifted the hand flat to him again and he glanced between her crotch and her palm. Bare skin between her thighs . . . vulva on the palm of her hand.

'If you take the sticking plaster off she might go home

again. She sometimes does, when she's a bit nervous, like today.'

'Then we'll try that, my dear.'

He pulled the end of the sticking plaster up and began to peel it off, watching the vulva move on her palm as though aware it was about to be released. *She* was about to be released.

'Ow,' she said. The last winding of sticking plaster was coming off, pulling up delicate hairs on her wrist.

'There,' he said, and dropped the length of sticking-plaster into the bin waiting by the couch.

'Yes, she's doing it,' she said, and he looked back at her palm. The vulva was moving slowly towards her wrist, and then, suddenly, with a jerk, it was sliding up her arm, riding over her skin like a three-dimensional shadow, curving to match the curves of her shoulder as it slid on to her torso and then down over her left breast to nestle in her breast-cleft.

'Go home,' she told it, poking a finger at it. 'That's where she goes first, sometimes, doctor. The safest nearest place, if you see what I mean, from the wrist.'

He nodded, watching the vulva slide over her skin, down from her breast-cleft, over her belly, to nestle between her thighs. She swung them closed.

'There, doctor. Home again.'

'Might I see?' he asked.

'All right, doctor. But be gentle with her, or you'll frighten her and she'll move again.'

She swung her thighs open and he bent to examine the vulva sitting between them. It looked perfectly normal, as though it had been sitting there since she came into his room, though perhaps . . . he tilted his head a little one way, then the other.

'Yes, doctor,' she said. 'She's sometimes doesn't come back perfectly straight.'

He nodded. The vulva wasn't quite vertical, sloping a little to the left.

'If I might, my dear?'

'Please do, doctor.'

He reached out and touched the vulva, then began to palpate it gently, and felt it quiver and slide slightly away from his fingers.

'See, doctor? She's very shy with strangers. A bit like a nervous filly, really, aren't you, Philly?'

Her fingers brushed his as she reached down between her thighs and stroked her vulva, crooning soothingly to it for a moment.

'There, there. Nice doctor isn't going to hurt you, Philly.'

It was too much: he couldn't wait any longer.

'When is your birthday, my dear?'

She looked up at him, dark eyebrows lifting in surprise into the smooth, creamy skin of her forehead.

'May seventeenth, doctor.'

'Can you tell me three words that rhyme with "May", my dear?'

She frowned now.

'Um . . . day, ray, say.'

'And say them in reverse order?'

'Say, ray, d –'

Her head fell back on the couch with a little sigh, her puzzled forehead smoothing, her dark lashes closing over her green eyes. He lifted his fingers away from her vulva, looked at her for a moment, his cock starting to stiffen inside his trousers, and then turned and walked to the sink. He would do it over lunch, he thought. He'd never risked it before, not taking the whole of lunch, because it was too risky, but if he could do what he thought he could do with her, it was worth it. When he'd dried his hands he went to his desk and pressed the intercom.

'Yes, doctor?'

'Mrs Williams, you can take an early lunch today. I'll see Miss Bleathington out myself, and then I need to write up her notes. Bring me back a sandwich, will you?'

'Yes, doctor. Thank you, doctor. See you at about one o'clock.'

'Fine.'

He released the button and looked up at the sleeping girl. Had he heard something just then? A pop, as though she had smacked her lips in her sleep? He shrugged and turned away to the window, watching through the thick curtains until he saw his secretary walk out of the front door of the surgery, shaking an umbrella open. He watched her walk down the path and turn left, then turned back to his office and began to loosen his tie. He'd tried hypnosis on his secretary too, several times, anxious to find his way into her well-upholstered bra, but she was a bad subject and on the last occasion he'd seen that she was starting to suspect something, so he'd stopped. And besides, he thought, as he pulled his tie loose and hung it over the back of his chair, why worry about thirty-two-year-old mutton when you can have eighteen-year-old lamb?

The thought made his cock jerk to full erection and he looked up at the sleeping girl and began to hurry his undressing. When everything was hung neatly over the back of his chair, he walked over to the couch and looked at her again. How many times had he had her like this? Seven? No, it was eight. Exactly eight. Not as many times as the Franklin girl, or the Ridge girl, or the Harper twins, but she was something special. The lord of the manor's daughter, and possessing her was almost ... revolutionary. Not that he had the slightest sympathy for the Russians, in the ordinary way of thinking, but he felt that he must be experiencing something of the excitement of the Bolsheviks storming the Winter Palace when he entered her. Something of the excitement of the sans-culottes. And perhaps all revolutions were, when you came down to it, just an expression of sexual envy. Lower-class men lusting for the smooth and scented daughters of the rich.

He grunted and sat down on the couch next to her.

'Sarah,' he said. 'Wake up. It's time for your throat medicine.'

She came awake with another little sigh, blinking up at him.

'Doctor?'

'Your throat medicine, dear. I've got the bottle ready. Sit up and drink it down like a good girl.'

'Yes, doctor.'

She pushed herself up on the couch, breasts quivering, and he turned towards her.

'Here it is, dear,' he said.

'Thank you, doctor.'

Her hair brushed his stomach as she bent forward and lowered her mouth to his cock. As she took hold of it and began to suck, he stroked the back of her head, marvelling again at the softness of her hair. The daughters of the rich, he thought. Exotic blooms grown in warm greenhouses, sheltered all their lives from the cold, desiccating winds of poverty and failure. No wonder they grew up so soft, so smooth, so . . . fuckable. He groaned a little. She was starting to rock her head on his cock, and her hand was cupping his balls, starting to squeeze a little. This was all he would have risked today, fellatio at the end of her appointment, if she hadn't revealed to him all she'd revealed, but now he had an hour to do much more. And he *was* going to do much more.

He grunted again, feeling his orgasm starting to build, and slid a hand between her thighs, feeling for her vulva. He grunted for a third time, but with surprise, because it had gone. He twisted his neck, trying to look at her body, and saw a flicker of dark movement down one of her flanks.

'Playing hard to get, are we?' he said. 'Don't worry, I'll catch you. I'll . . .'

He broke off as he began to discharge inside her mouth and she swallowed his sperm greedily. After he'd slid his cock out, he asked her, 'How did it taste, my dear?'

'Delicious, doctor. Pepperminty. My favourite.'

'Good,' he said. 'Now, lie back and go to sleep again.'

'OK, doctor.'

She lay back obediently and was asleep as soon as the back of her head touched the couch. He slipped off it himself and walked to the undressing screen for her belt, then walked to his desk for the roll of sticking plaster, then walked back to the couch.

'Now, where are you, you little . . . Ah, there you are.'

The vulva was nestling between her breasts again, quivering slightly, obviously nervous. He dropped the belt and roll of sticking plaster between her legs and reached in his pocket for the box of matches. Would this work? He opened it, took a match out, and struck it. His fingers were shaking slightly with excitement and he had to strike it twice before it lit. Now he lowered it to the sleeping girl's breasts, holding his breath . . . Yes, it had worked! The match was still three or four inches clear of her skin when the vulva moved, darting away from the heat of the burning match, sliding down her stomach back between her thighs.

He shook the match out and dropped it in the bin, then picked up her belt and looped it round her waist, having to lift her a little to slide it under her, then tightening the belt hard. Now it was trapped between the belt and her tight stockings, but he wanted to give it a little more room for manoeuvre. He undid the stocking on her right leg from her suspenders and slid it down, having to tug hard at first. Then he lit another match and lowered it between her thighs, and clicked with satisfaction as the nervous vulva darted away from the heat again, climbing the swell of her thigh and sliding down it to try and burrow under her buttocks. He pushed the match at it again and it slid back, then darted down her right leg and hid from him on the back of her calf.

He shook the match out and dropped it in the bin, then picked up the roll of sticking plaster. He wound it round her knee three times, pressing hard, then turned and walked to his desk for the scissors. He came back and cut the sticking plaster, then nodded with satisfaction. There. Now it was trapped on the lower half of her right leg. He lit another match and lowered it to her calf, driving the vulva relentlessly downwards. In a minute he was winding sticking plaster round her ankle and the vulva was trapped on her foot. The final stage would be tricky, he thought: he wanted it on her sole, but the vulva seemed to know what he was up to by now and he wasted three matches driving it futilely round and round her foot before an idea struck him and he went and fetched a bottle of iodine.

As he painted her upper foot he began to smile: the vulva was backing away from it and he soon had it trapped in a narrowing oval of iodine on her sole. There. Now he had it exactly where he wanted it and he bent over the foot, lifting it to his mouth and planting a kiss right on top of the vulva, feeling his cock beginning to restiffen after the fellatio. He returned the bottle of iodine to its shelf and fetched the jar of lubricating cream from his desk.

'Now, Philly,' he said. 'Are you going to be a good girl and let the nice doctor give you a thorough internal with his nice big cock? Yes?'

He began to massage the cream into the vulva, feeling it quiver under his fingertips, making little rushes backwards and forwards in the little pool of unpainted sole that was all he had left it. He smiled again as he felt the lips beginning to swell and leak juice. She had bowed to the inevitable. There. She was ready. He put the lid back on the jar and put it back on his desk, then returned to the couch and sat astride the end of it, sliding forward to lift her foot to his cock. He rubbed the head of his cock on the lips of the vulva, moistening it before insertion, then gripped the top of her foot hard and pressed forward.

He slid into her easily, delighted at her warmth and slickness, a little dizzy with the strangeness of it. There was a fully aroused vagina beyond the vulva, accepting the full length of his cock easily, though the head of his cock should have appeared on the other side of her foot almost immediately. He started to thrust and withdraw, working up pleasure slowly for his second orgasm, and when he felt it begin to build too quickly he distracted himself by thinking of where he would drive the vulva next, for his third orgasm and second fuck. Between her breasts? The centre of her forehead? Now that he knew about the iodine trick he could position it to the inch. He groaned. Oh. She was tighter like this than he'd ever known her before, squeezing deliciously on his cock as he withdrew, setting up a delightful resistance as he slid back in, squeezing ... Ow. Squeezing a little – ow – a little too ... a *lot* too hard. Fuck. What a thing to happen. Vaginismus. He reached a finger for her clitoris, meaning to begin stroking it, and then stopped dead, looking at the face of the sleeping girl.

Her eyes had opened. She was still sleeping, but her eyes had opened, surveying him unblinking. Then her lips moved.

'It is too tight for you, doctor?'

It wasn't her voice. Not Sarah Bleathington's voice. It was the voice of a much older woman, and its accent wasn't English, it was ... He lifted his iodine-stained fingers to his nose and sniffed hard, then put his thumb into his mouth again and bit down on it.

'No, doctor. Sarah has already told you. You are not dreaming. This truly is happening. You truly are caught in Sarah's foot. And you are not going to get out, *tu sais.*'

The sleeping girl's lips smiled oddly. French. It was a French accent. He took hold of the foot again, but pushed this time, trying to lever it off his cock. No use. He looked up at her face again.

'Who are you?' he said.

'I am one of Sarah's little friends. You know, you really knew so very little about her when you selected her for these ... games of yours. It would have been much better to confine yourself to other girls. Less *knowing* girls.'

He wrenched with his hips, trying to drag his cock out of her by main force.

'Who *are* you?' he said, starting to shout.

'Don't struggle, doctor. If you injure her, even in the slightest, it will go much harder for you.'

Now the lips laughed. It was like watching a very clever puppet, the eyes and lips being controlled by an invisible puppet master.

'Who are you?' he repeated, and he was shouting this time.

'Shut up,' the lips said, and the vagina tightened convulsively on his cock, making him whimper.

'If you are quiet, I will tell you. If you are not, I will punish you. Like that.'

He sighed with relief as the vagina loosened its grip on his cock, trapping him, but not torturing him.

'Very well?'

He nodded silently.

'Good boy. Now, you wish to know who I am? Or should I say: " 'oo I am"?'

The lips laughed again, then curled with pride and disdain.

'*Moi, mon bon docteur, je suis la putain du roi. La Marquise de Montespan.* I am the king's whore, my good doctor – the 'ore of ze keeng! – the Marchioness of Montespan. You know of me, of course?'

He nodded, dizzy with disbelief.

'Louis the Fourteenth,' he said.

'Yes, doctor.'

'But you . . . you died two hundred years ago.'

'Two hundred and forty-six years ago, to be precise, doctor. But what of it? Do you think *time* is any obstacle to those with true wisdom? Do you think a witch of the calibre of Sarah's mother would have any difficulty in calling up a spirit from ten times as far?'

His lips worked soundlessly.

'A witch?' he managed to say.

'A witch, doctor. Your innocent eighteen-year-old lamb is a witch's daughter. And now the witch has caught you out. With my 'elp, doctor.'

'I'm dreaming,' he said.

'Then wake up.'

He lifted his thumb to his mouth again and bit down on it hard, harder, then gasped as her vagina tightened on his cock again.

'Stop that, you fool,' the lips said. 'Neither are you to injure yourself. Those are her instructions.'

'Where is Sarah?'

'Sleeping, as you can see. She has willingly allowed me control of her body. I have been watching and waiting all the time. Waiting for you to begin.'

'When did you find out?'

'What, find out that you had been using her?'

He nodded.

'We learnt of it last month. She has been a medium for the coven here for nearly five years. An excellent hypnotic subject, is she not? Yes, precisely. That is why it was so easy for you to gain your dominance over her, but your block on her memory was laughably weak and the high priestess of the coven was able to remove it very easily when our suspicions were aroused by a semen stain we discovered on her collar. You were careless there, doctor.'

He nodded again, remembering how it had happened.

'And so, we laid this trap. With a story of green stars and cobwebs, so that you would think . . . of what? Of

45

little green men from outer space, doctor? Mr Wells's and Mr Wyndham's "science fiction"?'

'Yes.'

'Yes. But we knew that whatever you thought, you would not be able to look a gift horse in the mouth. Or a gift whore in the foot, *n'est-ce pas?*'

'No.'

'And now you are thinking, are you not, what is it they want with me?'

He nodded.

'A confession, doctor. A full confession to your crimes against the young womanhood of this delightful rural district. Names, times, acts. When Mrs Williams returns from lunch . . .'

He whimpered as the sleeping girl's limbs began to move, dragging at his cock as she pushed herself up on the couch so that her head could turn, looking towards the clock above the door. Then she dropped back to the position she had occupied before.

'When Mrs Williams returns from lunch in six minutes, you are going to call her into your office and, assuming she does not faint or have hysterics on the spot, you are going to dictate a confession to her. And sign it. Then, and only then, will you be released.'

'I won't call her,' he said immediately.

'Then don't, doctor. Stay here, trapped by the cock, and wait for her to buzz you and tell you she has the sandwich you asked her to get.'

Damn. He'd forgotten the sandwich.

'If you start now, you might be able to get young Sarah over to the desk in time for you to reply when she buzzes you. You can tell her you don't want the sandwich. But what are you going to tell her when she tells you the first of your afternoon patients has arrived and is ready for you? That you're not feeling well? That you're going home early? She'll want to see you, won't she, doctor? What excuses are you going to offer? No, you had best face it, doctor. Sooner or later that door is going to open and you will be found here with your cock buried in the foot of the lord of the manor's daughter. Far better that it be Mrs Williams in four minutes' time, with no patients on the premises, don't you think? After all, no one is going to believe her story, are they? Look at you. You've got your whole cock buried in her foot. That's impossible. Mrs Williams herself won't believe it. But she, and everybody else, *will* believe your confession.'

'It will ruin me,' he said.

'It will.'

'I'll pay anything you like. Do anything you like.'

'A signed confession is all we require of you. And then you can go free. Free to flee the country, if you want. But you won't be trying anything like this again in a hurry, will you, doctor?'

He looked up at the clock over the door, watching the second hand rotate with maddening efficiency and indifference, then reached forward and took hold of the sleeping girl by her thigh and began to pull her off the couch with him.

'Ah,' said the lips. 'So you haven't learnt your lesson. It's going to be the hard way. The hard way again, doctor. The hard way, as always.'

They laughed and he swore at them, starting to sweat.

3

Scentipede

'What I want,' he said, 'is one hundred women. For one night.'

She pursed her lips and nodded.

'You certainly conceive things on a grand scale, Mr Owen.'

'Can you supply them?'

She shrugged. 'If you can pay for them, I can supply them. You may have two hundred, if you wish.'

'No. One hundred is all I need. And I can pay.'

'Then of course, I can supply, Mr Owen.'

She picked up a small gold pen and made a note on a jotter in front of her.

'One hundred women, for one night,' she said. 'And what is it you wish them to do for you?'

'I want them to be a centipede.'

She looked up at him, frowning slightly.

'I am afraid I do not know the word, Mr Owen.'

'A centipede,' he said. 'It's an, um, I suppose you could call it an insect. With one hundred legs. One hundred feet.'

'An insect . . .? Ah,' she said, her face clearing. '*Stonoga*. You will forgive me. A centipede. Yes. But, please forgive me, will you not require only fifty women, for a centipede?'

He shook his head, smiling.

'You are an honest woman, Madame Mihailovic.'

She nodded, smiling too.

'No,' he went on, 'perhaps it would have been more accurate of me to say that I want the one hundred women to be *two* centipedes. Once with their right feet, once with their left feet. Coming, and going.'

'I thank you for your compliment, Mr Owen. But perhaps it would be more accurate of you to say that I am a woman, a businesswoman, who wishes to ensure complete customer satisfaction. So, one hundred women, for one night, to perform for you two centipedes.'

'Yes. But in fact there is a silent "s".'

'A silent "s", Mr Owen?'

'Yes. At the beginning of "centipede". May I see what you have written?'

'Certainly.'

She lifted her jotter, turned it, and held it out to him. He read: *100 f 1 n centipède.* He raised his eyebrows.

'You write in French?'

'Always. It is a tradition of the house.'

'Thank you. But the pun will not work in French, will it?'

'Hm? The pun?'

'The silent "s". At the beginning of "centipede".'

'Ah. I see.'

She pulled the jotter back and added a single letter, then raised her pen, looking at the word.

'Yes, the pun. No, it does not work in French. You wish them, I presume, to have . . . how shall I put it? . . . odorous feet?'

'Yes. All of them are to wear tight shoes constantly for one week on one foot.'

She had begun to write fast on the jotter, using shorthand this time, he could see.

'Fifty will wear the shoes on their right feet. Let us call them dextras,' he said. 'The other fifty will wear the shoe on their left feet. Let us call them sinistras. On the night, the other foot of each woman is to be carefully washed and perfumed. That is, the foot she has not worn a shoe on for a week. The centipede is to be composed of alternate dextras and sinistras, that is, each side will consist of alternately washed and unwashed feet. Very well?'

She looked up, nodding, then looked down at her jotter and read his instructions back to him, word for word.

'Good,' he said. 'Excellent. Now, the perfumes, for the washed feet. I want nine, in this order: rose . . . lemon . . . coconut . . . violet . . . cinnamon . . . sandalwood . . . vanilla . . . almond . . . jasmine . . .'

He stopped speaking. She had been writing at the same speed; now she looked up, eyebrows raised, waiting for him to continue. He took and released a long breath, and continued.

'All the women are to be naked, but I wish the belly of each to bear a representation in gold paint of the sole of the right or left foot of the woman directly in front of her in the centipede. When you are recommending women to me by email, please include photographs of the soles of both feet. When I choose a woman, I will also choose one of her feet for the belly-painting.'

'Very well. And the first woman in the centipede?'

'There will be no first woman, at the beginning of the session. The centipede will be circular. Now, the women will also wear jewellery: silver earrings, nipple-rings, and labia-rings from which will hang small gold feet. Women's feet. I will supply these. Would you read that back?'

He listened, nodding, as she read back his next set of instructions.

'Now, the setting. I will require a large hall, at least twenty metres by thirty. At one end there will be a black ramp shaped like a horse-shoe, rising, then falling. Set against the inner curve of the highest point of the ramp will be the heel of a giant *papier-mâché* model of the right foot of the Aphrodite of Cyrene. The foot will be hollow and large enough both for me and for a fellatrix. *Une fellatrice.* I will lie in it with my head resting in a groove on the surface of the ramp and have my cock sucked by the fellatrix. The scentipede will be created as a circle on the ramp, facing clockwise, with each woman joined to the woman in front of her by an anally inserted strap-on dildo. On my signal, the scentipede will begin to rotate clockwise and each member of it will rub her right foot on my face and then step onto my face at a rate I will set over loudspeakers. I will vary the rate as I please. Very well?'

She nodded. 'I read it back?'

'Please.'

She read it back to him.

'Excellent. Now, the scentipede will continue to rotate until I decide I have had enough. I may require it to rotate anti-clockwise, that is, to walk backwards, at some point. When I am satisfied, I will retire for an hour, perhaps taking with me one or more of the women in the scentipede. The remaining members of the scentipede will stay where they are on the ramp. When I have rested, I will return and take my place in a giant hollow *papier-mâché* model of the *left* foot of the Aphrodite of Cyrene set against the *outer* curve of the highest point of the ramp. The members of the scentipede who have retired with me, if any, will resume their places and the scentipede will rotate clockwise again, each member stepping this time with her left foot onto my face. As before, I will set the rate over loudspeakers, and may require the scentipede to rotate anti-clockwise at some point. Very well?'

She nodded and read his words back to him again. He listened, nodding occasionally, breathing heavily now, sweat shining on his forehead.

'Thank you,' he said when she had finished. 'That is the first stage of the ritual. The second stage will be more ... free-form. I will get out of the foot of Aphrodite and personally fit one hundred new pairs of stiletto shoes to the feet of the women in the scentipede. The shoes will be glass and have a steel heel exactly three and a third inches long. I will then return to the foot and watch the next stage of the ritual on monitors. The scentipede will dissolve and the women will walk off the ramp and onto the floor of the large room in which all this will be staged. Laid across the middle of the room will be contiguous rows of overripe fruit and vegetables and fresh eggs in this order: grapes ... larks' eggs ... strawberries ... plovers' eggs ... oranges ... hens' eggs ... pineapples ... ducks' eggs ... melons ... ostrich eggs ... pumpkins. The women will form a line parallel to these rows and then, on my signal, walk slowly over the fruit and vegetables and eggs. Very well?'

She nodded and read his words back to him.

'Good. When the women have reached the other side of the eggs and fruit, they will take off their stilettos and walk back *around* the rows to stand in groups of twenty at one end of these five rows: the row of the larks' eggs ... of strawberries ... of pineapples ... of melons ... and of ostrich eggs. They will then walk *down* the rows, coating their bare feet in whatever crushed eggs or fruit each row contains. This too will be filmed. I will then select two women in each group of twenty, and these ten will be carried to me where I sit in the right foot, where I will lick their feet clean. Very well?'

She nodded again and read his words back to him.

'Thank you. Those are my initial instructions. Do you have any questions?'

'One moment, please.'

She read silently through her shorthand notes, nodding slightly to herself, then looked up.

'The women first, of course. Have you any special requirements of race, of size, of hair colour?'

'Yes.'

She began to write in shorthand again.

'Sixty of them are to be white European, one third blonde, one third black-haired or brunette, one third redhead. Next, thirty of them are to be Asian, five apiece from China and Japan, ten from the Indian subcontinent, ten from South-East Asia. Indonesia, Malaysia, the Philippines. The remaining ten are to be black African, five pure black, five mulatto.'

'And languages?'

'No particular preference. Speech will not be required of them. As for size: a mixture, but I want most to be slim, so long as they are naturally slim. I want them to step on my face with as much of their weight as I can bear, but I do not want anoxerics.'

'Of course. I will include weight with a nude photograph of each woman I recommend. Do you prefer weight in imperial or metric?'

'Imperial, please.'

'Imperial. Very well. Now, supplies. You will arrange the jewellery, as I have noted, but all else is to be our responsibility? The fruit, the vegetables, the eggs? The shoes, the ramp, the *papier-mâché* feet of Aphrodite?'

'Yes.'

'Fine. And do you wish to indulge any other *fetiches*? Uro, copro, lac, perhaps? We have specialists in all three, and in all combinations of the three.'

He shook his head.

'No. You tempt me, but no. Only podo.'

'Only podo. And there is, of course, the question of when and where you wish for this to take place.'

'Location I will leave to you, Madame Mihailovic. The day on which I wish this to take place is May twelfth, the eve of St Lupus's Day. The scentipede must first begin to rotate on the stroke of midnight.'

She nodded.

'That is no problem. You have come to us in plenty of time. One more question, perhaps. The women you select from the groups of –' she glanced at her notes '– of twenty. How will you identify them? I cannot guarantee that all the women meeting your requirements will be fluent in English and it may cause some delay if you describe them.'

'I compliment you for your attention to detail, Madame Mihailovic,' he said. 'Let's see . . . shall we say . . . yes, please paste a small circle of paper between the shoulder-blades of each woman bearing a number from one to one hundred.'

'A circle of paper. How small?'

'Let's say . . . three inches.'

'And the colour of the paper and ink?'

'Again, I compliment you on your attention to detail, Madame Mihailovic. But I have no special preference. White paper, black ink.'

'Very well.'

'Ah. One more thing occurs to me. I would like the numbers to be in base five, not base ten.'

'Base . . .?'

'Base five. Counting one, two, three, four, ten, eleven, twelve, thirteen, fourteen, twenty. Et cetera.'

'Ah, yes, I see. Base five. Yes. Symbolic of the toes of a single foot, no doubt?'

'Yes. Symbolic of the toes. And I think that is it, unless you have more questions.'

'At the moment, I think, no. I am sure there will be some to raise by email, and over the telephone, but I see no obvious difficulties at present. I cannot cost the enterprise as a whole yet, but the hire of one hundred women for one night will be approximately £400,000, inclusive of interviews, photography, and training for those finally selected. I would advise you to choose an additional ten women as stand-bys, to cover possible illnesses and accidents.'

'That's fine. Perhaps you could include identical twins in the details you forward me.'

'I will be sure to do so. We have nearly thirty pairs on our books, with five sets of identical triplets also, and are negotiating the hire of a set of Venezuelan quadruplets to join the set from Morocco already on our books, when they reach the age of majority. A suitable set of quintuplets, alas, have so far eluded us, but the search continues.'

'I am impressed yet again, Madame Mihailovic.'

She smiled.

'The world truly is your oyster, Mr Owen, with *Meretrices Sans Frontières*. That is our motto, after all. And now, if you have no further points you wish to raise and we do not meet again before the day, may I wish you a good summer, and hope that our arrangements are completed soon and to our shared satisfaction?'

'No further points, Madame Mihailovic. I was promised I would not be disappointed by the service I received here, and I have not been disappointed.'

She nodded gracefully, and rose to offer him her hand across the desk. When he had kissed it, she pressed the button that would summon her secretary and he was shown out.

He saw her lips come together for a consonant, then open and round for a vowel, but the noise of the descending helicopter was too great for him to hear what she said, and he shook his head. She pointed downward through the window and he leaned over her to see what was there. Ah, it was the house, the manor house whose great hall she had hired for the night, rising out of the darkness in its leafy grounds, the lake gleaming with a silver streak of moon, the grove of lime that lined the western and southern sides of the house beginning to lash with the wind of the helicopter's blades. He leaned back, beaming at her, lifting his thumb, and she beamed back with professional pride.

When they had run, crouching, from the helicopter and listened to it hammer into the distance, she had said, 'Welcome to Fettlesham Manor, Mr Owen. I trust you will find everything to your satisfaction. The young women are now waiting for you.'

His cock had already been stiff in his trousers, and the lurch of excitement that went through him when she mentioned the women made him think for a moment that he was going to come there and then, spurting the seed he had been saving for the past week. But he swallowed the excitement back and followed her as she led him to the great hall. Soon she was opening a battered door of age-darkened oak and he was stooping to follow her in. He smelt the fruit and vegetables before he had straightened and looked round him, the rich essence of overripe strawberries, oranges, and pineapples contending in his nostrils. Now he straightened and looked, and his cock jerked in his trousers as he saw the gleaming rows laid on the oak-beam floor, the reds and greens and golds of the fruit and vegetables divided by the white and brown of the eggs, with a few black specks dancing above the fruit.

'They are fruit-flies, Mr Owen,' Mrs Mihailovic said, interpreting the angle of his gaze and his slight frown. 'You may remember I raised the possibility of their appearance in an email of . . . the twenty-third of March. Wild *Drosophila* species. You did not object at the time, but I have arranged for insecticide sprays to be available if you have changed your mind.'

'Ah,' he said. 'Yes. Fruit-flies. No, they are fine. More than fine. The fruit –' he sniffed deeply '– is exactly as I wished it to be.'

'Excellent. And you wish to inspect the ramp and the feet of Aphrodite?'

'Please.'

She led him to the ramp and they walked up it together, then down it to turn up between its curving arms and walk to the giant *papier-mâché* model of the right foot of the Aphrodite of Cyrene that rested against the highest point of its inner curve. He squatted to run his fingers over its gleaming perspex toenails, then peered inside the open ankle, humming a snatch of Elgar to hear the echo, then ran his fingers over the skin of the foot, then tested the pillow on which it had been decided the back of his head should rest.

'Perfect,' he kept murmuring. 'Perfect,' and Mrs Mihailovic nodded each time and murmured in reply, 'Thank you.'

Next she led him out of the curve of the ramp and round it to inspect the left foot, and he squatted to run his fingers over the toenails as before, and hummed into the ankle, and stroked the skin, with murmurs of 'Perfect' and 'Thank you' as before. It was then time for him to go to his dressing room, where he would strip, shower, and be wired for sound before he returned to climb inside the right foot and order the women in from their dressing rooms to form the scentipede. Footage of their preparations was being screened on a wall-screen as he undressed, and Mrs Mihailovic twice had to cough to bring him out of a voyeuristic trance, first when he stood with his fingers on his tie, watching the left foot of a tall strawberry blonde being bathed and perfumed, then when he stood, trousers off, in his shirt-tails watching the right foot of a golden-skinned *chinoise* being bathed and perfumed too.

He grunted and apologised each time, thanking her for reminding him that they had a strict schedule to keep, if the scentipede was to begin rotating on the stroke of midnight. Finally, stripped and showered, he was fitted with a light headset with a mouthpiece and walked out to meet the tiny Latvian woman who would climb into the foot before him and suck his cock when he got into the foot too. She was on a bonus of one thousand pounds per ejaculation, and laughed as Mrs Mihailovic spoke to her in Russian.

'I have told her she will put on weight if she is too successful,' Mrs Mihailovic said as the woman, with a pat on her bare bottom from the madame, climbed into the foot, 'but she says there are very few calories in semen.'

He nodded, not speaking now, his excitement beginning to mount as his months of waiting dwindled down finally to minutes. The madame caught his mood and turned serious, saying, 'Very little time now, Mr Owen, so I wish merely to congratulate you again for the grandness of your conception and breadth of your vision. If I might shake you by the cock?'

He nodded, and swallowed as the madame's cool hand, its fingers circled by cooler rings, took hold of his erect cock and shook it.

'Now, Mr Owen, the young women await and if Olga is positioned . . .'

She spoke into the shoe in Russian and he heard the tiny fellatrix squeak back, '*Da.*'

'Yes, she is ready. You may begin.'

He swung a leg into the open ankle of the foot, then the other, and cautiously sat down inside it, feeling the warm body of the fellatrix slide against his, then grunting with pleasure as her warmer mouth settled over his cock and began to suck. The madame was watching his face.

'She is good, is she not?'

'Excellent,' he croaked, and the speakers round the room croaked 'Excellent' with him.

'Now, head back, Mr Owen,' the madame said, and he put his head back into the groove that awaited it, settling it on the pillow there. The madame nodded.

'Then now I will leave you, Mr Owen. Call for the girls as soon as you are ready.'

He listened to her discreetly heeled stilettos tap away over the bare floor, staring up at the huge mirror fixed to the ceiling thirty feet above him and starting to sweat as the expert little fellatrix sucked him towards his first orgasm.

'I am ready,' he said, and heard doors opening further down the hall, then the hum of golf-buggies as the hundred young women were brought out of their dressing rooms and driven down the hall to the ramp. He watched in the mirror as the buggies halted at his end of the hall and the muscular drivers began to carry the women in twos, one resting on each arm, to the ramp. The women's feet, as Mrs Mihailovic had promised, would not touch the ground between dressing room and ramp, and would lose nothing of their scent until they were pressed to his face.

As women slipped off the drivers' arms and stood ready on the ramp, the first tendrils of foot-odour began to reach his nostrils and he started to come inside the fellatrix's urgently sucking mouth. The mirror was busy with movement now as the line of women formed on the ramp, long black strap-on dildos jutting from their groins, ready to create the scentipede. The drivers too had erections, he could see, and he smiled at the thought of how some of them would soon be masturbating their frustration away: Mrs Mihailovic had assured him that the stand-by women would not accede to any requests from any of the male personnel involved in setting up this fulfilment of his long-standing fantasy.

He gasped a little: the fellatrix was working hard on his cock now, trying to bring him to his second orgasm, but it was a little too soon. The hundred women were nearly ready and he licked his lips, moistening them. Yes. It was time. The last drivers set down their double arm-load of women and hurried off the ramp to drive the golf-buggies away, and he said, 'Spit on anuses.'

The hundred women were quite loosely spaced, and the line trailed off the ramp at both ends. Now its ends came together and the women moved closer to each other, bending forward, tugging the cheeks of their own buttocks apart so that each woman in the line could spit on the anus of woman directly in front of her. His cock jerked inside the mouth of the fellatrix at the sight and sound of it: one hundred young women spitting onto the anuses of one hundred young women.

Now he ordered, 'Tongue anuses,' and each woman lowered her head between the buttock cheeks of the woman directly in front of her and began to work the spittle in with her tongue. He glanced at the giant clock hanging on the wall and saw that they were running exactly on schedule: two minutes to midnight. His ears were filled with the sound of soft tongues busily licking warm anuses, and his balls started to ache, wanting to give up their juice again.

'Prepare to insert dildos,' he ordered, and the women straightened and moved closer together still, each woman taking hold of her strap-on dildo and guiding it into place over the gleaming anus in front of her.

'Insert dildos,' he ordered, and began to ejaculate for the second time, listening to the soft cries and squeaks as one hundred dildos sank between the firm buttock cheeks of one hundred naked young women. When he had finished coming the head of the tiny fellatrix crouched between his thighs started to pump gently on his cock, keeping it stiff for his third ejaculation. He stared into the mirror set above him, his eyes running round the circle of the scentipede, and ordered: 'Rotate.'

A red-haired woman was standing on the ramp directly above his head; now she moved inwards, putting her right foot on his face and beginning to rub the sole up and down. The scent of roses filling his head, the sight of the silky red hair curling round the pink lips of her cunt, the glitter of the piercings in her labia and nipples, the smoothness and warmth of her sole-skin, all these made his cock jerk inside the fellatrix's mouth.

Inside the foot, his right forefinger found the rot-rhyth button, paused, and pressed it. The over-amplified slap of a bare female foot on wet sand echoed through the hall, and the first woman ground her foot into his face, then lowered her weight onto it as she stepped away. He shuddered with pleasure, and then the next foot was descending on his face: a foot that had been crammed into a tight shoe for a week and never washed.

Its cheesy reek raped his nostrils before it even touched his face, seeming to force its way into his brain, and the heat of the sole glowed on his face like the sun. Then the sole was on his face, rubbing up and down, left and right, slimy, salty, richly and ripely stinking. His tongue came out, licking frantically, and his stomach rolled and tightened with perverted joy as his cock jerked again and again in the fellatrix's mouth, dry-firing him to erotic semi-delirium. He detected Camembert, Parmesan, Stilton in the caseous medley pouring into his senses, and could barely see the black triangle of hair between the thighs of the woman servicing him and the glitter of her gold piercings.

He pressed the rot-rhyth button and the woman ground her foot into his face and trod on him as she stepped away, crushing his nose and lips beneath what seemed like all of her eight or nine stone. The next foot descended, pure, clean, pink-soled, scented with lemon, and he shuddered with pleasure again as it began to stroke and soothe his face. His third ejaculation was building in his cock and balls, pumped out of him by the contrast between one foot and the next, by the lurch between sweet-scented purity and cheese-scented impurity, the descent from Heaven to Hell and ascent from Hell to Heaven. He pressed the button again and the lemon sole stepped onto his face and away, and his cock jerked as the next unwashed foot loomed above his face and descended, its cheesy reek raping its way into his nostrils again.

This was the foot of a slender Asian with large breasts and plump-lipped cunt, and his tongue probed and nostrils flared with added vigour, analysing the flavours and stinks that met them as she rubbed her foot on his face. His cock jerked again in the fellatrix's mouth, but it was still dry-firing and he pressed the rot-rhyth button again. Now another foot was descending on his face, clean, scented, smooth-soled, and soothing coconut was blowing through the cheese-raped galleries of his nose. This woman, a pale-skinned Scandinavian blonde, was more expert, more adept at pleasuring his face with her foot-stroking and sliding, and when he pressed the button and she stepped herself away, her release and re-gathering of weight was so well-timed and executed that her sole seemed to impress itself on his brain.

The third unwashed foot descended, and he could no longer hold back the sperm the blonde had provoked, spurting freely into the fellatrix's warm mouth, almost as though the cheesy reek of the descending foot was driving fluid out of him. He was fully into his erotic delirium now, seeming to mount on wide angel's wings with each washed-and-scented foot, God-blessed with sunlight, and plunge precipitously, white wings scorched to black ash, with each unwashed-and-stinking foot, restored and rejected, restored and rejected, as the wheel of the scentipede rotated on his scented-then-stinking, stinking-then-scented face. On foot seventeen, a jasmine-scented *chinoise*, he ejaculated for the fourth time, gasping with exhaustion, and even the reek of foot eighteen, his first true black, and sweetness of foot nineteen, another slender Scandinavian blonde, could not prevent his cock beginning to soften in the fellatrix's busily sucking mouth.

But his cock slowly re-stiffened as the scentipede rotated, blessing and blasting his nostrils over and over, and was fully erect again by foot forty-two, and spurting again by foot seventy-three. Here, perversely, so near to the final women in the scentipede, he ordered the rotation to reverse, and re-lived the scent-and-stink of the seventy-two feet he had already experienced before encountering, in reverse, the scent-and-stink of the final twenty-seven women. After that, exhausted, he ordered the scentipede to stop rotating and climbed wearily from the *papier-mâché* foot to take his hour's rest, accompanied by foot thirty-one (one of the Scandinavian blondes), foot forty-six (a Junoesque Romanian), foot fifty-eight (a petite Malay), and foot eighty-nine (a cream-skinned *irlandaise*). Paradoxically, he returned with a spring in his step, his cock re-stiffened and swaying before him as he walked to the *papier-mâché* model of the left foot of the Aphrodite of Cyrene, waited for the tiny Latvian fellatrix to climb in before him, and then climbed inside himself.

When he was ready, and the women he had selected to accompany his hour's rest had retaken their places in the scentipede, he ordered the rotation to begin again. Once more the feet passed over his face, scented and stinking, scented and stinking, but though his cock remained stiff, he did not ejaculate again and was able to enjoy two-and-a-half rotations before ordering the scentipede to rotate anti-clockwise and enjoying a further one-and-three-quarters. He then climbed from the foot, followed by a disappointed fellatrix, and prepared to fit the hundred pairs of stilettos for the fruit, vegetable, and egg trampling. Catching sight of the look on the fellatrix's face, however, and realising her disappointment at not increasing her bonus, he paused to whisper briefly in her ear, and she suddenly beamed and happily began to help him carry one hundred shoeboxes from where they were stacked in a bell-shaped curve against the wall nearest the ramp.

The shoeboxes were black, almost like little coffins, but when the sturdy lids were tugged away they were full of rustling white paper. Now he ordered the scentipede to disconnect, and dildos began to pop out of tight bottoms, as though dozens of champagne bottles were being uncorked. He and the fellatrix continued to unlid the shoeboxes as disconnected women began to unclip their dildos and tossed them inside the curve of the ramp, accompanying the popple of uncorked champagne with a rattle of dildos landing on the oak floor of the hall. Now women were beginning to sit on the outside edge of the ramp, feet dangling, and he and the fellatrix had finished unlidding the one hundred shoeboxes. He reverently unwrapped the first pair of stilettos and held them up, one in each hand, admiring their glittering transparency and the gleam of the three-and-a-third inch steel heel.

He turned and carried them to the ramp, knelt, swung the microphone of his headset away from his lips, and took hold of a pair of dangling feet, kissing them one by one, scented and stinking, before slipping each into its shoe. When he had finished, the fellatrix was at his shoulder with another pair of glass stilettos, and he slid sideways on his knees and took hold of another pair of feet. The champagne corks had long since ceased to pop and the last dildos were rattling onto the floor inside the curve of the ramp; a hundred pairs of feet were dangling over the edge of the ramp, ready for him to fit the one hundred pairs of glass stilettos. He worked steadily, quickly, kissing feet, slipping them into stilettos, and the little fellatrix scurried to keep him supplied from the opened boxes, occasionally losing a second or two by delving in a box that had already been emptied, but soon learning to tug the paper-padding completely out and drop it to one side.

He started to sweat as he worked, his cock dry-firing almost continuously at the sensation of handling and kissing so many beautiful feet, warm, smooth, and scented, warm, sweat-slimed, and stinking, and by the time he had completed the fiftieth he was having to knuckle sweat out of his eyes. He worked on, hearing the fellatrix pant now as she scuttled to hand him new shoes, occasionally glancing to his right to see a curve of completed feet, gleaming in their glass stilettos, then to his left to see a curve of uncompleted feet, swinging girlishly as the scentipedeans waited for his adoring hands and lips. When he had finished the hundredth foot, he pushed the microphone of his headset back into place, swung himself through one-hundred-and-eighty degrees, still kneeling, and nodded the fellatrix onto his straining, swollen cock. As she sucked him he stared upwards at the mirror, watching the full curve of gleaming glass stilettos, then ordered, 'Mexican wave.'

The scentipedeans began to swing their feet in staggered rhythm, making a wave of glittering light ripple round the ramp over and over, and he was soon spurting heavily inside the fellatrix's mouth. Now the fellatrix slipped her mouth off his cock and he stood up: it was time for the TV monitors and the trampling. A couch had been set up along the wall with a bank of monitors in front of it, and he lay on top of it on his face as the tiny fellatrix climbed onto the couch and began to foot-massage him, walking up and down his back, treading in circles on his buttocks, walking down one leg and up the other, as he watched the scentipede finally dissolve and the women form a line facing the rows of fruit, vegetables, and eggs.

He tested the control he was holding in his hand, zooming in and out, then gave the order for the trampling to begin. The glass-stilettoed, steel-heeled line began to move slowly forward, and he watched, cock solid beneath his belly, as the first grapes began to squash and burst beneath the toes of the stilettos, then be ground and crushed beneath the knifing steel-heels. He sniffed, almost able to smell the grape juice spilling from the row as the feet passed over it, listening to the over-amplified squelch and pop of destroyed grapes sounding over the room's loudspeakers. Then the stilettos reached the row of larks' eggs. The crunch of the breaking shells was continuous, like sustained volleys of rifle-fire, and whites and yolk splashed over the women's shins and calves, as though the eggs were ejaculating over them in their death-throes. He sniffed, definitely able to smell grape juice now, overwhelmed with the pleasure of four senses: sound, smell, sight, and touch, as the soft little feet of the fellatrix continued to work up and down his back, buttocks, and legs.

Next came the strawberries, mashed and pulped beneath the now-smeared and stained stilettos and their still-gleaming steel heels. Then plovers' eggs, crunching more loudly, splattering the women's shins and calves more thickly with glistening fresh whites and yolks. Then came the oranges, and he winced and shivered, watching the stilettos descending on the plump fruit, even catching the minute glitter of spraying zest as the steel heels pierced the thick skin and transfixed the oranges in their dozens. He shrugged his shoulders and the fellatrix jumped lightly off his back and he rolled over on his side, eyes still greedy on the monitors, so that she could suck his cock again. He ejaculated as the stilettos began to march over the hens' eggs, firing his own thick sticky fluid as the eggs cracked cataclysmically over the loudspeakers.

The pineapples made him wince even more than the oranges, for they were thicker, sturdier, and the women truly had to trample at them to break them open and leave the fruit divided and glistening in their wake. On the monitors showing wide shots the first rows were lying devastated, mashed and spiked beneath the women's relentless feet, glistening with fluids, while the final rows – the ducks' eggs, the melons, the ostrich eggs, the pumpkins – waited defenceless for destruction to fall upon them. And there went the first ducks' eggs, crashing open on the loudspeakers, spurting whites and yolk as high as the women's knees. He had switched the monitors to random-cycle now, and images came at him in flurries and spurts: a steel heel crashing through a curved brown shell; yolk and white spurting under the toe of a glass stiletto; a fragment of shell clinging to the thigh of a trampling woman.

Then, leaving the row of ducks' eggs crushed and glistening in their wake, they were on to the melons, and for the first time they had to work hard to destroy a row: even after a dozen stabs from steel heels the fruit remained intact, sugary juice spurting up from the wounds against the bare legs of the *stilettistas*, black melon seeds clinging to the women's shining skin like tiny parasites. They had to jump hard on the melons, kick at them, to destroy them, finally shattering the heavy bulk of the fruit and scattering the pink sweet pulp. Next, rising like a miniature range of close-packed mountains, the ostrich eggs waited; and here again the *stilettistas* had to work hard to destroy, for the heels were even sliding off the shells as the women tried to break them, and they had to raise their feet high and stab them down hard with grunts and gasps, their melon-splashed breasts bouncing with effort. Once broken, the eggs gushed like volcanoes, their yolk and white spurting like magma, soaking the women as high as their bellies and buttocks, and splashes even landed on the lenses of some of the cameras that were recording the scene.

His cock was still in the fellatrix's mouth, jerking as it dry-fired in tribute to what he was watching, and when the first stilettos reached the metre-wide pumpkins, sitting like a row of odd, orange-skinned, organic tanks, he started to come again, his weary cock releasing a few droplets of sperm. The destruction of this row was like watching a 70s disaster movie or Japanese monster movie: on close-up the glass stilettos looked like spacecraft crashing against a skyline of warehouses or sports-stadia, and the steel heels, flashing and falling, looked like death-rays or the weapons of some sequoia-sized monster, Godstilla or Gambera. And yes, some of the east Asian women among the *stilettistas* seemed to be enjoying this row most of all, their small teeth gleaming as they stamped and kicked and slashed the pumpkins open, the moist yellow pulp inside the heavy rind of the pumpkins spraying up over their legs and lower torsos like a blizzard of urine-mixed snow.

Eyes still eager on the screens, he reached down his body and tapped the bobbing head of the fellatrix, and her mouth came off his cock with a pop. She slid back on her knees as he rolled onto his stomach again, then stood up and stepped back onto him and continued the foot-massage as he watched the destruction of the final row, the steel heels stabbing into the final few pumpkins, most of the women smiling or laughing now, as though fantasising that they had their enemies under their deadly feet. He began to switch off monitors, leaving a mixture of close-up and long-view for the final moments of the trampling, ready to start choosing women for the final act of the ritual. The paper labels clinging between the women's shoulder-blades were flecked and splashed with egg, fruit, and vegetable, but very few were unreadable and he had already chosen most of the women he wanted.

There. They were passing finally off the row of pumpkins, their skin coated thickly as far as their bellies with a sheet of pumpkin and melon pulp over a glistening sheet of ostrich egg-white and yolk, with splatters of pulp and egg all over their upper bodies too. The stilettos were almost invisible and it seemed odd to watch the women taking them off, as though they were detaching their feet and leaving them behind as they walked to line up in groups of twenty at one end of the five rows he had selected for trampling with bare feet: the larks' eggs, strawberries, pineapples, melons, and ostrich eggs. The two women at the rear of each group turned to the wall and detached one of the hoses hanging from it, then flicked it on and sent a high-pressure jet of warm water spurting against her legs and feet, cleaning them so that he would taste only what she next walked on in the row.

When each of these women had finished her own legs and feet, she walked forward between the remaining eighteen women in her group, who had formed into two rows and turned to face each other. Their legs and feet sprung out startlingly clean as the pumpkin and melon was whisked away by the high-pressure jet of water, and he ground his hips against the couch hungrily as they lifted their feet to have their soles cleaned, giggling involuntarily at the ticklish feel of the water. When every woman's legs and feet had been cleaned and each group had turned to face its row again, he reached down and lifted a microphone to his lips.

'Walk,' he ordered, and the groups began to walk slowly forward over the trampled rows of larks' eggs, strawberries, pineapples, melons, and ostrich eggs. He watched the bare, clean feet come forward, stepping onto mashed egg or fruit, thin jets of it squirting between their toes, and soon becoming filthy, splattered, coated in egg or fruit pulp, large pieces of ostrich-egg shell tilting and throwing egg like catapults up the bare legs of the women walking down the ostrich-egg row. He had chosen eight of the women he wanted now from the groups, and was watching the monitors eagerly for numbers nine and ten. There. That slender *chinoise* . . . and that . . . yes, that tall black. The women continued to paddle and splash down the rows of crushed eggs and fruit, their legs coated in pulp or white-and-yolk as high as their calves now. His stomach rolled and cock jerked as he thought of licking everything off, raw egg and sweet fruit-pulp, his tongue passing over their soles, worming between their toes, spiralling round their ankles, climbing their calves in long sweeps.

The first of them were reaching the end of the rows, and he licked his lips, preparing to read out the base-five numbers he had chosen: 32 (a high-ankled redhead), 11 (a gap-toed Malay), 41 (one of the Scandinavian blondes), 30 (a *chinoise* with feet as tiny as a child's), 92 (another Scandinavian blonde), 103 (a narrow-footed mulatto), 122 (a prehensile-toed brunette), 140 (another high-ankled redhead), 210 (the slender *chinoise*), 233 (the tall black). There: they were all coming off the rows, feet splashing on the bare floor, forming circles, arms linked, and rotating for him again, displaying the numbers between their shoulder-blades. He puffed into the microphone and began to read out the numbers he had chosen as the circles continued to rotate.

'Thirty-two . . . eleven . . . forty-one . . .'

Women who did not recognise their number were told that they had been chosen by women who did, and the rotating circles broke apart one by one. Soon, very soon, ninety of the women would be walking away to their showers, and he would be licking his way up the feet and legs of the remaining ten. The fellatrix had hopped from his back and was busy setting up the long-legged chairs in which his chosen ten would sit.

'Two hundred and ten,' he said. 'Two hundred and thirty-three.'

The ten women were now chosen; all that was left was for them to be carried over to him by their comrades. A pair of the strongest women in each group stood behind each of the two women who had been chosen from it, and the chosen women were hoisted into the air, their arms slipping round the necks of the strong women, their bottoms on the strong women's clasped hands. They were carried to the chairs that awaited them, their dangling feet dripping egg and fruit pulp to the floor, and he finally snapped off the monitors and turned on the couch to meet them, his cock stiff and aching between his thighs. It was impossible that he would come again, but he was certain that somehow he would as he licked his way along the row of feet dangling in the chairs.

He took hold of the head of his cock and masturbated it as he watched the women slipping off their carriers' hands and twisting to land their firm bottoms on the seats of the chairs. The fellatrix walked down the row of chairs as each was occupied, dropping a broad wooden disc beneath each pair of dangling feet from the pile she was balancing on her forearm. He stopped masturbating, pushed himself off the couch, and went down on his knees to crawl to the nearest pair, glistening with the white and yolk of crushed raw larks' eggs.

He reached them and looked down the row impatiently, waiting for the final chair to be occupied and the final wooden disc laid beneath the dangling feet to catch drops of falling ostrich-egg yolk and white. Then he caught hold of the right foot in front of him, holding it by the ankle between thumb and forefinger, and swung it upwards and towards his opening mouth. The first stroke of his tongue over the sole made him groan with pleasure: the raw, slightly bitter egg was such a contrast to the smoothness and warmth of the soleskin, and the redhead shivered deliciously, tickled by his hot, sticky tongue. He licked the sole again, reaching between his thighs and beginning to masturbate himself with his free hand as he prepared to start tonguing and sucking the five pink toes.

The woman shivered again, and now he started on her toes, mining the white and yolk that had collected between them, spiralling them with his tongue, tugging at them, taking the big toe into his mouth and sucking it like a lollipop. His masturbating hand began to move faster, but his balls were exhausted and he knew it would be two or three feet down the row before he came again. He licked, lapped, sucked, kissed, nibbled his way over the foot, leaving the sole and toes clean behind him

as he began on its upper surface, working conscientiously towards the ankles, still savouring the contrast
between bitter egg and sweet skin, timing the movement
of his tongue on the woman to the movement of his
hand between his thighs.

When he had finished the foot, he slid sideways to
position himself midway between the redhead's larks'-
egg-soaked left foot and the Malay's strawberry-soaked
right foot, so that he could lift both simultaneously and
hold them together like a sandwich of warm footflesh,
sour and sweet, slick and pulpy, egg and strawberry. He
had to take his hand off his cock to do it, using both
hands to guide and direct the feet, and he didn't have to
look up and nod the fellatrix over to him, because her
small warm hand was already slipping between his
thighs and taking over, gripping the head of his cock
gently and beginning to masturbate him, her palm and
fingers wet with her professionally copious spittle. Now
he had a contrast not merely between egg and footskin,
but between egg and strawberry, strawberry and footskin, and his joy began to mount, moving him towards
his eight or ninth orgasm of St Lupus's Day.

4

Sole Music

Genesis, 8:9 But the dove found no rest for the sole of her foot, and she returned unto him into the ark.

'The oasis Veneris, little one,' she whispered in his ear, and strands of her hair brushed his sweating cheek like sparks. She kissed him, her lips light as falling petals, and tickled a fingernail between his breasts and down, down, down over his belly . . . and lifted it away. He heard the rich curtains whisper back into place: she must have slipped silently through them like the serpent of Hades she was, to torment him again as he lay bound and blindfold on the floor of the palanquin. He shuddered as her scent lingered in his nostrils, and bit his lip to suppress a groan. They had been travelling across the desert for many hours; now they had arrived at the oasis she had spoken of, and the worst of his torments was about to begin. The rack and the lead-mines held no fears for him, and he had laughed in the face of the sizzling brand and the air-bruising scourge, vowing never to repudiate his crucified Galilean god-man or to burn the slightest crumb of incense before the Emperor's image; and his Roman tormentors had seemed baffled by his obduracy and courage, flinging him back into his cell and leaving him there unfed and unwatered for two days.

And then, chained upright and naked against the wall, bruises and whip-tracks still livid in his skin, the stench of his own filth heavy in his nostrils, he had heard the rattle of the lock and the owl-like screech of the unoiled hinges of the door of his cell. He had not opened his eyes or raised his head, and he was puzzled to hear not the heavy tread of the guard, come to inform him of some new torment or of the final order for his execution, but the soft lisp of sandals and then the whisper of a silken hood being drawn back as his visitor stood before him. His nostrils had flared before he was consciously aware of the thread of scent that had reached them; and he raised his head and opened his eyes and gasped at what he saw in front of him.

Aye, the screech of the door had been owl-like indeed, for it was a priestess of Hecate come to practise her Satanic wiles upon him. Rising above the green cloth of her travelling gown, whose neck was deliberately cut and arranged like leaves, her face was like a flower, pale and moist, with a rosebud of a mouth and two large, slanting, leaf-green eyes framed between petal-like curls of poppy-yellow hair. She had smiled faintly, lifting her chin a little and staring him directly in the eyes, then lowered her gaze slowly down his naked body, her smile strengthening. It was though she were caressing him with her eyes, and a hot fresh sweat had broken out on his skin, half-dissolving the crust of salt with which it was caked. Her eyes fell lower, lower, till they reached his dangling *membrum virile*, and now he groaned aloud, for the tip of her tongue had slipped between her lips, trembled there for a moment like a snake's, and then withdrawn.

She had looked up at his face then, reading his agony, and smiling more broadly still. She looked back over her shoulder, calling out in a bell-like voice, '*Custos!*'; and the guard, shambling like a bear, had entered the cell, bowing to her as she ordered him to unchain his Christian prisoner. He had been unable to stand and the guard had to drag him from the cell to the eight burly, dark-skinned slaves and the waiting palanquin, where the young woman watched as he was bound with silk cords and laid blindfold on the floor in the rear compartment.

'A fine privilege you have earned, *filiole*,' the guard had rasped maliciously in his ear as he was lowered there. ''Tis the Emperor's own favourite whore, the Lady Nymphissa, come to purge you of your Galilean fever with a *cura amoris*.'

A flaming sword had seemed to strike him through the heart as he learned this; and the feet of the slaves followed the rhythm of the guard's final words as the woman climbed into the palanquin herself and gave the order for the journey to begin. *Cura amoris, cura amoris, cura amoris* . . . cure of love, cure of love, cure of love . . . What had the guard meant? What did the woman intend with him? But he had learned soon enough, for the curtains dividing compartment from compartment had whispered back and the scent of honeyed lilies was again in his nostrils.

'Iohannes,' she had whispered into his ear, her breath cool against his sweating skin. '*Sitisnum?*'

He had not answered her, but his withered tongue had moved involuntarily inside his parched mouth, and she must have read the movement, for a delicate hand slipped under his head and lifted him to push the spout of a *hydria* between his cracked lips. He had tried to spit out the trickle of water she had released into his mouth, but the spout had swung away and tormentingly cool and delicate fingers were holding his lips closed, forcing him to swallow. Then her mouth had been at his ear again, and a fingernail was tickling down between his breasts, over his belly, as she whispered: 'You must drink, Iohannes, for you must have strength for the ordeals ahead, in the temple of Aphrodite at the oasis Veneris.'

'*Scortum Satanæ!*' he had hissed.

'*Scortum sum,*' she had gravely agreed, her fingernail tickling through the first fringes of his pubic hair. '*Sed non Satanæ . . . Veneris.*'

And then, with a tweak at the hair, her hand had lifted away and the curtains had whispered again and she was gone, leaving him to become slowly and horrifyingly aware that his *membrum virile* was prickling with extra heat; indeed, that it was slowly, very slowly, beginning to swell and erect. The water had been drugged with some aphrodisiac. A sweat of shame and horror had broken out over his whole body, quite soaking the floor beneath him, and he had gabbled a prayer for divine aid and somehow forced the swelling down. After ten minutes the curtains had again whispered open and cool fingers had curled round his flaccid member. She had hissed faintly with surprise as she tightened her grip and lifted it, then she had released him and returned to her compartment. She had tried to give him more water again later, but he had turned his head aside and refused to open his mouth, even when she held his nostrils pinched shut until blood was roaring in his ears like the *bucinæ Josue*, and she had left him with a laugh and the whispered threat: 'The oasis Veneris, Iohannes.'

Now they had arrived, and her threat was about to be realised. The palanquin was lowered to the ground and after a moment he heard her voice outside, instructing the slaves in some language he did not recognise. The curtains were wrenched back by strong masculine hands, and so long had he lain in darkness that, even through his blindfold, his eyes smarted with the sunlight that flooded over him as he was seized and lifted out, his naked body suddenly cooling as hot sunlight fell and sucked the sweat from his skin. He held his eyes shut as he was held upright and the blindfold was untied and tugged away, and she ordered the slaves to open them for him. A strong hand clamped on either side of his

76

occiput and blunt fingers prised at his eyelids, pulling them open and forcing him to see. And there she stood in front of him in her green travelling cloak, smiling faintly, looking as cool and fresh as she had in his prison cell; and then she had stepped aside, holding out her hand and saying, 'The oasis Veneris, Iohannes.'

The first glimpse of what lay before him made him cease struggling, and the woman ordered the slaves to release him. The hands and fingers fell away and he gazed in wonder.

'*Paradisus voluptatis*,' he murmured involuntarily. She caught the phrase with her witch's ears, sharp as an owl's, and her bell-like laughter went chiming through the sun-scalded air. And it *was* a garden of delights: they stood on the lip of a bowl-like oasis set in rolling leagues of sun-flogged desert. It was no more than a few hundred paces from side to side, but was filled almost to the brim with heavily laden fruit-trees and flowers in all shades of the rainbow. Thick clouds of butterflies drifted in all directions, and he saw tiny, sharp-winged birds with gem-like breasts that sparkled as they flitted from tree to tree. He heard a deep humming beneath their joyous trills and roulades, and he noted huge, tigerishly striped bees moving from flower to flower. The first tendrils of scent met his nostrils, creeping forth from the sheltered bowl, and his ears sang for a moment with dizziness.

'Bring him,' Nymphissa said, and she turned to lead six of the eight slaves down into the oasis. It was as though a cloak of cold was thrown over him as he was pushed beneath the first trees, and the deep humming of the bees seemed to enter his bones as he grew dizzy with the scents of the flowers round him, hanging like invisible banks of mist on the undisturbed air. He saw the first silver glitter of the pool that lay at the heart of this pseudo-paradise, and caught the bone-white gleam of the marble hypaethral temple that stood on its shore.

Nymphissa paused in front of him, stooping to a flower that nodded like a scarlet trumpet blasting his perdition, and turned carrying on the back of her hand one of the huge bees. She picked it up between forefinger and thumb and lifted it to her mouth, watching his face with a smile. She nodded as though he had given his permission for her to continue and slipped the bee into her mouth like a furry date. Her mouth closed and she smiled at him, then opened her mouth and allowed the bee to crawl out and pause on her lips before taking to the air, the notes of its wings seemingly deepened with indignation.

'*Non pungent*, Iohannes,' she said, and turned back to lead them on. The pool glittered again through the trees, then again, and again, and then was there before him. A corner of the temple shouldered into view and was not hidden again, and when he could see the thing clearly he groaned with well-justified horror and disgust, for its eight marble columns were carved in the shape of *ithyphalloi*, with swollen bases counterfeiting heavy scrotal sacs and apexes in the shape of the *glans penis* holding up the roof. The temple was open to the air and contained a single tripod of beaten silver before a malachite copy of Heliodorus's *Aphrodite Untying a Sandal* and a long rectangular altar of white marble from whose corners golden fetters dangled. She led him to the poolside and pointed to the golden fish that crisscrossed its pellucid waters.

'Gifts from the emperor of far Sinœ,' she said. She turned to him, her face set with an unwonted seriousness. 'But it is not true, Iohannes, that they must eat human flesh or lose their colour. Or at least, not true that they must eat it *often*.'

At the look on his face her laughter went chiming through the air again. She turned and led him finally to the temple and up the nine steps to its white marble floor.

'Hold him,' she told the slaves, and went over to the tripod and the small chest of dark wood that stood between its legs. She swung the lid open and lifted out fire-making apparatus, three crystal jars of incense, and what seemed like rolls of white cloth. Soon the tripod was smoking, and simultaneous with the assault of pagan smells on his nostrils came an assault of pagan syllables on his ears, for she stood, head bowed, before the tripod and statue and prayed for success in her coming battle. Then, having sprinkled another handful of incense on the smouldering sandalwood coals with which the tripod was now filled, she turned and jumped lightly, catlike onto the rectangular altar of marble.

'Bring him closer,' she ordered, and he was carried closer. Now he could see clearly the carvings with which the sides of the altar were crowded, and indignant blood rose into his cheeks and whistled in his ears.

'Look at me,' she ordered, and he raised his eyes to see her shrug her travelling-cloak off. It sloughed from her white body like early-falling leaves, but at first sight of her white shoulders he squeezed his eyes shut and began to gabble a prayer.

'Open them for him,' she ordered, and strong hands clamped as before on his head as blunt fingers prised as before at his eyelids. He crossed his eyes as light again struck them, frantic not to see the soul-blasting nakedness before him, but despite himself his brain sharpened and reconstructed the blurred plains and curves of her body as she displayed herself with a harlot's shamelessness.

'*Non sum bella*, Iohannes?'[1] she asked mockingly. '*Corpus meum, non te placet?*'[2]

Her body was smooth and unblemished, like the innermost petals of a flower, and he caught the flash and glitter of the gold that hung from the pink nipples atop

---

[1] 'Am I not beautiful, John?'
[2] 'My body, does it not please thee?'

the breasts which she held and shook for him and from the pink lips of her shaved *pudendum muliebre*, her woman's shame, which she held open for him between splayed thighs before turning to bend and hold the marble purity of her *nates* apart and display the pink coin of her anus as she peered for his response between her thighs. The hands of the slaves on his head and eyelids shook faintly and the ham of his left leg was prodded by what seemed like a rod of iron: the slaves were responding to the poisoned sweets scattered so wantonly before them. He, somehow, with God's aid, managed to fight back his lust, spurring down his *membrum* with dread of Hell and hope of Heaven, and when she blew out her lips, seeing between her thighs that his *membrum* remained quiescent, he was filled with a great gladness. She let go of her buttocks, straightened, and turned back to him.

'Bind me,' she ordered now, kneeling on the marble altar with her upper body erect, arms held hard to her sides, and two slaves ran to stand on either side of her as another ran to the rolls of white cloth she had removed from the chest. The slave carried one to the slaves standing on either side of her, and they began to wrap her in the cloth, handing the roll back and forth as it unwound, wrapping her neck and shoulders and upper arms and her body, but leaving her gold-pierced nipples free and pouting at him. It was like a mummification, the Christian realised: she was being wrapped as though for the tomb, her arms bound to her sides in winding after winding of cloth. When they had bound her in three rolls of cloth as far as her hips, leaving her arms trapped but for her hands, she pushed herself off her knees and jumped lightly from the altar to the floor of the temple.

'Fasten him,' she said, and he was carried forward to the altar and laid on top of it face up. The slaves dragged his hands and feet into place and fastened them into the golden fetters as he turned his head aside from the vividly painted obscenities leering down at him from the temple ceiling between the brass-lined grooves of some Satanic mechanism. But his heart was glad, for in the midst of his despair a means of salvation had been vouchsafed him. He might be bound hand and foot, his body defenceless against the wiles she would now practise on him, but if no miracle supervened he could in his last extremity bite off his . . .

'*Linguam præterea*,'[3] she ordered, suddenly using Latin, and before he could react his mouth was wrenched open and a golden bit had been set between his teeth, cool at first against his tongue and lips, swiftly beginning to warm. The *lamia* – thus he had begun to apostrophise her – walked over to him now, her bound upper body swaying voluptuously, making the tiny silver bells hanging on her gold nipple-rings tinkle like the far-off laughter of water-nymphs.

'Last year,' she said. 'One of you escaped me by biting off his tongue. It shall not happen again. Wash him, and anoint him with the oils.'

The bare feet of the slaves pattered on the marble floor as they hastened to obey, and in few moments he was gasping beneath the impact of two heavy *situlæ* of water carried from the pool. The water was cool and refreshing, and the vegetable husks with which other slaves then began to scrub his body were harshly soothing on his bruised and cut skin. He smelt her scent again and then the spout of a *hydria* was again between his gold-levered lips and faintly spiced water was flooding into his mouth. He swallowed some despite himself, and she sighed with satisfaction as she lifted the *hydria* away.

'*Es meus*, Iohannes,'[4] she said. '*Meus, nunc et semper.*'[5]

---

[3] 'Also his tongue.'
[4] 'Thou art mine, John.'
[5] 'Mine, now and always.'

He shook his head, tugging at his golden fetters, writhing his body beneath the scrubbing husks.

'*Sum Dei*,'[6] he cried out in despair. '*Sum Dei, et Ejus Soli.*'[7]

'*Meum*,' she repeated, and then the husks were lifted away and two more *situlæ* of water were dashed on his body.

'*Satis*,'[8] she said. '*Unguete eum.*'[9]

A thick odour of spice was suddenly in his nostrils and he looked down his body to see four slaves, two on either side of him, tipping flasks slowly over him. Slow threads of oil fell from them, landing heavily on his skin and pooling there before beginning to trickle down his flanks. He heard a rattle of what sounded like rope, a jingle of brass straps, and heard her order, 'Lift me.' He opened his eyes to see her being hoisted in a leather harness that hung on a rope from a pulley in the network of brass-lined grooves in the temple ceiling. Two thinner ropes stretched from the pulley into the hands of slaves on either side of the altar, and when she was in the air, fluttering her hands like the wings of pale butterflies, they tugged in unison and she swung over him.

'*Sum angela*, Iohannes!'[10] she cried above him, still fluttering her hands. 'See how I fly!'

And in truth she was as beautiful as an angel, as beautiful as Lucifer must have been, that *angelus lucis*,[11] that son of the morning, falling from heaven like a star.

'Lower me,' she ordered, and the ropes twanged as the two slaves jerked on them and she began to descend upon him, treading the air with her exquisite feet, no larger than a child's, with soles as pink and smooth as rose-petals.

---

[6] 'I am God's.'
[7] 'I am God's, and His alone.'
[8] 'Enough.'
[9] 'Anoint him.'
[10] 'I am an angel, John.'
[11] Angel of light.

'More slowly,' she said as her feet approached his chest. He groaned and closed his eyes, feeling the drugged water beginning to work inside him, prickling in his treacherous *membrum virile*; and when her toes brushed his belly he began to mumble a prayer round the gold bit in his mouth.

'Cease lowering,' she said. 'Now, silence him.'

A moment later a spice-soaked cloth was stuffed into his mouth around the bit, beginning to fill his head with its odour as she ordered, 'Forward, but slowly, slowly,' and the slaves began to inch her forward as she massaged the spiced oil into his skin with her toes.

'Stop.'

She was over his nipples now and began to rub them with her toes, north-east-south-west over his right nipple, west-south-east-north over his left, and to pluck and tweak at them with her great and second toes, so that he groaned through the cloth filling his mouth and her laughter pealed down on him.

'Again, forward,' she ordered.

Her feet began to move again, travelling up his chest, tickling at his throat and chin, then stroking his face.

'Lower me a little.'

Now her soles were on his face, soft and smooth as silk, scented with honeyed lilies, softly treading him to delirium as he began to sweat heavily again with the horror of what she was doing to him.

'*Haec dicit, Domina,*' she said, and he writhed in his fetters to hear her pervert scripture so flagrantly, '*caelum sedis mea et facies tua scabillum pedum meorum!*'[12]

'*Domina mea!*' one of the slaves called to her; '*vide membrum ejus!*'[13]

---

[12] 'Thus saith the LADY, The heaven is my throne, and thy face is a stool for my feet!'
[13] 'My Lady, behold his cock.'

83

He felt one of her feet slide on his face as she twisted in her harness, looking back down his body, and laughing with glee at what she saw: his *membrum*, overheated by the drug now filling his blood, spurred to arousal by her feet gently treading at his face, had begun to lift and swell, rising to point like a huge blunt finger at the obscene paintings on the roof of the temple.

'Back!' she ordered, and he felt her feet leave his face as the slaves hauled her back down his body. He rocked his head from side to side, ordering his *membrum* down furiously inside his head, threatening himself with all the tortures of the *puteus abyssi*,[14] imagining his nostrils filled with the stink of sulphur, his ears filled with the screams and blasphemies of his fellow damned, his skin gnawed with tongues of undying fire; but it was no use: his *membrum* rose to greet her as she swung down his body, paddling at the oil on his skin as she went.

When she hung over his *membrum* she ordered the slaves to halt her there and to anoint him for massage; and when the heavy oils had been tipped over the head of his *membrum* and were trickling down its vein-crawled shaft, she began to work at him with her feet, sliding her soles down and up, rotating them as they went, massaging the oil into his cock-skin, and paying particular and careful attention to his *glans*, which she also tweaked and rubbed with her toes. His balls rose in their leathery sac, and he felt the salty liquor of his seed, which he had not spilled voluntarily since his earliest youth, beginning to boil up within them.

But even through her feet her whorish skill read his impending *fluxus seminis*,[15] and she began to work at him more slowly, more gently, allowing the vats of his pleasure to fill more deeply before release. She slipped the toes of one foot beneath his sac, lifting it against the

---

[14] The Bottomless Pit.
[15] Flux of seed.

toes of the other, testing the state of his arousal, then ordered the slaves to lower her further to him and to open his eyes, that he might watch what she purposed. A cushion was propped beneath his head, lifting it forward as the blunt fingers again prised his eyelids open and he saw her nakedness. There she hung in her leather harness from the white marble ceiling, her upper body wound in white linen, her pink-nippled, gold-pierced breasts on wanton display between the windings, quivering to her descent, and there were her small feet, still working at his swollen *membrum* as she splayed her thighs like a frog's and lowered the pink-lipped, gold-pierced mouth of her feminine sheath to the blunt red head of his masculine sceptre.

The heat that glowed from her struck him before her vulval lips touched him, like a breath from the gate of Hell, and then her vulva kissed the head of his *membrum* and she ordered 'Pause!', holding his *membrum* firm between the soles of her feet.

'Empty his mouth,' she ordered the slaves, and the spice-soaked cloth was plucked from between his lips. He instantly began to gabble his prayers for salvation, the sacred syllables uncouthly altered and deformed by the gold bit that had been forced between his teeth.

'Iohannes,' she said through his words. '*Es in limine paradisi voluptatis. Volesne entrare?*'[16]

She rocked herself a little on his *membrum*, lodging the head deeper between the heated pink lips for a moment as she rotated her hips on him, and his prayers took on a more frantic tone, directed now above all to Saint Anthony, who had triumphed, surely, over worse lascivities in the visions sent him by cunning Satan. His balls were aching fiercely, drawn hard to the root of his *membrum*, and he knew that a single thrust up into her

---

[16] 'Thou art on the threshold of the garden of delights. Do you wish to enter?'

would suffice to secure her triumph, for he would fountain like the *diluvium Noe*.[17]

'*Volesne entrare?*' she repeated through his words, and he felt as though he were hanging at full stretch from the lip of a precipice, feeling his fingers one by one lose their strength. But then, in the moment of his greatest extremity, even as his lips writhed against the impulse to shriek '*Volo!*',[18] the Lord seemed to answer his prayers. He heard a deep rumble as of subterranean laughter, and the altar beneath his sweat-drenched back bucked and trembled. '*In tonitru et commotione terrae!*'[19] he cried out in triumph as the witch who tormented him twisted in her harness, wailing with fright and calling upon her slaves not to desert her.

But his head and eyes had already been released, and he watched gladly now as she cast fear-heated eyes on the handiwork of the Lord enacted round her, her gateway of femininity still held to the head of his *membrum*. There was a crash as the malachite statue of Venus, rocking on its onyx base, overturned and shattered on the marble floor, and the two slaves who held her aloft released the ropes with cries of terror and fled. She gave another wail as she fell, and his hammering heart, filled with joy and thanksgiving to the Lord, lurched with horror, for his *membrum* impaled her as she fell, sliding to the root into her fear-tightened sheath. '*In tonitru et commotione terrae!*' he repeated, but the altar was quieting beneath his shoulders and the rumble was fading to a mutter, to a whisper, to silence, and the terror on the face of the witch was fading to fear, to doubt, to relief. There she sat, still upright in her harness, impaled on his still rigid

---

[17] Noah's flood.

[18] 'I wish!'

[19] Isaiah 29:6 [Thou shalt be visited of the LORD of hosts] with thunder, and with earthquake . . .

membrum; and now her mouth curled and she smiled upon him and spoke.

'*Es* in *paradiso voluptatis*, Iohannes,'[20] she said, and ground her rump slowly north-east-south-west, west-south-east-north, working her tight sheath upon his *membrum*. She looked away and spoke again in the unknown language, rebuking the slaves he heard returning to the temple for their cowardice; and she cut through their exculpations with a brisk nod at the floor of the temple and the order: '*Caput affere.*'

Bring the head. What had she meant? In the next moment he saw: a slave was lifting the head of Venus from the shattered statue and carrying it to her.

'*Non. Hosti osculum habet Dea.*'[21]

The slave turned and brought the head to him, pressing the smooth cool green face to his, setting the smooth cool lips against his own. He groaned, trying to turn his head aside, and Nymphissa's laughter echoed again under the marble temple roof; and when the head was lifted away he saw her setting her feet carefully to either side of his hips.

'*Hortum meum irriga, Galileæ,*'[22] she ordered, beginning, very slowly, to raise and lower herself on him. '*Irriga me . . . irriga me . . . irriga me . . .*'

---

[20] 'Thou art *in* the garden of delights, Iohannes.'
[21] 'No. It is for our guest the goddess has a kiss.'
[22] 'Water my garden, Galilean.'

5

Footing the Belle

'One moment, gen'lemen, please.'

The three men turned and saw the girl at the clothes-counter holding out, one dangling from her left hand, two from her right, what seemed like three muzzles. Muzzles for dogs with long, slender snouts.

'Ah,' said Ashby, scratching at the hair on his chest for a moment. 'Sorry, fellers. In my eagerness to get aboard and join in the fun, I clean forgot.'

He led them back to the counter and took the muzzles from the girl, handing one to Freeman, one to Neruda, keeping one for himself.

'What are they?' Neruda asked, holding his up and examining it. It was made of glass, with no breathing holes, and its bulbous end seemed to be graduated, as though to measure some liquid.

'Cock-muzzles, sir,' the girl said. Freeman looked at her, marvelling again at the freshness of her complexion.

'Cock-muzzles?' he said.

'Yessir. You slip 'em on an' every time you come it stays safe an' snug inside. Then, on the way out, you can watch me make a cocktail of 'em an' drink the lot.'

She beamed happily. Neruda lowered his cock-muzzle and whistled.

'*Cariña*, 'ow old *are* you?'

'Eighteen, sir. An' I sure love drinkin' come. It's great for the skin. Cain't you see?'

She rested an index finger on either side of her chin and pushed her face first one way, then the other, then licked her lips with an 'Hmm-*hmmm*' and beamed again. Freeman felt his cock rising in salute of her unashamed sluttishness. Neruda, his thick cock already fully erect, grunted and said, 'If you'd like some now, *cariña*, your oncle is ready.'

The girl shook her head, her lips quirking sadly.

'Sorry, sir. House rule. No penetration of orifices on board ship with cocks. You can watch, but you cain't touch. Not with your cocks, that is.'

Neruda frowned.

'Then 'ow the fock do we come?'

'You'll come, all right, Nero, old buddy,' Ashby said. 'Trust Brother Ashby on that. Here, let's get 'em on and get into the action. Dice game sound OK?'

He unbuckled the strap and slipped it round his buttocks as he guided the muzzle itself over his erect cock, then tightened and re-buckled the strap.

'Dice? Sure, why not?' said Neruda, following suit, and Freeman echoed him as he slipped his own cock into his muzzle. 'But when do we get to see the girls?'

'The girls *are* the dice game,' said Ashby. 'You'll see. Can you whistle them we're coming, honey?'

'Right away, sir.'

The girl turned and tugged a speaking-tube from the wall behind her, then turned the pointer on what looked like a clock face set beneath it till the pointer was pointing at XI. She whistled sharply into the tube.

'Mai-Wu, sweetpah, there's a party o' gen'lemen on their way.'

'Thanks, honey,' Ashby said. 'Now, fellers, all we need do now is stock up on cigars and we can proceed to what I promise you will be the finest and most uniquest game of dice you've seen in all your born days.'

He moved along the counter and swung open the lid of a silver cigar-box, taking out a handful of slender cigars and slipping them into the loops that Freeman now saw ran round the strap of each cock-muzzle.

'Makes me feel like a gon-fighter,' Neruda said as he took a handful himself and began to fill his own belt.

'You'll be doing plenty of firing tonight, Juan, ole buddy,' Ashby said. 'It's a guarantee.'

But Neruda had paused and was sniffing suspiciously at one of the cigars.

''Ey, this is no –'

'No ordinary cigar,' Ashby said, plucking it from the Mexican's fingers and pushing it between his lips. 'And that's why you'll be firing so much tonight. Honey, if you could light us up, we'll be on our way.'

He pushed another cigar into the bemused Freeman's mouth and bent over the burning wick the girl was now holding up for him, sucking hard to get the cigar lit, then stepping back to allow his two friends to get their cigars lit too. Neruda lit his cigar then stood back, and Freeman's cock jerked against the cool glass of the muzzle as he bent over the wick and saw the delicate blue veins in the girl's slender white wrists. Ashby and Neruda were waiting for him over by the door, already puffing busily at their cigars.

'Thanks,' he said, lifting his head and nodding at her.

'My pleasure, sir,' she said, then, lowering her voice. 'Be sure an' come loads for me, won'tcha, now?'

He drew on his cigar and blew smoke silently into her face, watching her nostrils flare as she drew it in. He took another draw on his cigar, feeling a singing begin in his ears.

'For you, honey, I'll come like an elephant.'

Her laughter followed him as he walked to Ashby and Neruda and Ashby led the two of them down the red-carpeted corridor leading from the clothes-counter to the rest of the ship, cocks sticking ahead of them in the glass muzzles. They paused at the first few of the oil paintings that lined the oak-panelled walls, then walked on, cocks stiffer than ever.

'That redhead,' said Ashby, jerking a thumb over his shoulder, 'she is painted from life. The blonde too. You'll see some visit.'

They were walking towards the first doorway, and Freeman heard a sudden outburst of applause from the room beyond it as wisps of smoke curled round its jamb. Ashby led them past and he had time only to glance inside, seeing through a haze of cigar smoke a party of naked men seated two-deep round a low platform of red velvet atop which two naked young women were strangely entangled. He looked up at the scroll in fancy lettering above the door. *Footing the Belle*. He caught up with Ashby.

'Say, Jack, what's footing the belle?'

'Wait. You'll see some visit.'

'*Hombre*,' complained Neruda, 'that's what you keep sayin', an' we ain't seen a thing so far.'

'You're about to,' said Ashby. 'Gentlemen, prepare to place your bets.'

Almost beginning to trot, he led them past two more doorways, one on the left (*Yellow Rose of Texas*), one on the right (*Prime Assets*) and then stopped at a third. Above this door it said *Holey Trinity*. He led them in. The singing in Freeman's head had died away but he felt as though he was a mile high, somehow, towering over the room even as he stood inside it and walked towards the triangular table of green baize in the centre of the floor and the three identical-looking Chinese whores in black silk dresses waiting barefoot by the broad, four-foot marble post at each of its three corners.

'Mai-Wu!' Ashby cried, moving towards one of them and bending to embrace her. She shook her head slightly and one of the other whores said, 'No, Mistuh Aspee, I Mai-Wu.'

'Ah.'

Ashby moved round to her, stooped, and tried to kiss her without taking the cigar out of his mouth. The whore ducked her head aside sinuously as the glowing tip of the cigar stabbed at her face and Ashby chuckled ruefully.

'Sorry, honey.'

He took the cigar out of his mouth and lowered his face again. The whore puckered her lips and they kissed. Ashby turned back to his companions.

'Fellers, I want you to meet Mai-Wu and her sisters.'

He began to jerk his cigar one by one at the other girls.

'This here's, this is, uh –'

'Li-Tan,' Mai said.

'And this little cutie's –'

'Chu-Sai.'

'Yep. You might find it hard to tell 'em apart, and the fact is, *I* do, but that ain't so surprising, considerin', is it, Mai-Wu?'

'No, Mistuh Aspee.'

'No, they ain't just sisters, they're triplets. Mai-Wu is the oldest, by about a minute, ain't it, now, Mai-Wu?'

'Yes, Mistuh Aspee.'

'That's why she gets to undress last. Chu-Fan goes first, ain't it, Mai-Wu?'

'Chu-Sai, Mistuh Aspee.'

'Yeah, Chu-Sai. 'Cause she's youngest. So, honey, if you'll begin. Fellers, prepare to fire your first ten-gun salute.'

He moved away from the table and turned back to face it, drawing deep on his cigar and blowing out a smoke ring that dissolved slowly, hanging over the table. Mai-Wu looked towards one of the other girls, Chu-Sai, Freeman realised, and said something in what he presumed was Chinese. The girl bowed her head deeply, then took a pace backwards and wriggled her hips and shoulders. Her black dress slid off her with a rustle of silk, and her pale body seemed to spurt upwards like a flame, her firm, symmetrical apple-sized breasts quivering for a moment. Freeman, cigar between his lips, groaned so loudly that he drowned the sound of Ashby's and Neruda's groans, and then he heard a faint, repeated squirting. He looked down, tottering slightly on weakened knees, and saw that his cock was spurting heavily inside its glass muzzle, like the cocks of Ashby and Neruda. Neruda took his cigar out of his mouth and looked at it in wonder.

'*Madre de dios*,' he said. 'What is *in* this thing?'

Ashby chuckled and took another long drag on his cigar.

'I told you you'd see, Juan, ole buddy. Now, Chu-Sai, honey, if you'll just git up on your post.'

The girl bowed her head again and stepped up onto the marble post standing at her corner of the table in one easy movement. Freeman, his cock as stiff as ever, felt his balls tighten again as the lips of her pussy, capped with a neat triangle of black pubic hair, gaped between her thighs, shining as though she were already beginning to leak, but it was too soon for even his cigar-stimulated cock to fire again in salute. The girl was standing on the post now, staring ahead expressionlessly as she faced the black ring on the centre of the baize and waited for whatever came next. As Freeman looked at her bare feet, almost invisible against the white marble, he noticed for the first time that the posts weren't circular but . . . nine-sided in cross-section. Nonagonal?

'Thanks, honey,' Ashby said. 'Li-Tan, your turn.'

Mai-Wu spoke again and the second girl shrugged herself out of her dress, her pale body spurting flame-like with its firm, symmetrical apple-sized breasts.

'And on your post, honey.'

The girl stepped up onto her post, her pussy gaping momentarily between her slender thighs, and Freeman heard himself groan with lust.

'And now, last but not least, Mai-Wu herself.'

This time, as Mai-Wu stepped back and wriggled out of her dress, Neruda swore softly in Spanish and, looking down, Freeman saw that he was coming again, his thick cock spurting inside its glass muzzle. Ashby chuckled and took his cigar out of his mouth, waving it as he said, 'Good stuff, ain't it? Mai-Wu, up on your post, honey.'

Mai-Wu stepped back, then up onto her post, and Freeman felt his balls tighten hard as her pussy gaped momentarily between her thighs, and when he looked down he saw his cock spurt twice into the pool of come that had collected in the bulbous end of his cock-muzzle. Ashby chuckled again and walked forward to the table now framed by three identical Chinese girls standing atop nonagonal marble posts. He picked something up from the table and turned and Freeman saw that he was holding a green silk bag that had lain unnoticed on the green baize inside the black central ring. Ashby pulled the bag open and reached inside.

'Riddle for you, fellers. Here, catch.'

He threw something to Neruda, then reached inside the bag again and threw something to Freeman. Freeman caught it and looked at it. It was a die of green jade, but an odd one, like a little triangular pyramid, with four triangular faces and rounded corners. He turned it over, looking at the symbols on each face. One face had two black strokes inlaid into it, one had one black stroke, one had three, and one was blank.

'Chinese numbers,' Ashby said. 'One to three. The blank face means zero. And get this, it's the face that lands *down* that wins. Crazy, huh? But the dice couldn't work otherwise.'

Freeman grunted, realising he was right.

'They're a special shape, too. What's it called, Mai-Wu, honey?'

'In Chinese, si^4 $mian^4$ ti^3, Mistuh Aspee. In English, tet-la-he-da-lon.'

'Yeah. That's it. Tetrahedron. Symbol of eternity, ain't that right?'

'Yes, Mistuh Aspee.'

He turned back to the table.

'OK, Mai-Wu, math lesson over. Git ready to play.'

She nodded and issued another brief order, and in almost perfect synchrony each girl knelt on the top of her post, knees pressed firmly together, took hold of her delicate ankles, and leaned back in an arc until the back of her head was resting on the marble, her small, delicate-nippled breasts tightening and riding on the ribs that rippled beneath her pale skin. Freeman groaned again with lust.

'Couldn't you just eat 'em up, every bit, eh, fellers?' Ashby said. 'If I could have 'em back? Tom?'

'Huh?'

Freeman gaped at him, feeling his cock and balls straining to fire again.

'Your dice, ole buddy.'

'Oh.'

He threw his die back.

'Thanking you. Juan?'

Neruda threw his die back and Ashby walked forward to the table and dropped them on the baize before tipping another die from the bag beside them. Freeman noticed that the dice had different coloured strokes: black, white, and red.

'Now, fellers, the riddle. How we gonna play dice?'

Neruda grunted.

'In the general way.'

'No. The rule of the game is that we can only pick them up, we can't throw them.'

'Then the girls.'

'OK. How? They have to stay in that position. Ain't that right, Mai-Wu?'

'Yes, Mistuh Aspee,' Mai-Wu said, speaking without apparent strain, her nipples dancing slightly. Freeman swallowed as he watched them.

'Tom?' Ashby said.

He looked away from Mai-Wu's nipples.

'What?'

'Any ideas?'

'On what?'

'How we play, for Chrissake. Ain't you been listening? We can't throw 'em ourselves and the girls can't move from that position. So how do we do it?'

Freeman looked at the table. Green baize, with a black ring on the middle of it. Three identical Chinese whores kneeling, backs arched, on three nonagonal posts round the table, their closed knees pointing at the black ring. He lifted his cigar to his mouth and drew on it, frowning a little as he tried to dig out a memory. But Neruda was there before him.

'*Hombre* . . .' he began.

'Yeah?' Ashby said.

'These 'ores, they 'ave a special talent, no?'

Ashby nodded, beaming, his cigar clenched between his teeth.

'Very special, ole buddy.'

'Then I think they 'ave – 'ow you say it? – a *trick* with the *coños*, with the pussies. And that is 'ow they throw the dices.'

'Juan, ole buddy, you got it in one. Look.'

He picked up one of the dice and stepped round the table to the girl on the far side.

'Test-firing, honey,' he said round his cigar, and took hold of one of her nipples and squeezed. She swung her legs smoothly apart and Freeman lurched forward and clutched at the table for support as his cock began firing again in salute of the shining-lipped pussy revealed between her smooth thighs. Ashby leaned forward over the table and twisted his head so that he could watch as he pushed the die into the girl's pussy. Then he leaned back, still holding her nipple.

'Watch, fellers. She's loaded and ready to fire when I tweak her tit. You ready?'

Freeman pushed himself back from the table, breathing hard. He nodded.

'OK.'

He watched Ashby's blunt fingers tighten on the nipple again. The girl tensed, arching her back even more, and then with a small grunt fired the die from her pussy high into the air. It landed bouncing in the black ring on the middle of the green baize and Ashby leaned forward, smiling, as he peered at it.

'Three,' he said. 'Now, you wanna go?'

Juan groaned and his cock began to squirt inside his cock-muzzle. Freeman reached forward over the table and picked up a die, then turned to the nearest girl and squeezed one of her nipples. It was warm and soft under his fingers. Her legs swung apart and he leaned forward as he had seen Ashby do, keeping hold of the nipple as he reached between her thighs, feeling it begin to harden a little, and pushed the die between her gleaming pussy lips. They were oiled, lubricated for the game, he realised.

'No need to ram it in, Tom,' Ashby said. 'She can suck it in herself, less chance of bruising her pussy on the corners like that, and I'm not sure I'd care to risk a finger too deep anyways. Might lose the skin, nail, everything, the suck they've got on 'em, ain't that right, Mai-Wu?'

Freeman withdrew his finger reluctantly from the girl's warm pussy, leaving the die lodged between the lips, and his cock jerked again as he watched the die suddenly move backwards, pulled inside by a contraction of the girl's pussy-muscles.

'You too, Juan,' Ashby said. 'Not too deep. Let her do the work. That's it. OK, ready, fellers?'

Freeman had leaned back and stood waiting with his fingers on the girl's nipple.

'OK, then, fire when ready.'

He and Neruda squeezed their nipples in the same instant, and his cock jerked again as his girl tensed,

97

arched, and fired her die with a faint grunt, sending it arcing through the air to the black ring in the middle of the table. The die fired by Neruda's girl's landed simultaneously with it, bouncing with his, rolling, coming to rest. Ashby leaned forward over the table.

'Two and blank, meaning zero. I would've won that one, fellers. OK, now the rules and aim of the game. Rule one: the dice must land in the black ring in the middle of the table. But I ain't never seen one of 'em miss yet, so I don't think we need worry 'bout that. Rule two: highest score wins round, first to win nine rounds wins game. Rule three: winner of game gets to do what he likes with all three girls, short of causin' harm or distress or penetrating her with his prick. And it's as simple as that. OK? Yep? Then we can begin. Retrieve your dice and load 'em up.'

Freeman reached out over the table and picked up his die, feeling the slight slickness of the oil with which his girl's pussy was lubricated.

'Load 'em,' Ashby said.

Freeman took hold of his girl's nipple, leaning forward over the table and looking between his girl's splayed thighs. He pushed the die between the lips of her pussy, then released it and felt his cock jerk again as he watched it sucked inside.

'OK,' Ashby said. Freeman leaned back. All three girls were loaded, ready to fire when their nipples were squeezed.

'Fire,' Ashby said, and Freeman squeezed his girl's nipple. The girls tensed, arched their backs, and fired with a grunt in the same instant, and three dice were spinning through the air to land and bounce in the black ring. Ashby leaned forward over the table, peering.

'Is that a three, Juan?' he asked.

'*Si.*'

'Then you win. Load 'em again, gentlemen.'

They loaded their dice again, and this time Neruda groaned as he watched his die being sucked back into his girl's pussy, and Freeman heard his sperm squirting inside his cock-muzzle.

'OK. Fire.'

The three dice arched through the air, landed, bounced, came to rest. Ashby leaned forward over the table, peering.

'Zero to you, Tom, two apiece for me and Juan. No winner. Load 'em.'

The next game was a draw, and then Ashby won with a three. His cigar was now a stub in his mouth and he turned his head away from the table and down and spat it to the floor before reaching down to the strap of his cock-muzzle and pulling out a new one. He pushed it into his mouth and walked over to one of the gas-lights and lit it before returning to the table. Neruda pulled his cigar out and examined it, then threw it over his shoulder and pulled out a new one before lighting it in the same way. Ashby waited impatiently for him to return to the table, then said, 'Load 'em.'

They loaded their girls' pussies.

'Fire.'

Ashby leaned, peering. Another draw, all three dice resting on their blank faces.

'Load 'em . . . Fire.'

And finally Freeman won, with three to Ashby's and Neruda's twos. A win apiece. Next Neruda won again, then there was another draw, and another, and then Ashby won again. Freeman was sweating now, his balls aching as they strained to release sperm down his swollen cock into his cock-muzzle. The room seemed to swim round him, as though heat and humidity was pouring through the pussy lips of the three identical Chinese girls as they fired the dice onto the centre of the table, and he half-expected to see a white spurt of steam as they fired and hear a moist, sharp hiss of released pressure.

'Load 'em . . . Fire.'

They played, smoking their cigars fast, replacing them from the straps of their cock-muzzles, wiping beads of sweat off their flushed foreheads, wincing as they leaned forward over the table now and looked back to watch themselves pushing their dice between the lips of their girls.

'Load 'em . . . Fire.'

They went to three wins apiece, then drew five times in a row before Freeman edged ahead to four. After another draw Neruda caught him, then Ashby joined them on the next throw. Four apiece, and then Neruda went ahead with five, and the glowing tip of Ashby's fifth or sixth cigar was shaking slightly as he chewed on it, frowning with concentration. The bodies of the three girls were beginning to flush: and their nipples were hardened under the fingers of the three men. The repeated insertion of dice into their pussies had excited them, and pussy juice was oozing down their thighs, to drip to the post and slowly pool there. Ashby was dipping his die into his girl's pool before he inserted it now, muttering to himself as he did so, and Neruda had swapped hands to squeeze his girl's nipple with his left hand, crossing himself with his right before he fired.

It worked when he took the lead with five and held it for another round before Freeman caught him and then took the lead back with six. Ashby was still on four, then matched Neruda on five before Neruda matched Freeman on six. Then Freeman took the lead again with seven, then went to eight and groaned more with pain than pleasure as his cock began to squirt into his cock-muzzle. This, surely, was it. The next round was a draw, and the next, and then Neruda nudged to seven and Freeman's heart was thudding in his chest. On the next round, his heart twisted with fear, because Neruda had drawn level with him on eight.

'Load 'em,' Ashby croaked, a dead cigar waggling in his mouth. 'Fire.'

The dice shot from the girls' pussies with a faint spray of pussy juice, landed in the ring, bounced, settled. Ashby leaned forward, one eye shut as a stinging droplet of sweat rolled into it, then the tension in his body relaxed.

'Zero for you, Juan . . . one for me . . . three for you, Tom. You win. 'Gratulations. Place your order with Mai-Wu whenever you're up to it.'

Freeman, who had been clutching the edge of the table hard enough to make his knuckles ache, nearly slumped forward over it. He pushed himself back, sighing with relief, shaking his head to try and clear it. He said something.

'What was that?' Ashby asked.

'Footing the belle,' he said. 'I wanna see 'em footing the belle.'

'Mai-Wu?' Ashby said. 'Are you up for it?'

'Yes, Mistuh Aspee,' Mai-Wu said from the corner where Neruda had been firing her. She raised her head, issuing another sharp order in Chinese, and all three girls came out of their firing posture, raising their upper bodies and letting go of their ankles so that they were kneeling on their posts again. Their nipples were sticking out hard, like little brown tongues.

'But first, let's bring 'em off, fellers,' Ashby said. 'Reward 'em for their efforts.'

He got behind his girl and took hold of a nipple with one hand as he reached down into her pussy with the other. Her mouth came open and she gasped as he started to manipulate her clitoris, dead cigar wriggling hard in one corner of his mouth. Neruda and Freeman copied him, squeezing a hard brown nipple as they manipulated their girls' clitorises too. Ashby's girl was squeaking now, a second or two from orgasm, but Freeman's shifted uncomfortably, her thighs half-closing on his hand, and he realised he was hurting her. He let go of her clitoris and started to stimulate it indirectly, squeezing round it, and her thighs came apart again.

Ashby's girl came with a long groan, and Neruda's joined her. Freeman squeezed more gently, then put the tip of his index finger over his girl's clitoris and began to brush it very lightly in time with gentle tugs and tweaks of her nipples. She started to gasp harder and faster and he drew hard on his newly lit cigar, leaned forward and round, and released a long plume of smoke into her face.

It was enough: her half-closed eyes, almost invisible above her flushed, sweat-moistened cheeks, went to black, eyelash-fringed strokes as she drew the smoke in with a whistle through flared nostrils and began to come with piggletty grunts of pleasure, thrusting her pelvis at his hand as he slipped his middle finger between her pussy lips and slipped it deep between her lust-slimed pussy-walls.

'She who comes last, comes hardest,' Ashby said.

'Who is she?' Freeman asked, his finger locked into the girl's pussy, squeezed over and over by her spasming pussy-walls.

'That's ... Well, I couldn't rightly tell you,' Ashby said. ''Course, 's'either Li-Tan or Chu-Sai. Mai-Wu?'

Mai-Wu, still gasping on her post, shook her head as though trying to clear it.

'Who, Mistuh Aspee?'

'That 'un there. Tom's dice-thrower.'

Mai-Wu blinked and peered across the table.

'It is Li-Tan, Mistuh Aspee.'

'Yeah, Li-Tan. I'd forgotten.'

Freeman pulled his finger free with a moist pop and sniffed it.

'Now, ole buddy, what was it you wanted?'

Freeman pulled the finger reluctantly from his nose and shook his head.

'Footing the belle,' he said.

'Yeah. Mai-Wu, table-top OK?'

'Yes, Mistuh Aspee.'

'And all three of you?'

'Yes, Mistuh Aspee. But please, you must lick our feet, for, how is it? Lublication.'

'Sure thing, honey. Fellers, the ladies require a little assistance.'

Mai-Wu issued another order and the three girls slipped their knees from under them simultaneously, sat down with soft squelches in their pools of pussy-juice, and slid forward on their bottoms to the green baize of the table-top. Mai-Wu's smooth face had creased with a moue of distaste when she sat down on the post and Ashby asked, 'What's wrong, honey?'

'My pussy-juice, Mistuh Aspee. It was cold.'

They were on the table now, beginning to arrange themselves for the foot-licking, each as the apex of a triangle with legs wide apart. Now Mai-Wu took Li-Tan's tiny right foot, hardly bigger than a child's, and lifted it and propped it on her right shoulder, ready for Ashby's tongue; Li-Tan took Chu-Sai's right foot and propped it on her right shoulder ready for Neruda's tongue; Chu-Sai took Mai-Wu's and propped it on hers ready for Freeman's. Ashby threw his dead cigar away and moved forward.

'OK, fellers, let's not keep the ladies waiting.'

His large tongue came out and he licked the sole of Li-Tan's foot from heel to toes, then began to insert the blunt tip of his tongue between her toes from little toe to big toe. Freeman paused, watching Li-Tan's face tighten with pleasure, then put his face forward and licked the sole of Mai-Wu's foot. It was warm and smooth and soft and tasted faintly and deliciously of sweat and sandalwood. He licked it carefully and conscientiously, moistening it thoroughly before beginning on her toes, pushing into the gap between each pair, probing for the stronger, faintly cheesy flavour of sweat that had ripened here, then began to suck her toes individually one by one, coating them thoroughly before beginning on the upper surface of her foot.

To his right, Neruda, who was probing between the big and second toes of Chu-Sai's foot, groaned and began to come again, his sperm squirting into his cock-muzzle. Ashby had finished the upper surface of Li-Tan's foot now and was sucking at her heel, taking almost half of her foot into his mouth, puffing and blowing and flubbering his lips on it as he licked, making her quiver with pleasure and reach a small hand down into her pussy-triangle, probing at her clitoris with a slender forefinger. Ashby came off the foot with a sigh.

'Enough, fellers. I'm about to come again if I carry on, and I druther come while I'm watching the show. Fellers!'

Neruda came reluctantly off Chu-Sai's foot, planting a kiss on the spittle-slicked sole before stepping back to stand waiting with Ashby and Freeman.

'OK, you both ready? Then prop your muzzles on th'edge of the table, like this.'

Ashby raised his muzzle and propped it on the edge of the table, sperm running away from his cockhead. Neruda and Freeman followed suit and Ashby asked, 'You ready now too, Mai-Wu?'

'Yes, Mistuh Aspee.'

'Then go to it, girl. Let's play belle!'

Mai-Wu nodded and issued another order. Spittle-lubricated feet slipped off shoulders and then were pushed forward into the triangle of splayed thighs, where small hands took them up and began to tug them into place over the gaping pussy lips that awaited them.

'You mean . . . ?' said Neruda.

'Yep, *amigo*. Up they go.'

Chu-Sai gasped. Li-Tan's clenched toes had begun to enter her pussy, sliding forward a fraction of an inch at a time. Then Mai-Wu gasped too, beginning to accept Chu-Sai's foot into her pussy, and Li-Tan, beginning to accept Mai-Wu's.

'Hang on, fellers, we need to lend a helping hand here,' Ashby said. It was true: the girls were slipping backwards as the toes slipped home and the bulk of the foot tried to enter their pussies, their bottoms sliding on the pussy-juice-slicked surface of the table. Ashby reached down behind Mai-Wu, taking hold of her buttocks and pushing her forward as Neruda and Freeman did the same for Li-Tan and Chu-Sai. The girls stopped sliding backwards and grunted again as the feet pushed harder on their pussies, then began to enter fully. Ashby whistled.

'Isn't this just the horniest thing you've seen in your *life*?' he said. Sperm began to squirt and splash inside his cock-muzzle, and Freeman grunted with pain as his balls tightened and tried to discharge. Not just yet. The feet slid deeper, deeper, binding the three girls together in a triangle.

'*Hombre*, how deep can they go?' Neruda asked.

'Whole foot,' Ashby said, shaking his head and sighing deeply as his orgasm ended. 'Maybe th'ankle too. Leastways, that's what the girls in the specialist foot-belle room can do. But maybe –' he spoke provocatively '– these girls ain't up for it.'

Mai-Wu's head had gone back and her eyes had closed with strain; now she lowered it, blinking as she said, 'No. We can do it. Ankle. Watch.'

Freeman clutched at the edge of the table for support with one hand as another inch of foot disappeared into each pussy and his cock and balls began to discharge for the seventh or eighth time that night. The feet sank deeper, almost up to the heel now, glistening with pussy juice and spittle, and the girls were grunting and murmuring almost continuously, while Li-Tan seemed to be repeating a prayer under her breath between grunts.

'What's Li-Tan saying, honey?' Ashby asked Mai-Wu.

'She pray to Kwan Yin, Mistuh Aspee . . . Chinese goddess of Love and . . . compassion.'

'And quite right, too.'

There was another simultaneous jerk and grunt and the three girls slid close enough to lift their hands from the feet between their thighs and reach out for one another. Their stretched fingers hooked together and they began to tug themselves closer.

'No more need for our help, fellers,' Ashby said, and lifted his hand away from Mai-Wu's bottom. Mai-Wu shook her head.

'No, please, Mistuh Aspee. Put finger . . . up ass. Help us with ankle.'

'Well, OK, honey. Fellers, you heard the lady.'

Freeman's cock jerked as he rubbed his middle finger down Chu-Sai's spine, feeling the smooth knobbles of her vertebrae under her silken skin, coating the finger in sweat so that when it reached her buttock cleft and slipped beneath her he was ready to push it into her ass. Her hairless little sphincter irised open as his finger probed at it, then closed as he pushed it inside, and his cock jerked again at the warmth of her interior and tightness of her ass-walls. The girls began to bounce slightly on the middle fingers of the three men as they pulled their sisters' feet fully into their pussies, and Freeman heard the cock-muzzles rattle on the edge of the table, seismographing the faint repeated shock.

'Game little battlers, ain't they?' Ashby said. 'Looks as though they're gonna make it.'

With another jerk each pussy had accepted the heel of the foot that was sliding inside it, its swollen lips splayed wide, their inflamed colour heightened against the white skin of the foot. Freeman's cock was jerking almost continuously, his balls contracted tight to the fork of his thighs, aching fiercely as they strained to release sperm in tribute to the foot-belle being played on the surface of the table. The feet were still sliding into the slick pussies, but more slowly, a fraction of an inch at a time, and the girls were having to rock harder on the fingers inserted in their tight bottoms.

'Nearly there,' Ashby said, his eyes fixed on Mai-Wu's foot as it slid deeper into Li-Tan's pussy. 'Nearly there. Come on, girl. Another tug . . .'

All three girls groaned and tugged, dragging each other a fraction of an inch closer, accepting each other's feet a fraction of an inch deeper into their pussies, then suddenly gasped: with a jerk, the whole of each foot had entered its fleshy foot-sheath beyond the ankle. The three men groaned aloud too, their cocks jerking inside their cock-muzzles, straining in vain to release sperm in tribute to the girls' success.

'We're drained, fellers,' Ashby said, gasping. 'Cain't do it.'

All the heads of all three girls had gone back, eyes closed in an ecstasy of strain as their pussies accepted the final inch of foot and ankle; now Mai-Wu lowered hers, shaking it, then crying out in Chinese. There was a rattle from above and the three men raised their eyes in surprise to see a section of the ceiling sliding back, revealing a narrow crescent of black that widened until there was a huge black circle directly above the table. Mai-Wu looked upwards and cried out again. There was a loud click and the black circle suddenly turned completely over, swinging on hinges at two diametrically opposed points.

On the other side of it was a huge convex mirror reflecting and magnifying everything that lay below it, and as the three men saw the table and the three Chinese girls atop it, melded in a triangle of sex-flushed flesh, small feet buried between slender thighs, they groaned again on a rising note that broke as their exhausted cocks and balls began to spurt for the final time. When their orgasms were over, Ashby, knees still trembling, one hand still clenched on the edge of the table, one still pressed to Mai-Wu's buttocks, holding his middle finger up her ass, said, 'Thanks, Mai-Wu. That was ... that was some experience.'

Mai-Wu nodded.

'We can uncoupaw now, Mistuh Aspee?'

'Yes, honey. Uncouple and go and get yourselves washed down. You've earned it, girl.'

He slid his finger free of her and raised it to his nose, sniffing, then licking it.

'Fresh as a daisy, fellers,' he said. 'You're a good clean girl, Mai-Wu.'

'Yes, Mistuh Aspee,' Mai-Wu said. 'An' I go get clean again, now.'

Neruda and Freeman had slid their fingers free of Li-Tan's and Chu-Sai's asses, and watched, groaning again as the three girls began to slide their feet free of each other's pussies with squelches and pops, pussy-juice running in rivulets to the surface of the table. Neruda clutched at the edge of the table, looking as though he was about to faint.

'*Madre de dios*,' he said. 'Jack, this is a 'ore'ouse *I* will not forget in a 'urry.'

Soaked with pussy juice, the feet came free with a final pop and squelch, and the three girls broke their triangle, each moving gingerly as she turned over and began to crawl on hands and knees for her corner of the table, her thighs shining with pussy-juice.

'That baize is gonna need replacing,' Ashby said. 'Look at it, fellers. Soaked with some of the finest pussy-juice a man could taste.'

He put his middle finger into one of the pools of pussy-juice shining on the table-top and put the finger to his mouth, sucking at it. The three girls were climbing off the table onto the floor, picking up the dresses discarded there and then forming a line in front of the three men as they waited to be dismissed. Ashby watched them with a fond smile, his cock-muzzle sitting filled with sperm on the table in front of him.

'Yes, Mai-Wu, you can go now. There'll be a big tip waiting for you today, y'hear now? From all three of us, unless I'm much mistaken.'

'OK, Mistuh Aspee. Thank you. We see you again soon.'

'Count on it, honey.'

The three girls turned and walked through a curtained doorway in the wall behind them that Freeman had not noticed before.

'Prime ass, fellers,' Ashby said. 'Prime Oriental ass. Shall we make our way home, stopping off for cocktails on the way? Or should I say, cocktail?'

Neruda laughed and he and Freeman followed Ashby as he walked a little unsteadily to the door and led them back down the red-carpeted corridor to the clothes-counter and the waiting eighteen-year-old. Her eyes widened happily as they walked through the doorway and up to the counter, fixed on the three cock-muzzles and the thick sperm that swirled in the bulbous ends.

'My, gen'lemen!' she said, raising her eyes to their flushed, smiling faces. 'You have bin busy tonight!'

'Sure thing, honey,' Ashby said. 'You gonna unstrap us and lick us dry?'

'Quick as I cain, sir.'

She raised a section of counter-top and slipped through the gap, her bustled hips brushing its sides with a whisper of cloth, and trotted eagerly to Ashby. As she knelt in front of him and began to unstrap his cock-muzzle, she looked up at him and said, 'You wanna be gettin' the shaker ready for me when I'm done here, sir?'

Ashby nodded as the cock-muzzle fell free from his hips and was carefully pulled off his now flaccid cock. The girl crawled to the counter and dropped the muzzle bulb down into one of a row of metal loops fastened along its edge, then turned back to Ashby and lifted his sperm-wet cock to her mouth. Neruda rumbled in his throat as she swallowed the cock noisily and began to suck it clean.

109

'*Hombre*,' he said to Freeman. 'I never thought I watch something like that one day and stay limp as a wet *tortilla*, you know?'

Freeman nodded.

'Me neither.'

The girl pulled Ashby's cock free and examined it, then turned and crawled for Neruda. Ashby glanced down at his cock and then across at his companions. It had barely begun to stiffen, despite its insertion seconds before into the girl's warm mouth.

'Shameful, ain't it, fellers?' he said. 'But I'll be mightily surprised if either of you do any better. Even you, Juan.'

The girl was unstrapping Neruda's cock-muzzle and sliding it free of his dark, flaccid cock. As she turned and crawled with the muzzle to the counter, Neruda took hold of his cock and squeezed it.

'I try my best, *amigo*,' he said. The girl looked over her shoulder with a smile.

'It's a poor compliment for a poor girl, ain't it, sirs?'

She slipped Neruda's cock-muzzle into its loop and crawled back to his waiting cock.

'A girl does her best, an' what does she get?'

She opened her mouth and lifted the cock into it, mumbling round it as she sucked it in.

'What was that, ole buddy?' Ashby asked.

'I reckon she said "Limp cocks",' Freeman said. Neruda was staring down hard at her dark head as she sucked his cock clean, but the expression on his face told the other two men that he was not stiffening. The girl pulled his cock out of her mouth and shook it sadly, making it flop and bend.

'Limp cocks,' she said. 'Nothing but limp cocks, all day long. Still,' she continued, turning and crawling for Freeman and his cock muzzle, 'there are compensations.'

She unstrapped his cock-muzzle and carried to the counter.

'What are they, honey?' Ashby asked.

'Sir?'

She turned with mock innocence, Freeman's cock raised in her hand, presented to her opening mouth.

'What are the compensations, honey?'

'Oh, that,' she said. 'Well, sir, the limper the cock —' she shook Freeman's too, making it flop and swing '— the fuller the cock-muzzle an' the creamier the cocktail. Hmm-*mmm*.'

She pushed Freeman's cock into her mouth and began to suck it clean.

'*Dieciocho*?' Neruda said. 'This *chica*, she is a born *puta*. I never thought I live to see the day when a girl talk like *this* to me and my cock stay like *this*.'

He shook it again sadly.

'But what may I do? My *huevos* are as dry as the desert.'

'You and me both, ole buddy,' Ashby said. 'You and me both. Hang on, I near went and forgot the little lady's request.'

He walked over to the counter and leaned over it, reaching for something on a shelf underneath it. Behind him the girl pulled Freeman's sucked-clean cock out of her mouth and shook it with mock disapproval and disappointment, lips pursed sadly.

'You too, sir. You too.'

She pushed herself back to her feet and walked back to the counter, slipping back through the gap and lowering the raised section of counter. Ashby had lifted up a tall glass and a silver cocktail-shaker and put them on the top of the counter.

'Slide 'em along, sir,' the girl said. He slid them along the counter one by one and she stopped them with a small hand before tugging the cocktail-shaker apart.

'Now, gen'lemen, if you'll hand me your cock-muzzles, I'll get ready to shake.'

The three men walked eagerly to the cock-muzzles hanging ready in their metal loops.

'Did you note your numbers, fellers?'

His two companions shook their heads. Ashby lifted the strap of one cock-muzzle and showed them a small brass plate stamped with the number *127*.

'Each muzzle's got a number on the strap, like this, see? Something to remember for next time, fellers. This ain't mine, so you can take pot-luck.'

'I think it's mine,' Freeman said. 'I remember that loose stitching.'

'OK.'

Ashby lifted the muzzle free and handed it to him and he carried it down the counter to where the girl stood waiting with her cocktail-shaker. Behind him he heard Ashby say, 'Fifteen's mine, ole buddy, so sixty-three must be yours.'

He handed his muzzle to the girl and she took it and tipped it over the shaker, licking her lips as she watched the sperm slide thickly from it and fall in long sticky strings into the shaker.

'You sure did come like an elephant for me, sir,' she said.

'How about us, honey?' Ashby asked, walking down to them with Neruda. Still holding Freeman's muzzle over the shaker, the girl reached out and accepted his cock-muzzle too, tipping it over the shaker and licking her lips again as the sperm inside it began to slide out.

'You have too, sir,' she said. She shook Freeman's muzzle, emptying it of its final few drops, then laid it on the counter and reached for Neruda's. The three men watched her hold the two muzzles over her shaker, eyes shining as she watched sperm sliding into it, and marvelled at the continued limpness of their cocks. Now she was shaking Ashby's muzzle free of its final few drops and laying it to the counter.

'*Elefante?*' Neruda said proudly, watching sperm still pouring from his muzzle. 'No, me, I came *como ballena*. Like a whale.'

'You're Catholic,' Ashby said. 'Quantity over quality.'

'No, quantity *and* quality,' Neruda said. The girl was
finally shaking his muzzle free of its final few drops.
'You effete *protestantes*, there is less of quantity, less of
quality both.'

Ashby laughed.

'It's all the same now, *amigo*. Cain't tell it apart when
it's mixed, and I bet *she* cain't taste the difference, eh,
honey?'

The girl laid Neruda's cock-muzzle on the counter,
shaking her head seriously.

'No, sir. I love to drink come whatever the cock it
comes out of. Now,' she went on, slipping the top on
the cocktail-shaker, 'you gen'lemen like to watch mah
tits too, while I'm shakin'?'

'Fellers?' Ashby said, his eyes suddenly fixed on her
chest. Neruda and Freeman both laughed.

'I think they want to, honey,' Ashby. 'And you don't
need to ask if I do.'

''Kay. No sooner said than seen, gen'lemen.'

She reached behind her neck with both hands. There
was a soft click and she tugged at the throat of her
dress. It peeled away and she tugged a section of cloth
away over her chest, revealing her firm pink-nippled
breasts. Picking up the cocktail-shaker, she said, 'Tweak
'em too, if you like.'

She started to shake the cocktail, holding the shaker
carefully to one side so that they could watch her tits
bounce and wobble. Ashby sighed happily and reached
out to tweak one of her nipples and she beamed even
more widely as his fingers closed on it and squeezed.

'You too, sirs,' she said to Neruda and Freeman.

'*Amigo*?' Neruda said. 'May I?'

'Be my guest,' Freeman said. He watched Neruda
reach out for the remaining nipple and tweak it. Neruda
lifted his hand away.

'Your turn,' he said. Freeman reached for the nipple too and closed his fingers on it. It had begun to harden, jerking faintly away from him as the girl continued to shake her sperm cocktail, beaming more widely still.

'*Dieciocho*,' Neruda said wonderingly. 'Pray God and the Virgin she continue to ripen and do not harden as so many do. Such a 'ore as this is worth an emperor's ransom.'

'Thanks, gen'lemen,' the girl said. Ashby and Freeman let go of her nipples and she put the shaker on the counter, panting slightly, her breasts quivering. She tugged the top off the shaker and sniffed happily as white foam spilled down its sides and the air filled with a strong odour of sperm. Freeman could hear the continuous hiss of exploding bubbles of sperm, and when the girl lifted the shaker and tipped its contents into the waiting glass, he saw that the sperm had been turned almost completely into a thick, sticky foam.

The girl held the shaker in place until it was empty, then put it down on the counter and picked up the glass. She held it at eye level, licked her lips twice, then closed her eyes and swung it to her opening mouth. Ashby's and Neruda's hands were suddenly gripping the edge of the counter and Freeman felt his knees weakening and his cock, impossibly, stir and stiffen a little as the glass met her lips and she began to drink in long, slow gulps, her long throat noding and smoothing over and over. Neruda was groaning deep in his throat as he watched the girl's head tilt back, and when her head was horizontal and her long pink tongue was darting into the glass, meeting the last draining traces of sperm, he swore under his breath and snatched a single glance at Ashby before staring back at the girl.

''Ow much, Jack? 'Ow much to buy 'er? For 'er, I pay five thousand dollars.'

The girl's tensed shoulders relaxed and she lifted the glass away from her mouth, lowering her face and sighing with deep satisfaction as she licked her lips. The bottom of the glass met the counter with a clunk and she chuckled to herself, then belched. Freeman groaned too as her spermy breath wafted to him, and Neruda crossed himself and looked upwards.

'For 'er,' he said. 'I pay ten thousand dollars.'

The girl belched again, then lifted the glass back towards her mouth, opening her mouth in a narrow 'o'. Her breasts shook; she belched for a third time; retched slightly; and then sperm was squirting from her mouth back into the glass. When it stopped squirting she blew sperm off her lips and looked up, eyes sparkling with mischief.

'Twenty thous . . .' Neruda started to say, then stopped as the girl's eyes slowly crossed, straightened, and she dipped her head slightly nearer the glass and squirted sperm in twin streams from her nostrils into it. When the glass was nearly full again, she stopped and looked up at them. A bubble of sperm grew in one nostril, swelling, swelling, and burst leaving shining splatters across her cheek. The three men watched her, cocks slowly re-stiffening, as she lifted the glass to her mouth and prepared to drink it again.

6

High Society

Holding the camera to his eye, he worked himself forward on his elbows through the last few stems of rhododendron, hardly daring to breathe. The earth was dry and filled with sharp little stones that cut him through the sleeves of his shirt, but he barely felt them, he was concentrating so hard on what he was about to see. Ah! Yes! Yes! There they were! His heart was suddenly thumping in his chest and his groin arrowed instantly to erection, as it always did when he was successful after a long stalk. He carefully adjusted the focus and the slightly blurred figures sprang sharply into view: the circle of naked women interrupted like an hour hand by the naked figure of the elderly tycoon lying face down on the sun-scalded concrete of the poolside.

He swallowed hard, his hips almost lifted off the ground by his erection as he scanned the circle of women. It was true, every word of it, every word of what his informant had told him: some of Hollywood's hottest female stars – my God – *all* of Hollywood's hottest female stars. There was the 'Blonde Comet' Moira Huxley, tits out to *here*; the 'Scarlet Queen' Jane Wilding, red pubic triangle trimmed in the shape of a heart; Gayle Connor, legs that didn't quit; Tania Vandon, Maria Best, Sylvia Fairley, Amber Freeman – all naked as nature made 'em, but for black stilettos

116

with glittering leather calf-straps. What *was* the old fuck paying them for this, and what the *fuck* were they . . . ?

He swallowed almost convulsively, stomach lurching with excitement. Amber Freeman had just put the heel of her right stiletto onto Howard's withered left buttock, and lifted herself clear of the poolside on it. The tycoon's bark of pain reached the sweating *paparazzo*'s ears a couple of seconds later, drifting up the hill from the glittering blue rectangle of the pool. Now Amber stepped off him and the circle of naked women turned a notch, bringing Maria Best forward. And what . . . His finger stabbed for the camera-button. My God, she was *pissing* on him! The golden droplets glittered in the sunlight as she sprayed his back and buttocks, which he noticed now were already sheened with liquid, then put the heel of her right stiletto onto his left buttock and stood on him too.

That's what Howard's kick was. High heels and California sunshine. Finger working frantically at the button of his camera, he slipped his other hand down his body and beneath the hem of his trousers, groping for his swollen cock. The voice just behind his head and the heel descending into *his* left buttock were simultaneous.

'*That* is enough of *that*.'

He stifled a scream of pain and twisted his body hard, turning away from the heel and pushing himself forward with his feet. But his feet were suddenly seized and he couldn't move, lying twisted on his side and staring upwards, learning that not all of Hollywood's hottest female stars were in the circle of naked flesh down by the pool. One of them was standing and looking down at him. She licked her lips and said, 'What's a worm like you doing in a place like this?'

'Yolanda,' he said. 'Honey, I can expl–'

. Yolanda Helcutt snorted, her delicate nostrils flaring in perfect black triangles as she tossed her famous blonde curls.

'I'm sure you can explain everything, Jake,' she said. 'But we need a bigger audience. Joe, Harry, get him on his feet.'

Only now did his eyes drop from the beautiful blonde standing above him in a blue swimsuit to meet those of the two kneeling gorillas who had hold of his feet.

'Sure thing, Miss Helcutt,' one of them rumbled. Their hamlike hands reached up his legs and he was hauled unceremoniously to his feet by his belt.

'Take his camera, Joe.'

'Sure thing, Miss Helcutt.'

The camera was jerked from his hand.

'OK, now follow me,' Yolanda said, slipping her high heels off and holding them in one slender hand as she led the way downhill in her bare feet to the pool, her high buttocks rolling in the tight blue cloth of her swimsuit. The photographer followed reluctantly, losing all feeling in his forearms as his elbows were clamped in the vicelike grip of the two gorillas, his feet barely brushing the grass. Another bark of pain drifted up the hillside to them, and over Yolanda's shoulder the photographer could see Tania Vandon balancing by one heel on Howard's left buttock. The star's shoulder shook as Yolanda raised her arm and slipped two fingers into her mouth. The photographer flinched as she whistled loudly and heads turned at the poolside.

'I've got him!' Yolanda carolled, and the photographer heard excited shouts and laughter drift up to them. When they reached the pool, he *had* lost all feeling in his forearms. Hugh Howard was sitting in a cane chair by the pool, his thick grey chest-hair protruding through a hastily donned dressing gown of yellow silk. The circle of women he had seen from the hillside was standing behind him, still naked, watching him unselfconsciously as he was brought to them, firm breasts staring at him too with blind nipple-eyes. Howard pushed himself to his feet with a grunt as Yolanda led the two gorillas in front of him. He took her hand, raised it to his lips, and kissed it.

'Thank you, my dear,' he said. He sat back down, and his softened face hardened again as he looked at the photographer.

'What was he doing on my property?' he asked.

'Listen, Mr Howard, I can expl –'

Howard swung a hand briefly and one of the gorillas seized the photographer by the throat.

'Well, my dear?' Howard said. Yolanda was putting her high heels back on, lifting her feet, left, right, slipping the shoes on, lowering her feet with little clicks, left right.

'Spying,' she said. 'Here's his camera.'

One of the gorillas held out the camera on its strap. The photographer's ears were starting to buzz with lack of air.

'Give it to me,' Howard said to the gorilla. He let go of the photographer's elbow and walked forward to hand the camera to the tycoon, who raised it, reading the counter.

'Seventeen shots,' he said.

'Maria was pissing on you,' Yolanda said. 'He seemed to find it . . . *exciting*.'

The world was going black in front of the photographer's eyes and the buzzing in his ears had turned into a drumbeat, a thump-thump of slowing blood.

'Did he?' Howard said. He lifted the camera and took a photograph of the photographer's now crimson face, then lowered it and said, 'Let him go, Harry.'

The gorilla's hands released his throat and forearm and he fell forward onto his knees, whooping for breath.

'You liked watching me be pissed on, eh, Jake?' the tycoon said. The photographer raised a deprecatory hand, holding his throat and croaking, 'Listen, Mr Howard, I can expl–'

'Shut up.'

The photographer shut up.

'You can explain, can you? Well, I'm very pleased to hear it. And so are these ladies. Aren't you, my dears?'

'Yes, sir, Mr Howard.'

'Yes, sir.'

'Yes, sir, Mr Howard.'

'Sure am, Mr Howard.'

'Yes, sir.'

'Yes, sir, Mr Howard.'

Their replies rippled outwards from the cane chair, left and right. The tycoon listened, nodding with satisfaction, then said, 'You see, Jake? They're all pleased to hear that you can explain. Because each of them, as you may know, has something she would like explaining. Haven't you, my dears?'

More ripples of agreement came from the circle behind the tycoon. He twisted in his seat, looking behind him, holding an exquisitely manicured hand out to one of them.

'Sylvia, here, for example. She has something she would like explaining, have you not, my dear?'

The porcelain-featured blonde nodded. 'I sure do, Mr Howard.'

'And what is it, my dear?'

'My first divorce, Mr Howard. I'd like to know how those pictures were taken, and who by.'

'By whom, my dear. By whom. And you, Gayle, you would like something explaining too, would you not?'

'I do, Mr Howard. That photograph of my apartment in Rome. I'd like to know how it was taken, and . . . by whom.'

'Thank you, my dear. And you, Moira, you have something you would like explaining, I believe?'

'My sister's wedding, Mr Howard. That photograph of one of the guests and I in the shrubbery. I'd like to know how it was taken, and by whom.'

'One of the guests and *me*, my dear.'

He went through the women one by one, and as each mentioned some compromising photo of some moment of indiscretion or promiscuity, the photographer's heart sank further. When the recital from behind his chair was over the tycoon turned back and looked past him, to the woman standing behind him on his left.

'And you, my dear Yolanda, you have something you would like explaining, have you not?'

'The photographs of my yacht-party in the Caribbean, Mr Howard. I *long* to know how and by whom they were taken.'

The tycoon nodded, smiling bleakly.

'And who can blame you, my dear? Who can blame you?'

He looked at Jake and his smile faded.

'And I, Jake, I too have something I would like . . . *explaining*. The photographs of my second wife and her chauffeur, taken two years ago as they . . . *dallied* by this very pool. It was easy enough to calculate *whence* they had been taken –' he nodded back up the hill to the rhododendrons '– and even, by the length and angle of shadows, *when* they had been taken. But I did not know by *whom* they had been taken. And *why*. So I . . . no, I do apologise, ladies. So *we* decided to lay a little trap. A little honeytrap for a little fly. Knowing that the fly could not resist and that it was highly likely, in its greed and eagerness, it would even select the same point of vantage from which to observe proceedings. And now here the fly is, ready to buzz its little explanation for all of us . . . *spiders*.'

A titter ran through the women standing behind his chair.

'So buzz, little fly. Buzz for us.'

'Mr Howard, look, I can . . .' He trailed off hopelessly.

'But I *am* looking, Jake. I also wish to *hear*. So buzz. Buzz. Buzz. Buzz.'

He watched the photographer's face.

'Well?'

'I did it . . . I did it for the money.'

'Yes? And was that all? Yolanda notes that you were *excited* as you watched, therefore we can safely deduce that money is not all there is to it. So what else is there for you to explain?'

'I do it for the . . . the excitement too.'

'The excitement? Such a pedestrian word. Would it not be better to say you do it for the . . . *thrill*?'

The photographer nodded silently.

'Well?' the tycoon snapped.

'Yes, Mr Howard. For the thrill.'

'So you do it for the money and the thrill. First things first. The money. We would like to know how much you earned, Jake. In Yolanda's felicitous phraseology, we *long* to know. So tell us. How much did you earn for the photographs of my second wife and her chauffeur?'

Jake muttered something.

'I did not catch that, Jake. Say it louder.'

'Ten thousand dollars.'

'Ten thousand dollars, was it? And how much to destroy Sylvia's marriage?'

'Twenty-five thousand dollars.'

'Twenty-five thousand? I am covered in chagrin to learn this. But of course, Sylvia is a much bigger star than dear departed Carol ever was, aren't you, my dear? But we will not go on and embarrass anyone else with a similar revelation. So let us take an average. Ten thousand and twenty-five thousand. Thirty-five thousand in total, for an average of seven thousand, five hundred. An average of seventeen thousand, five hundred dollars to destroy a marriage and cause much distress and disruption to many lives. Would you say that is about right?'

The photographer nodded, then said, 'Yes, Mr Howard.'

'Seven thousand, five hundred dollars. But how much *thrill*, Jake? That is what we want to know now. How much *thrill* did you get out of it? Let us begin again with my second wife. How much *thrill* did you get out of photographing her . . . dalliance with her chauffeur?'

The photographer blinked and licked his lips.

'Come on, Jake. Surely you can remember. How much *thrill*? Only a little? Or a lot?'

The photographer swallowed. His mouth opened, closed.

'Well? A little, or a lot?'

'A . . . a lot, Mr Howard.'

'We want you to be more precise than that, Jake. Let's give you a unit of *thrill*. The . . . *placet*. One placet being equivalent to the pleasure of the finest *fuck* you can imagine.'

The photographer winced at the obscenity embedded in the tycoon's precise, pedantic diction.

'So tell us, Jake, tell us how many placets it was. How many placets did you earn taking those photographs of my second wife and her chauffeur? Less than one?'

The photographer shook his head.

'More than one?'

The photographer nodded.

'How many more? Two? Three? Ah, not so high as that. Somewhere between two and three. Shall we say . . . two-and-a-half placets? Yes? Does that sound roughly correct? Two-and-a-half of the finest imaginable fucks to take those photographs of my wife and her chauffeur. That's about right? Good. And how about Sylvia's marriage? How many placets did you earn to wreck that? More than two-and-a-half?'

The photographer nodded.

'How many more? Tell us.'

'Maybe . . . maybe four.'

'I am covered in chagrin again. But of course, Sylvia is considerably more beautiful than the dear departed

123

Carol, are you not, my dear? Still, that gives us our average again. Two-and-a-half placets to destroy my marriage and four to destroy Sylvia's. A total of six-and-a-half placets for an average of three-and-three-quarters placets per marriage. Three-and-three-quarters of the finest imaginable fucks to destroy a marriage. Somehow, you know, somehow it seems . . . very little. Very little indeed. Do you not think? Seventeen thousand, five hundred dollars and three-and-three-quarters of the finest imaginable fucks to wreck a marriage and cause all that distress and despair for so many people for so long. Well? Don't you think?'

The photographer swallowed.

'Well? Yes or no?'

'Yes, Mr Howard.'

'Ah. So even you agree that it was very little. To take so much from us – from all of us – and sell it for so little. So very little for so very much. There is an imbalance, is there not?'

'Yes, Mr Howard.'

'And the imbalance must be redressed, must it not?'

The photographer's head started to hang.

'Look at me,' the tycoon said. 'I asked you a question. You admit an imbalance, therefore the imbalance must be redressed. Must it not?'

'Yes. Yes, Mr Howard.'

'Excellent. We are in perfect accord. Let us see if we can maintain it. Tell me, Jake, how do you suggest that we redress the balance? How, to coin a phrase, shall we tip the scale?'

Silence.

'Not one thought occurs to you, Jake? Let me make a suggestion then. Poetic justice. You are familiar with the phrase?'

'Yes, Mr Howard.'

'Then define it for me.'

'It's when . . . it's when someone does something to

someone else, and the –' he swallowed '– the same thing happens to him.'

'Inelegant, but adequate for our purposes. So Jake, tell me, what have you done to us?'

'I've . . . I've taken photographs of you, Mr Howard.'

'That is so. But by taking those "photographs", what else have you done? No suggestions? Then I shall tell you. You've humiliated us, Jake. You've caused us all considerable pain and suffering. Would you not agree?'

The photographer nodded.

'I said, "Would you not agree?" '

'Yes, Mr Howard.'

'Then what poetic justice should entail in your case, Jake?'

The photographer blinked.

'Humiliation, Mr Howard.'

'Yes. Humiliation. And?'

'Pain and –' he caught a warning flash in the tycoon's eyes '– considerable pain and suffering. Mr Howard.'

'Excellent, Jake. Excellent. But to make the poetic justice complete, what refinement should be added to this humiliation and this *considerable* pain and suffering? Can you suggest something?'

The tycoon clicked his fingers loudly.

'That was not for you, Jake. Just answer the question.'

'It . . . it should be photographed, Mr Howard.'

'Ah, I can promise you more than that, Jake. Not merely photographed, but –' he nodded over the photographer's shoulder '– *filmed*. Yes, please look.'

There was a buzz of excitement and surprise from the film-stars watching over the tycoon's shoulders, and the photographer turned and saw a black glistening mass rising in the middle of the pool. It was a movie camera swathed in black waterproof cloth, he realised, ridden by a cameraman in scuba gear.

'Yes, Jake,' the tycoon said from behind him. 'You're going to be filmed as you are humiliated and subjected

125

to considerable pain and suffering. We're going to film a three-hour feature and we're going to call it – Gayle, dear, what was your suggestion? Ah, thank you. We're going to film a three-hour feature and we're going to call it *High Society*. And you, Jake, you are going to be the male lead. Indeed, you are going to be the only star in the picture. Ladies, if you would all don your dominoes. Joe here will circulate and hand them out to you. Yolanda, you are script supervisor. Please take Jake through his opening lines of dialogue while Gayle supervises his costuming.'

The stars came out from behind Hugh Howard's chair, chattering happily as one of the gorillas, Joe, walked among them in his black suit, like a whale nudging through a shoal of angel fish, handing out dominoes from one of his pockets. Gayle Connor slipped hers on and came over to him as he heard whispers of cloth to his right. He glanced there and saw Yolanda stepping out of the ring of her discarded swimsuit, then walking over to him too.

'Give Yolanda her script, Harry,' Howard said. Jake swallowed and started to get an erection as the two women reached him and stood in front of him, naked but for their black high-heels and black dominoes. There was a rustle of paper and Harry handed Yolanda a sheaf of typescript.

'Thanks, Harry,' she said. Gayle glanced over her shoulder at the tycoon, the sunlight striking glittering highlights from her honey-blonde hair.

'I can begin, Mr Howard?' she asked.

'You can begin, my dear. Hand her the scissors, Joe, then fetch some more.'

Joe handed her a pair of large steel scissors and she stood working them for a moment, staring into Jake's face.

'Is that a light meter in your pocket, Mr Green? Or are you just pleased to see me?'

She thrust the scissors with a snap at the bulge in his trousers and his hips jerked away from them involuntarily.

'Hold him, Harry,' said the tycoon, and two hands clamped over his shoulders and held him steady as Gayle tugged one of his sleeves open and inserted the hem between the open blades of her scissors.

'Here are your opening lines, Jake,' said Yolanda as Gayle began to cut steadily up the sleeve.

'The scene is the poolside. Thanks, Joan.'

Joan Meadingley had handed her a domino and she slipped the typescript between her knees and held it there while she put the domino on.

'Right,' she said, retrieving the typescript. 'The scene is the poolside. I walk towards you in high heels. Click, click, click, click. When I reach you, I say, "Now, down. Down on your face." You go down on your face. I continue, "Yes, like that. Now, what do you want?" Your reply is, "To kiss them, Mistress." My heels, that is.'

Gayle had reached his armpit with the scissors and was now cutting in a circle.

'Repeat it, Jake,' Yolanda said. 'Repeat your line.'

He swallowed. Gayle finished cutting, took hold of the sleeve with her other hand, and tore it away.

' "To kiss them, Mistress." '

'That's right. Then my line is, "You must grovel first." And you grovel. I continue, "Yes, like that. Grovel for me. Grovel, you worm. Now, repeat. What do you want?" And your reply is the same as before: "To kiss them, Mistress." Then I say "Then kiss them, worm," and you kiss my shoes. Right? Repeat that line.'

Gayle had started on his second sleeve, steadily cutting through the cloth to his armpit.

' "To kiss them, Mistress," ' the photographer said.

'Good. OK, let's run through it. Poolside. I come towards you on high heels. Click, click, click.'

His erection jerked in his trousers as she started acting.

' "Now, down. Down on your face. Yes, like that. Now, what do you want?" '

He opened his mouth.

' "To . . . to kiss them, Mistress." '

Gayle wrenched at his sleeve and pulled it away, dropping it to the ground with the first.

' "You must grovel first," ' Yolanda continued. ' "Yes, like that. Grovel for me. Grovel, you worm. Now, repeat. What do you want?" '

' "To kiss them, Mistress." '

' "Then kiss them, worm." And you kiss them. Right?'

He nodded. The line of beautiful women who were watching him, naked but for black high heels and black dominoes, clapped ironically, drowning the faint click of shirt buttons meeting the concrete of the poolside as Gayle cut them off one by one.

'The next scene, you don't have any scripted dialogue. But I'm sure you can improvise a few . . . noises.'

The women, knowing what was in the script, tittered. Gayle had moved behind him, murmuring an order to Harry, who released him and let her begin cutting his shirt up the back.

'You might like to help her, some of you,' Howard said. Joe was moving along the line of women with a tray, and one by one the women were advancing on the photographer, working the scissors they had picked up from the tray.

'But please, ladies, please be careful of his manhood.'

The first two, Moira Huxley and Jane Wilding, reached him, high heels clicking on the concrete, and began cutting at his trousers with their scissors. Soon he was the centre of six or seven pairs of busily working scissors and strips of clothing were falling off him in a steady shower. He tried to swing his hands protectively over his erect cock as his underpants were cut open, but scissors clacked warningly at his fingers and he pulled his hands away. Soon he was naked and the women moved back, leaving him standing in a circle of strips of clothing.

'Excellent!' Howard said with a clap. 'Is it in the can, William?'

The scuba-suited cameraman raised a black thumb, and the photographer realised that he had been being filmed as the final pieces of his clothing were cut away.

'Now, your scene with Yolanda, Jake,' Howard continued. 'Harry will show you where to stand. Yes, that's about right. Yolanda, if you'll just get into position.'

'Yes, Mr Howard.'

'And ladies, if you'll begin fitting your, ah, instruments.'

Harry let go of Jake's shoulders and moved back, out of shot as Yolanda positioned herself on one corner of the pool. Jake heard a click, then a hiss of amplified breath as the tycoon raised a loudhailer to his lips.

'And . . . action!'

Yolanda began to walk down the pool towards him, her high heels clicking on the concrete of the poolside. His erection ticked higher, but his mind had gone blank. What was it he had to say? She reached him and stood staring at him for a moment with a look of superb contempt on her face.

'Now, down. Down on your face.'

He went down on one knee, then the other, then stretched himself full-length on the poolside, feeling the heat of it sear into his skin as he stared ahead of him at her black high heels. His line clicked back into his head.

'Yes, like that,' Yolanda said from above him. 'Now, what do you want?'

He twisted his head upward, trying to see her face.

'To kiss them, Mistress.'

'You must grovel first. Grovel.'

He rode the contempt in her voice, allowing it to guide his limbs as he drew them up and grovelled before her, groaning a little as she rewarded him for his skill by letting satisfaction creep into her voice as she continued: 'Yes, like that. Grovel for me. Grovel, you worm. Now, repeat. What do you want?'

'To kiss them, Mistress.'

'Then kiss them, worm.'

He crawled forward and began to kiss her shoes, feeling his cock leak pre-come on the scalding concrete.

'Cut!' Howard yelled. 'Jake, you're a natural. Ladies, are you ready?'

A chorus of 'Yes, Mr Howard' and 'Yes, sir, Mr Howard' went up and Jake turned his head sideways. He gasped with horror: the line of stars was now equipped with large, black, strap-on dildos.

'Very well, then please take your positions for scene three.'

They advanced on him menacingly, the dildos ticking off their steps as their high heels clicked on the concrete.

'Jake, spread-eagle.'

The photographer tried to push himself up and look towards the tycoon.

'Spread-eagle, man. Hands and feet wide from your body. Hands palm-down, feet turned to one side. Do it.'

He understood and spread-eagled, putting his hands palm-down, turning his feet to one side.

'Moira, you take his left hand; Gayle, you take his right. Fiona, his left foot; Tania, his right. The rest please line up and prepare to pull the train on him. Joe, the cushion, if you please.'

The high heels clicked round him and his head jerked left and right, trying to watch him. Suddenly he cried out in pain. A high heel had descended on the back of his right hand, pinning it into place. He cried out again. Another high heel descended on his left hand, then one on his left ankle, quickly followed by one on his right. He was pinned down like a butterfly. Heavier footsteps shook the concrete faintly beneath him and he heard a male grunt and smelt harsh sweat as Joe knelt beside him. A strong hand grasped his right hip and lifted it, and a fat cushion was pushed beneath him, trapping his cock up against his belly, leaving his balls dangling between his spread thighs.

'Thank you, Joe,' Howard said. 'Ladies, are you ready?'

Another chorus of 'Yes, Mr Howard' and 'Yes, sir, Mr Howard' went up.

'And . . . action!'

High heels began to click on the poolside behind him, getting nearer and nearer and his balls crawled with dread, tightening to the fork of his thighs. The high heels reached him and he heard a sigh of pleasure, then quivered as the star lowered herself to him and two silken knees brushed the back of his thighs. Who was it? Who was about to ass-fuck him? He quivered again. Sharp-nailed fingers were prying his buttock-cleft open, exposing his sweat-moistened asshole. The knees slid against his skin and then he felt the head of the dildo being put to his asshole. He cried out again as the four heels holding him down dug harder into him: the women were making sure he did not move when the ass-fucking began. He groaned as the dildo-head was pushed at him experimentally, then began to exert an increasing pressure, slowly forcing its way into him for his first anal rape of the day.

7

Paces of Eight

'There,' he said through his habitual mouthful of tobacco, pointing with a black-nailed forefinger. 'Can ye see 'im?'

His taller companion followed the gesture down, narrowing his blue eyes against the harsh glitter of tropical sunlight on the disturbed water of the *Geraldine*'s wake, and saw what he had been brought here to see: the blunt-headed shape perhaps thirty or forty feet deep, darker against the dark blue of deep ocean.

'Aye,' he said. 'I see him.'

Maggot triumphantly discharged a gobbet of tobacco to the water, where it lay like a splot of blood for a moment before dissolving.

'Did I not tell ye so? Twen'y foot, if 'e's an inch, an' worst of bad luck fr'all on us.'

His companion leaned back from the rail, shaking his head.

'No, he'll be after ship's offal, deck-scourings and the like. They're foul omnivores, these creatures and –'

'Noa,' Maggot interrupted with a scowl. 'I'll 'ave none of your book-larnin' when I *knows* the truth on it. 'E's a devil-fish, an' the devil rides with 'im. Was I not with Captain Samuels, but a day out from Tortuga, an' one of 'em attaches 'isself to our arse jus' like this one 'ere 'as done, an' two days later, were we not . . .'

He broke off, and spat into the water again, landing the gobbet of tobacco this time directly above the dark, restless shape, as though to defy it. His companion shook his head with a laugh.

'And do ye not have the scars to prove it, young Maggot?' he said, imitating the other's accent with a grin. Then, in his habitual voice: 'No, you're a superstitious old devil, Maggot, and that's only devil we have in these parts. This devil-fish of yours obeys natural laws and knows no more than what he sees and smells, as you'll see in two days' time when we're putting safe into –'

But he was interrupted again, for ringing down from the crow's-nest far above them came the lookout's cry.

'Ship ho! Ship ho on the starboard bow!'

Maggot gaped upward, black teeth glinting in the sunlight, then flung a look of mingled triumph and terror at his interlocutor.

'Did ye 'ear 'im? Did ye 'ear 'im?' he gabbled. ''Tis the *Amazon Maid*, the cursed *Amazon Maid*, sure as Captain Samuels 'as been dead an' drownded these thirty-one years past.'

Then he was scuttling up the deck for the starboard bow, leaving the words of his companion's reply still-born on his lips. And indeed, within five minutes it was plain to see that the sighted ship was no lumbering merchantman: she was flying over the waves light as a gull, and there could be no doubt that she was intent on intercepting them. Maggot's young companion had followed the aged seaman up the deck and was shielding his eyes as he stared out over the water. Now he turned to the ship's captain where that worthy stood at the now crowded rail, gazing at the mysterious ship through his telescope.

'What ensign does she carry, Captain?' he asked.

The captain, a tall, hollow-cheeked New Englander, grunted and lowered his telescope.

'See for yourself, Mr Adams,' he said, handing the device over. Adams took it and raised it to his own eye. As he touched the focusing screw the white sails of the ship sprang out at him, white and curved as the breasts of a giantess. Then he had lifted the telescope and the foreshortened ship's ensign was flapping silently in the telescope's field. He swore softly, and Maggot, who was muttering two places along the crowded rail, caught the word and cried out with fear. He lowered the telescope and turned to meet the captain's sardonic gaze. The captain nodded.

'You told me you'd like to see action this trip, did you not, Mr Adams? It seems you'll see some. Perhaps more than you'll have a taste for.'

Mr Adams nodded silently himself, feeling a pulse throb in his tightened throat. The ensign had shown crossed whips beneath a pair of male buttocks and it was the *Amazon Maid* all right, sure as Captain Samuels had been dead and drowned these thirty-one years past. But as he handed the telescope back a cheer of relief went up from the men: the scudding progress of their pursuer had faltered and it was apparent that the wind, still fresh enough where they sailed, was dropping fast those couple of miles across the water. The captain sent all available hands aloft to pile on sail, and they went up chattering happily, confident that the extra distance they gained would see them shake off the pursuit for good when night fell. As the extra sail took effect and the *Geraldine* began to surge through the water, Maggot alone remained at the rail watching the dwindling shape of the *Amazon Maid*, and his was the first voice raised when the wind began to desert them too. Mr Adams joined him again, clapping the old man on the shoulder and pointing out that they had gained another couple of miles and were surely now safe. Maggot shook his head and spat over the rail.

'Noa. See, they's already got 'em at it, poor bastards.'

His dirty fingernail came up again, pointing out over the water, and Mr Adams stared after it, noticing suddenly that the hull of the distant ship was now surrounded by a glittering halo, as though sunlight danced there off broken water. He frowned.

'What in God's . . .?'

'Rowin'. They's got 'em rowin', an' they's ticklin' their arses to encourage 'em along. Ye'll see soon enough.'

He spat again, and Mr Adams could only stare in the hope that he was wrong. But soon there was no doubt that the *Amazon Maid* was creeping nearer, and when next he looked through the captain's telescope he saw with a renewed tightening in his throat that Maggot had been right: the *Amazon Maid*'s sails were as flat and empty as their own, but long oars rose and fell on the water round her hull, pulling her inexorably closer. In half an hour a faint drum-beat was audible, echoing across the shrinking stretch of water between the two ships, and as it grew louder the waiting seamen on the *Geraldine* began to catch the faint repeated crack of whips. The *Amazon Maid*'s ensign was clearly visible now, stirring atop the mizzen in fugitive breezes that concealed and revealed its buttocks-and-crossed-whips to the seamen now crowding the rail again with their captain and officers.

'Here they are,' said the captain, and Mr Adams turned to see him lowering his telescope and lifting a long forearm. He turned and followed the gesture and saw that tall figures in an odd uniform of half-black, half-white had appeared on the deck of the *Amazon Maid*, driving smaller figures before them to the rail.

'You will see something now, Mr Adams,' the captain said. 'Half my crew will be lost within the hour.'

Mr Adams looked back at him and saw to his astonishment that the captain was squeezing a large bulge in his breeches as he lifted the telescope back to his eye with his free hand. He turned back to the approaching ship, straining his eyes to see what was taking place on deck, then turned back to the captain.

'Will you not fight, captain?'

The captain lowered the telescope and held it out to him.

'No, Mr Adams. And you can see for yourself why I shall not.'

Hands trembling faintly, he took the telescope and raised it to see for himself, and suddenly he too was conscious of his cock beginning to stir and thicken in his breeches. The tall figures on the deck of the *Amazon Maid* were women naked but for thigh-boots and shoulder-high gloves of black leather, and the smaller figures they were driving before them with flashing whips were chained and cringing men with oddly pale skin. The captain's voice sounded again beside him.

'I'll not order my men to fight women, and there's precious little chance of any such order being obeyed even if I could bring myself to make it. They'll go willingly enough, when the time comes.'

The chained men on the *Amazon Maid* had been driven to the rail now and were being strapped into a species of stocks that waited for them there. Adams's cock was fully erect now, straining in his trousers in salute to the firm breasts and shaved *montes Veneris* that filled the field of his telescope, and when he lowered it he saw that the crew of the *Geraldine* had responded to what they could see of the preparations on the deck of the *Amazon Maid*: twenty or thirty cocks were straining in the breeches of their owners. A breathless silence had now taken hold of the ship, and the splash of the oars that dragged the *Amazon Maid* nearer was clearly audible. The men on her deck were strapped into the stocks now, and two of the women were at work in front of them.

When the *Amazon Maid* had drawn up beside them and the oars were rattling back into the hull, the effects of their work was plainly apparent: the *Geraldine*'s crew was confronted by a row of erect cocks sitting along the rail and pointing at them like a row of guns where the men were strapped upright into the stocks. One of the thigh-booted and shoulder-gloved women jumped up on the rail beside the straining cocks, stroking idly at her shaved pussy with one hand as she cupped the other round her mouth and hailed across the water.

'A'oy, sheep-mates!'

A murmur had gone up from the *Geraldine*'s crew as she jumped and began to stroke her pussy; now, as it became apparent that she was French or Spanish, another murmur went up, and Mr Adams heard the first groans of lust as she paused, lifting the glove from her pussy and sniffing idly at its fingertips one by one before returning it to her pussy and continuing thus: 'A'oy, sheep-mates! We 'ave need of fresh cock aboard ze *Amazon Maid*. Will you not join us an' supply some? We promise you much pleasure in return for ze loan of your members.'

More groans sounded as she levered her pussy lips apart and flapped them like butterfly wings, and several of the younger members of the *Geraldine*'s crew were now leaning forward hard over the rail with open mouths. But now there came a sound of spitting and looking down the line of seamen Mr Adams saw Maggot shielding his eyes with a trembling, liver-spotted paw as he croaked his warning: 'Don't listen to 'er, ship-mates! 'Tis not pleasure ye'll be 'avin', but torment if you step aboard that hell-ship, an' not one on you will lay so much as a finger's tip to that bitch's quim. She flaunts it to entice, nothin' more!'

The woman lifted her gloved hand from her pussy with a laugh and stroked and fondled one of her breasts, tugging hard at the nipple, leaving smears of pussy-juice on its firm curves that flashed and winked in the sun when she lifted the hand away and drew in breath for another shout.

'Do not listen to 'im, sheep-mates! 'E is old an' 'is sap is dried in 'is wizzered balls. I, Captain Charlotte of ze *Amazon Maid*, promise you pleasure an' pleasure is what ye shall 'ave, as now you see.'

She looked away from them, nodding to the women who stood behind the row of stocks, and they stepped forward to the buttocks of the naked men fastened there. Evidently testicles were being grasped and squeezed, for the men suddenly groaned and their cocks jerked and bounced on the rail. The woman atop the rail now walked forward in her boots over the lines of cocks, standing carefully atop each as she passed, then turned and stood ready to walk back again. The cocks were stiffer now than ever, and the woman pointed at them proudly as she hailed the *Geraldine* across the water again.

'Do you see, sheep-mates? Zese stiff cocks might be yours, an' shall be, if you 'ave ze courage of men an' not of mice. Now watch again an' see ze 'eights to which you will lifted.'

She bent and began to tug off one of her thigh-boots now, but her words had already convinced two of the *Geraldine*'s crew, who leapt atop the rail and dove clumsily into the sea. One, it was apparent at once, could not swim, for he rose shouting in the water and then sank in a thrashing of limbs. Still tugging her thigh-boot down, the captain of the *Amazon Maid* issued an order in French, and one of the ball-squeezers deserted her post, tugged off her own thigh-boots in two swift jerks, jumped atop the rail, and threw herself into the sea in a clean, expert dive. The captain of the *Amazon Maid* had her thigh-boot off and was balancing on one leg; now she handed the boot to one of the ball-squeezers and began to tug down the second. The woman who had dived overboard had vanished beneath the waves now, evidently swimming after the sinking sailor while his companion swam clumsily to the hull of the *Amazon Maid* and clung to it. As a rope was dropped to him and he began to haul himself up, the sailor who could not swim reappeared, struggling on the surface, clasped from behind by the woman who had dived in to rescue him, and the captain was handing her second boot to a ball-squeezer.

'See, sheep-mates!' she cried, pointing at the rescued sailor, 'even whezzer you can sweem matters not, for we will bring you aboard zus! She 'as 'er hand in 'is trousers an' manipulates 'im to a joyous spurting of ze sperm even as she sweems 'im to ze Paradise that awaits 'im 'ere, aboard my sheep.'

It was evidently so: the rescued seaman had ceased to struggle as he was guided to the hull of the *Amazon Maid* and a waiting rope. His rescuer, apparently well aware of the eyes that were fastened on her, was swimming with extravagant frog's strokes of her well-rounded thighs, concealing and revealing her shaved pussy over and over, and one hand was busy in the breeches of the rescued sailor, who was gasping with pleasure.

'Yes!' cried the captain of the *Amazon Maid*. 'Such pleasure awaits all of you.'

And now, with a nod to the ball-squeezers, one of whom, replacing the rescuer, apparently had a pair of balls in each hand, she began to walk back down the rail in her bare feet over the line of cocks that rested atop it, standing on each as she passed it. It was enough: as her bare foot lifted from the first cock it began to discharge, firing thick shafts of white sperm high and far into the air to fall with tiny splashes into the sea. Now her bare foot was lifting from a second cock and it too was discharging; then from a third and fourth, and they too discharged; and fifth and sixth, and seventh and eighth, till she had walked down the line of cocks and brought all but one to its discharge. The rescued sailor was being hauled aboard the *Amazon Maid*, limbs loose and trailing, for the expert hand of his rescuer had been busy in his breeches till the last moment and he had evidently experienced his own heavy discharge.

'Do you see, sheep-mates!' cried Captain Charlotte, pointing down the line of cocks she had just brought to copious orgasm. 'Join us, or for ever suffer ze reproaches of your cocks.'

Then she began to walk down the line of cocks again, standing atop each again as she passed, pausing at the one that had not discharged and beginning to work at its head with her toes. To cries of horror from Maggot, more seamen aboard the *Geraldine* obeyed her summons, leaping atop the rail and throwing themselves clumsily into the sea. Some rose threshing in the water and sank, and Captain Charlotte jerked her head in command to the ball-squeezers as the cock she was working on with her toes began to discharge, its jets of semen falling into the sea almost in synchrony with the dives of the ball-squeezers.

The captain of the *Geraldine* watched his crew flinging themselves overboard with no more than a raised eyebrow, and even Mr Adams's leap atop the rail and plunge, fully clothed, into the sea prompted him to no more than a tut of surprise. The young man disappeared beneath the water in a neat circle of bubbles, then reappeared nearly at the *Amazon Maid*'s hull, reaching up for one of the ropes thrown by the women. When he hauled himself over the rail and clambered on deck, he found the crew of the *Amazon Maid* welcoming the new arrivals, who were being lined up and stripped of their soaking clothes as chains were passed over their wrists. Captain Charlotte had jumped down from the rail and was putting her thigh-boots back on; now she swaggered over, fingering at her pussy again. When they had all been stripped and chained she strolled down the line, wafting the shining fingertips of her hand under their noses to giggles from her own crew, for the men's cocks jerked almost vertical as the musky aroma of her pussy entered their nostrils.

'Fresh pussy, *mes garçons*,' Captain Charlotte said as she reached the end of the line and turned to survey the row of cocks she had set ticking with heightened lust. 'But I am afraid zat, as your aged sheep-mate so correctly forecast, you will not sample eet during your stay aboard my sheep. Are zey bound, *mes filles*? Zen stretch zem on ze deck, face down.'

A ball-squeezer yanked at the chain that had been looped round his wrists and Adams took a last look across at the *Geraldine*, seeing how old Maggott was struggling furiously at the rail with two young Puritans who, for all the forty years' advantage of youth and strength they possessed over the old man, were barely able to keep him from flinging himself into the sea and re-joining the crew of the *Amazon Maid*. And then he was down on his knees on the deck, lowering his tingling nipples to meet its sun-warmed wood. He heard Captain Charlotte stamp on the deck and announce again: 'No pussy, *mes garçons*. But,' she continued, and he heard one of his ship-mates suddenly groan with pleasure, 'we will always do our best to bring you to your paroxysms by other means.'

More groans, coming nearer. He tried to raise his head from the deck and see what the large-breasted captain was doing, but a ball-squeezer stamped warningly at his feet. But he learned without looking, for a groan had sounded from immediately beside him on the right and in the next moment he felt the captain's boots sinking into his buttocks as she walked on top of him. She paused, bouncing up and down, grinding his cock against the deck, and he heard another voice groan in acknowledgment: his own. Then she was stepping off him and passing to the man immediately beside him on the left.

'E 'oo leaves ze smallest patch of ze sperm,' the captain announced conversationally, 'will leek ze deck clean of all patches of ze sperm. Zerefore my advice is to 'old yourselves back, *mes garçons*, an' discharge at ze last of possible moments, when I 'ave stroden atop your fine 'airy backsides once more, before I bring you to such pleasure as you w –'

But she broke off with a click of exasperation and a muttered '*Ah, mais les jeunes!*'

Mr Adams heard the groans of a prematurely ejaculating seaman, and gathered himself to try and hold his sperm back as the captain turned and began to stride back down the line of clenched male buttocks, pausing atop each to bounce on it thoroughly. Another seaman ejaculated prematurely on her second pass, unable to control his sperm as her boots landed atop his buttocks one by one and sank deep into his flesh. Mr Adams gritted his teeth as she stepped on him for the second time and bounced, feeling his balls lift hard to the fork of his thighs, aching fiercely as his cock was crushed against the deck again. Then she stepped off him and stood atop the seaman on his right, and he felt a trickle of sperm leaving his cock head and moistening the deck. More groans as she strode and bounced to the end of the line of prostrate seamen.

'Vair good, *mes garçons*, you 'ave ze most of you 'eld back wiz admirable restraint. But I sink, per'aps . . .'

He heard her boots land on the deck, then, after a moment, there was a jingle of metal, followed by another. What was she doing? He blinked as she spoke again, crying out to the men left aboard the *Geraldine*, stamping on the deck with a renewed jingle of metal.

'Do you see, my timid ones? Do you see what pleasures await you, if you but pluck ze courage to sample zem? *Les éperons de capitaine Charlotte!* The spurs of Captain Charlotte!'

This time, as she stepped back atop the first pair of buttocks, there was first a groan, then a yelp of surprise and pain.

'Come, *mon garçon*,' the captain murmured, provoking further yelps of pain; 'come for your captain. Come for your captain, my little one. Ah, zat is so, zat is it, my pretty boy.'

Mr Adams waited, sweating in the strong sun as he listened to the captain working her way down the line of buttocks. Two further seamen jumped overboard from the *Geraldine* as she worked: he heard clumsy splashes in the sea; then the subdued splashes of two neat dives as ball-squeezers dived in to rescue them; then the sound of the men clambering aboard and the clink of chains as they were bound by their wrists and laid flat on their faces at the far end of the row. But a moment later his attention was focused entirely on himself, for the captain had stepped from the seaman immediately on his right and her boots were planted firmly atop his buttocks again.

She bounced, asking, 'Are you ready, *mon petit chou?*' and then he bit his lip with agony, feeling blood trickling fast on to the deck, for his right buttock had suddenly lanced with pain as she spurred him for the first time. She bounced again, rocking slightly so that his cock rolled against the deck, and then spurred his left buttock.

'Pain, *mon petit chou*,' she murmured, 'pain for you, an' for you alone, which shall not cease until you discharge for me.'

He couldn't restrain a yelp of pain this time, as she spurred him simultaneously in both buttocks, and then bounced harder than ever.

'Come, my little one. Come for your muzzer. Come for muzzer Charlotte.'

He struggled to hold himself back, but it was too much: the hardness of the deck beneath his crushed cock; the heat of the sun on his back and legs; the weight of the woman bouncing on and dominating his buttocks; the repeated, merciless spurts of pain as she spurred him; the instructions she issued in her cock-maddening accent: he could restrain himself no longer and felt sperm positively hosing up against his belly and chest as he came in eight or nine heavy spurts.

'Ah, *mon petit*, but zat, I believe, was 'eaviest of all,' she murmured through the roar of blood in his ears; and then she stepped off him, ready to begin work on the next pair of buttocks. He lay gasping, feeling the sun sucking greedily at the sweat that had sprung out down his back as he came and that was gathering to trickle down his buttock-cleft; and when the captain had finished the row of buttocks and jumped lightly to the deck with a cry of ''E comes!', he was still recovering from his orgasm. He heard her spurs jingle as she strode to the rail and hailed the *Geraldine* for the last time.

'Sheep-mates, your final chance 'as come! Join us now, an' enter Paradise, or for ever suffer ze reproaches of ze cocks which even from 'ere I can see salute us poor weemin of ze *Amazon Maid*.'

He lifted his head, blinking as he tried to focus through the blaze of sunlight. There she stood at the rail, thighs splayed, round firm buttocks jerking in time with her words, black-fringed pussy fingered lovingly by a gloved hand working slowly between her thighs.

'Ze choice, sheep-mates, it is yours, an' yours alone! Come to us, an' you will find us not ungrateful.'

He heard a splash as another seaman leapt overboard from the *Geraldine*, and the captain's buttocks tightened with pleasure.

'Ah, but zere is one man of courage left aboard, I see! One man 'oo wishes 'is cock to leeve as it deserves to leeve! Can it be zat 'e is truly ze last?'

Then, as an aside to one of the ball-squeezers, in a lower voice: '*Non, Judith, ce n'est pas nécessaire pour lui. Tu vois qu'il sait nager.*'

She paused, waiting as he heard the seaman clumsily splashing across the gap that separated the *Geraldine* from the *Amazon Maid*.

'No, sheep-mates? 'E is ze last? Zen farewell, foolish ones. You will 'ave plenty of stories to 'ear of what you 'ave missed, from our old crew.'

The dripping head of the final seaman appeared above the rail of the *Amazon Maid* and as he was hauled aboard by a pair of ball-squeezers Captain Charlotte turned with a lip-fart of contempt and a wave of dismissal with the hand she had lifted from her pussy.

'Get zem up from below an' srow zem overboard with *zose*,' she said, a gloved finger stabbing out at the line of chained men at the rail; 'an' get zem *zere* –' the finger stabbed at the line of men belly-down on the deck '– on zeir feet. I wish to inspect ze patches *spermatiques*.'

Boots rattled on the deck as ball-squeezers hurried to obey her command, some running to the line of men face down on the deck. What had she meant about 'srowing zem overboard'? he wondered as he was pulled to his feet by his hair and ears, listening to the ball-squeezers giggle as his cock swung into view again. He learnt soon enough: the other ball-squeezers had run below deck; now they re-emerged, dragging with them chained men who blinked and squinted in the sunlight and whose cord-like muscles and pale, whip-marked skin told of long weeks on the rowing-benches.

'Farewell, my little ones!' the captain called to them as they were hustled across the deck to join the men in the stocks; 'you 'ave served us well, an' 'ere is your reward: your freedom at last!'

But it was apparent that the men, despite the suffering they had obviously endured, did not wish to leave: they struggled as one by one, erect cocks swinging, they were unchained and hoisted atop the rail, ready to be pushed overboard. Captain Charlotte chuckled.

'But do you not wish to leave us, *mes petits*? Alas, you must, for we 'ave grown bored of your cocks zese past weeks an' 'ave need of ze fresh ones. *Oui, poussez-les.*'

And the first two went shouting over the rail to land with heavy splashes in the sea. Captain Charlotte strolled across to peer overboard and watch them struggling in the water.

'Sweem, my little ones! *Non*, do not try to get aboard again. Elaine, Judith, Suzette, *dissuadez-les.*'

Three ball-squeezers left the unchaining and ran across the deck to pluck whips from the row that circled one of the masts, then went running back to the rail where the two seamen had been pushed overboard. They leant over, swinging the whips back over their shoulders, then lashing them down. There were cries of pain and the sound of whips meeting flesh.

'*Continuez*,' said Captain Charlotte, turning from the rail and strolling back towards the line of new arrivals as the whips cracked again behind her and two more men were pushed overboard.

'Now, *c'est le temps de voir*,' she said, fingering her pussy again as she stood at one end of the row of stiff-cocked men, each standing above the patch of sperm he had spurted as she stood in her spurs atop his buttocks. 'Which one of you 'as left ze smallest patch of ze sperm?'

She strolled down the row, peering, pouting, squatting to examine an irregularly shaped patch, whistling softly to herself at the size of the patch left by the far-from-exceptional cock-and-balls of the next man; then, reaching the end of the row, turning on her heel and strolling back again. Half the men at the rail had been dropped overboard and the whips were flailing continuously now, keeping them in the water. The captain squatted again at the patch she had examined previously, and nodded her head.

'*Je regrette, c'est toi, mon petit*,' she said, raising herself to her full height again. Two ball-squeezers instantly seized the seaman by the shoulders and began to force him down on his face.

'And the others, captain?' asked one of tallest ball-squeezers, evidently a mate or second-in-command. Captain Charlotte swung on her heel with a squeak of leather.

'As for ze uzzers, get zem below an' chain zem to zeir oars. Wiz ze exception, of course, of . . . *notre espion*.'

Mr Adams blinked, wondering whether he had heard right, praying that he had not. But ball-squeezers were tugging the men on his left and right away, leaving him standing alone as the seized man was forced finally down on his face and an expert hand slid between his thighs from behind, gripping his balls as Captain Charlotte ordered: 'Leek. Leek ze deck clean, you miserable specimen. I will teach you to come with such paucity when you are pleasured an' pained by ze captain of ze *Amazon Maid*.'

The seaman yelped with pain as the hand tightened on his balls, his face and nose pressed into a sticky patch of sperm, and Captain Charlotte nodded with satisfaction, then turned away and began to stroll towards the man who had been left standing on his own as the others were dragged away below deck.

'Yes, *mon petit espion*, you 'eard right. Or should I say, my not-so-little spy?'

She reached him and her gloved hand dropped and took hold of his still-erect cock, squeezing hard at the head. Despite his six feet, she was looking directly into his eyes as she continued, her hand tightening and relaxing on his cock to the rhythm of her words.

'Welcome aboard, Mr Adams of the British Secret Service. We 'ave been expecting you for some time.'

The man ordered to lick the deck screamed as his ball-squeezer grew impatient at his continued refusal to obey and discarded refinements for a brutal wrench and twist of his balls. A smile flickered over Captain Charlotte's face and her chin tilted upwards as she continued, 'How negligent of ze creator, was it not, to provide each man wiz such vulnerable organs, so accessibly placed for ze 'and of ze torturer.'

The man screamed again, and Mr Adams could not stop himself from swallowing uneasily. Her smile grew stronger as she looked away.

'Is 'e leeking ze deck, Antonia?'

'*Si, capitana.*'

'Good.'

She looked back at Mr Adams, pouting thoughtfully.

'Well, Mr Adams? Are you prepared to reveal ze details of your mission, or must we . . . what is ze word? Must we *wring* it out of you, wiz cruel hands on your fine beeg balls?'

He blinked, swallowing again as he heard the man yelp, and slowly shook his head. Captain Charlotte laughed.

'Ah, but you are ze brave one, *mon pas-si-petit espion*. But neverzeless, I assure you, you would not have wizstood much of it. *Mes filles*, zey are most expert at zeir trade of ball-torture. But for Mr Adams of ze British Secret Service we shall not stoop to such *crudités*. For you, we must have only ze most sophisticated of ze tortures. Jenny 'as told us ze way to unlock your mous.'

He blinked with shock. Jenny? His beloved Jenny? Jenny, whose portrait lay in the locket discarded with his clothes on deck? Captain Charlotte laughed again and turned her head.

'*Cécile, apporte le médaillon.*'

A ball-squeezer scampered to his discarded clothing and tugged it to and fro, turning and scampering back with Jenny's locket dangling by its delicate gold chain from her hand. Captain Charlotte took it from her and turned to him as he blinked back stinging tears.

'*Mais oui, Monsieur Anglais*, your little Jenny, your little Devon 'ore, she is one of our agents an' 'er report 'as been waiting in my cabin zese past two mon's.'

She flicked the locket open and swung it in front of him, and the faint sweet smile on Jenny's face, framed by her blonde ringlets, grew crooked first one way, then the other, one way, then the other, as though he were suddenly recognising the sardonic pleasure that had been hidden there all along.

'Yes, my not-so-little spy, we 'ave 'ad a spy of our own. She 'as informed us fully of your . . . tastes. Of your . . . perversions. An' zere is not a sheep in ze world, not one, zat is so well-equipped to meet zem as my *Amazon Maid*. Cécile, Teresa, take 'eem below an' prepare 'eem in my cabin.'

She jerked the locket away from him as he was seized by his shoulders and hustled away. The cool below deck was almost a physical shock after the blazing sunshine above, and it was nearly a minute before his eyes adjusted and he began to see clearly again. By then he was in Captain Charlotte's cabin, being chained into a curious wheeled framework that left him hanging tilted downwards, balls dangling between his splayed thighs, erect cock nudging at the now crusting sperm on his belly. The soft hand of Cécile-or-Teresa stroked at his balls for a moment, but Teresa-or-Cécile admonished her and the hand left him. Blood was starting to pool in his head and he was becoming dizzy. The two ball-squeezers walked back a little and stood by the cabin door behind him, whispering and giggling. They went quiet a moment before he heard boots coming along the corridor leading to the cabin, and then Captain Charlotte was striding into the cabin.

'Excellent, *mes filles*. We will be under way shortly, so you, Teresa, go an' assist ze *flagéllatrices*.'

'*Sí, mi capitana*,' he heard Teresa reply as the captain came forward and threw herself with a sigh onto the couch that waited beside the framework into which he was chained.

'*Les bottes*, Cécile,' she said, as Teresa scampered from the cabin. He heard the captain's boots pulled off and dropped to the floor one by one.

'*Présente-le à mes pieds. Vite.*'

The ball-squeezer's own boots sounded on the floor as she moved behind him and began to pull the framework backwards before swinging to the left and pushing it to the couch where the captain's long, slender feet awaited his face. For a moment he caught a glimpse of the captain, thighs apart, fingering her pussy with a gloved hand, and then his face was pressed to within an inch of her feet. As his nostrils filled with an aroma of fresh foot-sweat and leather he felt his cock jerk up against his belly, almost digging into him, so stiff had it suddenly become.

'Shall I tell you, *mon espion anglais*, what now awaits you? Or shall I demonstrate? Boce, I sink. Cécile, *suce-le pour cinq secondes.*'

The ball-squeezer walked behind him and he heard her lower herself to the floor and shuffle on her knees beneath him. He almost cried out when hair brushed his stomach and a warm, moist mouth closed on the head of his cock and began sucking.

'*Un,*' said the captain. '*Deux. Trois. Quatre. Cinq. Et arrête.*'

The mouth came off his cock with a slow pop and he gasped with frustration, drawing the scent of the warm, moist female feet in front of him deep into his lungs.

'*Et maintenant, lèche ses bals.*'

Cécile shuffled backwards a little and a warm tongue was suddenly on his balls, licking them slowly and carefully.

'*Et arrête.*'

The tongue left his balls, leaving them coated with spittle.

'*Et maintenant, souffle ses bals.*'

He felt Cécile blowing gently on his balls. Heat was being drawn out of them.

'Do you see, my English spy? We 'ave presented you wiz a bargain. An exchange of goods. You give us what we wish to know, an' we will give you what you wish to 'ave. Cécile will suck you, zen gently lick your balls, zen gently blow zem, zus cooling zem an' denying you ze release for which you are already longing, *n'est-ce pas?* Zen she will suck you again, an' lick your balls again, an' blow your balls again, an' zis will repeat until you tell us what we wish to know. An' as she does zis, I will be most gently stroking your face wiz my feet, for I know from Jenny 'ow much it is you love zis. Cécile, *encore.*'

The cool breath ceased to blow over his balls as the captain pushed her feet forward and began to rub them gently against his face as Cecile's warm, moist mouth again closed on the head of his cock and sucked. His head was roaring with dizziness and pleasure and he could feel his balls already beginning to ache with denied orgasm.

'*Un*,' said the captain. '*Deux. Trois. Quatre. Cinq. Et arrête.*'

The mouth came off his cock with a pop.

'*Et léche-le.*'

The tongue began to lick his balls again as the captain gently tweaked his nose between her big toe and second toe. He groaned, hearing the oars rattle as they were lowered again into the sea, ready to set the *Amazon Maid* under way, sailing back into the dark legends from which it had emerged.

'*Et arrête.*'

8

Breast and Circuses

The dressing room was soundproofed, but when Jocasta sat down to put her ankh on she could feel the stamping shudder in the bench beneath her buttocks. Over by the door leading to the tunnel Jemima had revived one of her old pre-match superstitions, heading the ball a hundred times against the wall, and the repeated double slap of ball against wall-and-forehead ran unvarying beneath the bustle of players changing all round her: the twang of bra-straps, the snap of shorts being adjusted at waists, the rattle of ice-cubes as Hilary delved in the bucket of champagne that was all their minimalist manager Basil Amberson had given them as a team-talk, carrying it silently into the dressing room, silently putting it down, silently walking out again, confident that they understood. But Jemima was nervous, Hilary was nervous, she, Jocasta, was nervous, the whole team was nervous. It was understandable, on the day of the PA Cup Final.

She slipped off the bench, turned, and put her bare left foot on it, ready for her first boot. Created especially for her by Antonio Gripelli, one of the finest modern Italian footwear designers – her commercial agents were still negotiating with the world's two largest sports firms for marketing rights – they were made of an advanced silicon-fibre composite that was even more transparent than glass, so that her slim feet would be clearly visible as she ran and passed and shot. The left boot incorporated a foot-cam using the front curves of the boot itself as a lens and compensating for astigmatic distortion using a program written by a rogue computer genius at the Slovakian Ministry of Defence; the right boot incorporated an electronic thermometer and hygrometer that would beam temperature and humidity continuously in hundredths of centigrade and tenths of per cent to dedicated sports-fetishist channels as the match proceeded, supplementing the less detailed figures that would sit beneath the score on the stadium's giant laser display-board. For some of her fans, the readings would be far more important than the result of the match, because neither boot was ventilated and her feet would sweat copiously for ninety minutes and maybe half an hour of extra time, soaking the strips of ultra-absorbent nano-foam waiting in the soles of both boots. The strips would be divided into squares after the match and sold by auction over the Internet with numbered and signed certificates of authenticity: the same Slovakian computer genius had programmed the machine that would cut the sole-shaped strips into squares with minimum waste, and square left-sixteen had already been reserved in his name.

There were even bets being laid on how hot her feet would get, and pedological experts had argued for hours on the sports-fetishist channels, hands flexing models of her boots, erections often clearly visible in their trousers. Many thought that the temperature would depend partly on her emotional state: on whether she had a good game or a bad; more crucially still, on whether she scored, and when, and how often. She blinked at the thought of it, slipping her left foot into the boot, letting her hands run on by themselves as they looped the lace under the sole three times and then began to tie the knot. Her girlhood dream, and now she might be minutes away from fulfilling it. To score in the PA Cup Final, with two hundred thousand fans in the stadium itself, and maybe two billion viewers watching round the world, bright-eyed at midday or bleary at midnight, swigging cold beer or sipping hot coffee. The ice-cubes rattled again, as though Hilary had caught her thoughts, and she started to put on her right boot. This time the lace went only twice round the sole before it was tied: one of her old superstitions, like the silver ankh now warming between her breasts. The slap of ball on wall-and-forehead had stopped now, and studs were beginning to rattle on the floor behind her as the team lined up, ready to be led out of the dressing room, down the tunnel, and on to the pitch.

She took her booted right foot off the bench and turned to join the line herself, exchanging a smile with Jemima, but no more. The rest of the team knew that she didn't like to talk before a match and left her alone. Hilary, crunching on a final ice cube, her lips wet and shining, trotted across the floor to pair with her and now they could hear Amberson's deep voice rumbling faintly just outside the door as he fended off an importunate journalist with two words. Then the door swung open and the noise of the stadium was inside the dressing room with them: the chant and counter-chant of rival fans and the double clap and single stamp of waiting foot-fans, already kept up for nearly twenty minutes. Amberson stepped into the dressing room and she caught a whiff of his new aftershave, only a month old but already earning him millions in the Far East and Americas.

'Right,' he said. 'Ready?'

Jemima nodded silently and Jocasta saw her shoulders bulge as she pressed with both palms on the ball she was holding.

'Good. Let's do it,' Amberson said, and turned to lead them down the tunnel. Now, as it always did, her stomach turned over and her sphincter loosened for a moment, and then the studs of her boots were clashing against the floor with the studs of twenty other boots and she felt herself absorbed into the team, a unit in a greater whole as the clash of their opponents' boots greeted them and the two teams were trotting side-by-side down the tunnel. The clash of boots cut off as they passed above the first buttock-pavement, then began again as they moved towards the ocean of noise waiting on the open pitch. The sunlight that flooded down on them as they emerged from the tunnel seemed to seize hold of them, warring on their eyes as the noise warred on their ears. The chants and double-clap-and-stamp were lost in acclamation as they reached the pitch and the whole stadium could see them, and then she suddenly had her individuality back, smiling as the cheering increased and chants of 'Jocasta! Jocasta!' began to ring out in acknowledgment of the sudden two-degree jump in the foot-temp figure sitting beneath the 0–0 on the display-board.

They trotted over the second buttock-pavement, the studs of their boots sinking into the flesh of another fifty or sixty masochist fans who had paid as much as £150,000 for the privilege, and passed on, the white-and-tanned surface of the pavement now mottled with red stud-marks. The band was marching out to meet them from its separate tunnel, and Hilary was lining them up for the National Anthem. Charles and Camilla were here today on the advice of their spin-doctors, fresh from their coronation, and she wondered whether the BBC was filtering out the Tampax chants beginning to start up again in the crowd. The air throbbed against her body as the bass drum in the band signalled the first bars of the anthem, and the chants were lost as the stadium began to sing. Time already seemed to be moving much faster and it seemed as though the band was marching away after only half a minute. In the

Royal Box she saw the doll-like figures sitting again, wondering whether the one with the pinkest face was Camilla, and now the handcuffs were clinking behind them as the members of each team, goalkeepers excluded, were cuffed before the captains blew for ends. She put her hands behind her back, crossing them wrist over wrist on the swell of her buttocks as she waited. Her stomach usually hollowed and sphincter flickered again when the handcuffs were slipped over her wrists, but today she seemed invulnerable, riding high on adrenalin and excitement, barely even noticing the 'cuffs go on.

Hilary, wrists cuffed behind her back, was already trotting out to the centre circle where the first-half referee and identical male twins stood waiting. The cameras would be zooming in on her breasts as they bounced in her copyright sports-bra beneath her white shirt, and computerised breast-models would already be rotating on millions of TV screens as they were compared for size and elasticity with those of Maria, the rival captain. Heavy betting had taken place on this contest-within-a-contest too, of course, and for weeks Hilary had only emerged in public in loose dresses and oversized T-shirts. One enterprising tabloid had even tried to bribe staff at the team hotel to conceal a chemical sensor in the lavatory of Hilary's room, to try and determine from her urine where she was in her menstrual cycle. A roar went up from one end of the stadium as the results of the mammary comparison came in and fans in the crowd read them off the screens of their mobiles a fraction of a second before they sprang up on the giant stadium screens.

Hilary, competitive as ever, pouted as the first-half referee followed the regulation introduced by UEPA that season and carefully smelt her breath before slipping a thermometer into her mouth. Captains in some of the European leagues had been caught cheating in the choice-of-ends, swilling their mouths with scalding coffee or chewing on tissue-inflaming *habañero* chilis beforehand. The referee counted off thirty seconds on his watch, then slipped the thermometer out, glancing at it and raising his eyebrows for a moment before he nodded OK and moved to María, who was still beaming at her success in the breast-to-breast.

Freezing the mouth beforehand was still legal and Hilary had always sworn by it before summer matches, arguing that the shock of first entry could cut as much as ten or fifteen seconds off the time. The referee slipped the thermometer from María's mouth, glanced at it, nodded OK, and stepped back as the two captains moved towards the identical male twins waiting to either side of the centre spot. As the two women stopped two metres in front of them and lowered their knees to the lush grass of the pitch, sprayed for the past month with urine donated by all the teams in the Premier League, the twins reached down and prepared to unzip. The crowd fell silent, watching the giant screens in each corner of the stadium as the referee checked that each captain was two metres back, then raised the whistle to his mouth and blew. The buzz of the zips going down was lost in the roar of the crowd as Hilary and María, their hands cuffed securely behind their backs, knee-sprinted towards the tanned lengths of nine-inch cock jumping to meet their already gaping mouths.

María was a fraction of a second faster to her cock, but Hilary closed her eyes with apparent unconcern as she rammed her mouth over her cock and began sucking. María was already mouth-pistoning, her knees lifted clear off the pitch as she levered herself on her cock completing the in-stroke. The huge cock slid in and out of her mouth, gleaming with spittle down almost two-thirds of its length. Hilary had begun her mouth-pistoning too, working less frantically than María, more scientifically, her black lashes flickering over the closed slits of her eyes in extreme close-up. The twins' faces were already beginning to work with pleasure and the crowd was chanting encouragement from both ends, then bursting into roars of surprised approval from one end only as the mouth of Hilary's twin broke open in a groan and Hilary pulled her mouth off his cock, leaning backwards and pushing her breasts up and forward to catch the semen already spurting from him, flashing in the sun.

It was a new PA Cup Final record, excited commentators were already announcing, and the whole crowd roared as Hilary shuffled backwards on her knees, jerked herself upright, and turned to face it with the message revealed by alkali-sensitive patches in the cloth over her breasts. '<30' the message read in bright pink, and Jocasta smiled at the confidence Hilary had shown, hearing chants of 'Half-mo! Half-mo!' start to go up from groups of Hilary fans scattered in the crowd. Behind Hilary, María's mouth was sliding off her twin's cock and she too was catching spurts of semen on her breasts, scowling with chagrin now, her darkening of mood as sudden as her pleasure over her success in the breast-to-breast. The referee was supervising one of the lineswomen as she examined the patch of semen on Hilary's breasts, rubbing her fingers in it, sniffing it, licking it, before nodding to the referee, who pronounced it genuine with a peep of his whistle.

Hilary trotted back over to her team, the bright pink figures on her breasts beginning to fade as her team's sponsors activated her logo. They would play away from their fans in the first half, keeping it tight at the back and trying to reach the turn-round level or a goal to the good. The lineswoman, having swilled her mouth out with a glass of urine freshly supplied by one of the eighteen-year-old ball girls, was examining the glistening patch of semen on María's breasts, putting her nose close to it, sniffing hard, then licking directly at the soaked cloth. She put her head back, nodding OK, and

Jocasta's stomach hollowed again for a moment as Hilary dribbled the ball to the centre spot and waited for the whistle.

The referee glanced out to the wings, watching as the two lineswomen sprinted into position, then took a careful look round the field and the twenty young outfielders who were waiting to begin play, hands cuffed securely behind their backs so that their large breasts would be on constant display, bouncing and wobbling, recording every nuance of their exertions. He looked up into the air, assuring himself that the ten pigeon-sized robo-drone chopper-cams were in place, hanging twenty metres above the pitch, lo-noiz rotors whirling invisibly and almost inaudibly; checked that his discreet black earpiece was firmly in place; tested the release on his Viagra hip-pouch; then, obeying the first instruction through his earpiece, fingered the erection in his shorts with the same hand while he raised the whistle to his lips with the other and blew.

The Fifth Annual Pornball Association Cup Final, Slottenham Hotslits vs Mamchester Clitty, was under way. Hilary touched the ball to Jemima, who turned easily away from an early challenge by one of the Mamchester forwards, feinted to begin a midfield run and sent a long ball curving sweetly out to Jocasta. She caught it up in her stride, already racing down the wing in her imagination, when the stadium suddenly whirled round her and she found herself on the pitch, the warm smooth legs of a Mamchester midfielder tangled in hers. The Slottenham fans roared their disapproval of the illegal tackle, setting up a chant of 'Off! Off! Off!'

Jocasta slid her legs free, rolled onto her stomach, and used her knees to lever herself back to her feet. She winced theatrically as she flexed her left leg, hoping for a white card, for the referee was racing over, whistle in his mouth, one blunt-fingered hand reaching into his back pocket. He blew hard, but the card he raised was blue. The Mamchester midfielder, a tough Scot called Rachel, shrugged as she tugged at the quick-release of her shorts with her cuffed hands, wriggling her backside so that they slid smoothly down her thighs and dropped round her boots in a neat circle. She stepped out of them, turning her head back and spitting neatly into the circle of her shorts before she ran back into position in her tight white knickers. One of the ball girls was sprinting in from the touchline, racing to retrieve the shorts before the ball was rolled into position for the free kick. She hooked the shorts up with one hand still running, continuing across the pitch to the touchline on the opposite side. They would be loaded into one of the compressed-air catapults and fired into the crowd at half-time.

Jocasta received the ball direct from the free-kick, evaded another lunging challenge, this time from a Mamchester forward, and was finally off on one of her trademark runs, breasts bouncing as she heard the double-clap-and-stamp of her foot-fans start up in the crowd. A gap appeared in the Mamchester defence ahead of her, enticing her on a run into the box, but she knew it would stay open for only a second or two. She feinted as though to run into it, then swerved outfield again, her breasts recording the sudden change in speed and direction. She beat the Mamchester right back for pace, glancing up to see if Hilary and Jemima had started their runs. Yes. Her brain interpreted another roar from the crowd before she was consciously aware of it, and she pushed the ball ahead of her and jumped as Rachel slid in, apparently careless that she was on a blue card. Air rushed against her legs as the midfielder passed beneath her and she carried the salty tang of the twenty-three-year-old's fresh sweat with her as she raced after the ball, caught it, and began to run down the wing, beating another challenge and looking up to see Hilary just arriving in the Mamchester box.

As Rachel rolled onto her stomach, wormed herself to her knees, and climbed to her feet, white knickers streaked with green over the swell of her firm buttocks, Jocasta struck her cross, knowing even before it left her boot that it was perfect, curving fast and low in between the lunging boots of the Mamchester defence to meet Hilary's diving header at the near post. The ball arrowed into the net past the despairing dive of Mamchester's Italian goalkeeper Cecilia, and Hilary landed full-length on the pitch, her breasts absorbing the full impact of her body. Jocasta raced towards her as she drew her legs up and knelt to push herself back to her feet, mouth open and yelling exultantly into the roar of the Slottenham fans that had reached her with a second's delay from the opposite end of the stadium. Jemima reached Hilary first, almost knocking her back to the pitch as she thrust her own ripe body against Hilary's, their two pairs of firm breasts juddering between them as Jemima kissed Hilary's cheek, then began to munch on one of her ears. A moment later Jocasta reached them, absorbing the shock of impact with her own breasts, and pressed her lips over Hilary's yell.

They kissed and tongued each other as the Mamchester goalkeeper picked the ball out of the net and moodily kicked it upfield. Then they broke the hug, trotting back to their half for the kick-off. Footage from Jocasta's foot-cam was being played on the giant stad-screens, and she smiled happily as she watched it, making her steps a little higher so that her breasts jogged up and down to reward her foot-fans, who were counter-chanting 'Jocasta! Jocasta!' against the 'Half-mo! Half-mo!' of Hilary's fans. They reached their positions and the referee blew for the re-start. Mamchester attacked hard at once, hoping to catch the Slottenham defence off-guard in the exultation of an early goal, and as Rachel got on the end of an inch-perfect long ball from María and shaped for a shot, Slottenham's redhaired left back Sandra eagerly seized the chance to avenge the earlier foul on Jocasta, sliding in on the Scot from behind. Hands cuffed behind her back, legs scythed from under her, Rachel hit the pitch full on her breasts. The pitch, seeded with grass genetically engineered for thick, lush growth, had been certified fit for breast-impacts by the PA's medical team earlier in the day, but Rachel's grunt of pain testified that Sandra had more than lived up to her reputation for breast brutality.

The referee sprinted over, blowing his whistle for the physio as he reached inside his back pocket. Sandra was disentangling her legs from Rachel's and sliding free to stand up, but the Scottish midfielder was still lying on her stomach, breasts pressed hard to the pitch. The Mamchester fans roared their approval as the referee reached her and flourished a white card high in the air over her buttocks as he stared sternly at Sandra. The physio was running on to the pitch with his black bag and the Mamchester fans were chanting 'Off! Off! Off!' A blue card meant the removal of one item of clothing; a white card meant the removal of one item of clothing and the bestowing of a blow job on the referee, and all over the world sports editors on non-interactive channels were switching to split screens so that fans could watch Sandra slide off her shorts and kneel on the pitch to receive the referee's thick, vein-crawled 10-inch cock as a couple of metres away the physio helped Rachel to sit up so that he could lift her shirt, unclip her bra, and sponge her breasts with ice-water. By a lucky chance Sandra welcomed the referee's cock between her lips at the very moment at which the physio unclipped Rachel's bra and her large breasts fell free, quivering like firm jellies.

As the referee slid his cock deeper into Sandra's mouth the physio began to sponge Rachel's breasts, lingering over each nipple, encouraging it to erection so that it jerked free as the sponge passed away from it, quivering like a little pink tongue. The referee's shorts and the physio's sponge were both wired for sound and some split-screen shots were accompanied with the thick slurping of the blow job, others with the splatter of water and Rachel's moans and grunts as the physio, stopping occasionally to re-moisten his sponge, worked at her breasts. Under the headline 'Pay per Phew!' one tabloid newspaper had reported how a subscription channel had even paid for the installation of experimental odour-mics in the ref's and physio's clothing, and osmo-cards on the computers of a few tens of thousand technophiles were struggling to reproduce the subtle odours of a combination of bruised grass and Sandra's and Rachel's sweat. The mics were supposed to screen out the background smell of the referee's and physio's own sweat, but many technophiles later complained that their masturbation had been disturbed by male odours.

When Rachel's breasts had been thoroughly sponged and the referee, as excited as any player by the big-match atmosphere, had slid his cock from Sandra's mouth and come over her face with seven drenching spurts of salty thick semen, the game resumed. Rachel took the free kick awarded for the foul committed on her with water still dripping from beneath her shirt, chipping an excellent ball to the far post of the Slottenham goal, where María, fighting off a challenge from a still glistening-faced Sandra, forced an excellent save from Sofiya, Slottenham's giant Ukrainian goalkeeper, with a sharply directed downward header. It was the beginning of a sustained period of Mamchester pressure, with María forcing Sofiya into two more fine saves with another downward header and a run-and-shot-on-the-turn before Alison, the leggy Mamchester midfielder, made strenuous claims for a penalty after she was tumbled by Cathy, the Slottenham right back, in the box. The referee, still recovering from his blow job, turned her appeal down, but produced his card twice in quick succession shortly afterwards, awarding blues for another illegal tackle on Jocasta, this time by Juliette, the Mamchester right back, and for an attempted trip on María by Zoë, the Slottenham right back.

Four players were now running up and down the field in their knickers, their shorts loaded and waiting in the compressed-air catapults facing the crowd, and commentators were excitedly anticipating the first player to lose her shirt and bra. Perhaps predictably, it was Rachel, for a petulant foul on Jemima on the edge of the Mamchester box. The referee blew for a free-kick and flourished his blue card not once but twice: it was evident that if the foul had taken place even a few minutes later he would have shown her the white card. From the way he fingered his cock as he watched a scowling Rachel trigger the fibre-dissolve on her shirt and then turn to allow him to unclip her bra, it was also evident that he was regretting his leniency. The microphone in his shorts caught the pop of the bra coming free an instant before the excited roar of the crowd announced that Rachel's breasts were on full display – or almost: a few strands of dissolving shirt still clung to their firm curves and between the deep tit-cleft as she ran to take her place in the wall.

Jocasta, long rumoured to be one of Jemima's lovers, took the free-kick and afterwards refused to comment on whether she had deliberately curved the ball direct not merely against the wall but against Rachel herself. The meaty thud of ball-on-bare-breasts was later the rhythmic sampled foundation of a basement-sleaze single by the tit-fet duo Mamma's Boyz, with treated samples of the disapproving or congratulating roar of the crowd used in the chorus and bridge. Another Mamchester player, the Venezuelan left back Claudia, was blue-carded in the protests that took place above the supine figure of Rachel as her breasts were sponged anew by the Mamchester physio, and it was only when the referee threatened them with a white card by ostentatiously taking out and triggering his Viagra inhaler into both hairy nostrils that the Mamchester players subsided.

Snorting and blowing as he returned the inhaler to its pouch on the hip of his shorts, the referee ordered the free-kick retaken: Rachel had been running forward when she was struck on the breasts. The Mamchester supporters howled their outrage and chants of 'The referee's a faggot! The referee's a faggot!' began to echo from their end. Trotting backwards, whistle in his mouth, the referee smiled, hearing in his earpiece that cameras were zooming in on the growing bulge in his shorts. The Mamchester physio had sponged Rachel's breasts, helped her back to her feet, and was sprinting off the field; Jocasta was dribbling the ball back into position for the free-kick; now she took two strides back from it and two to the left. The referee blew and she took one slow breath, then ran forward and struck the ball in a tight curve round the wall and into the top right-hand corner.

In the protests from the Mamchester players that followed, almost inaudible in the storm of noise raging from both ends of the stadium – the Mamchester fans outraged, the Slottenham fans exultant – the referee issued two more blue cards, one to Rachel, the other to her fellow midfielder Yolanda, and his first pink, to the cultured French Mamchester left back Virginie. A ball girl ran on to the field to pull Rachel's knickers down, justifying the bookies' odds of 2–1 on for her to be the first player completely stripped, then trotted over to pull Virginie's down too: the right back had already triggered the release on her shorts. The referee sent the ball girl scuttling off the field with a firm buttock-slap and squeal, Virginie's shorts and knickers clutched in one hand, then nodded to two of the bigger Mamchester players to hold Virginie up between them, her elbows hooked round their necks, her thighs splayed and supported by their hands. When she was up and ready, he walked forward and lifted the hem of her shirt which, after the fashion in the French league, she wore long, and ordered her to hold it between her teeth. Now her flat tanned stomach and the neat hollow of her omphalos were on display and, beneath them, her pussy, a black-capped vertical pink slit between her slim but muscular thighs.

The earpiece buzzed minutely in the referee's ear and he stood a little to one side as he rubbed his fingertips in the clear droplets of sweat trickling down the midfielder's stomach and began to finger her pussy open, revealing the deeper shining pink of her *labia minora* and inner pussy. Most channels were on split-screen again and the giant stad-screens were even broadcasting a tri-view of the referee's blunt fingers, huge as tree-trunks, working in the small valley of the French girl's moistening pussy, flanked on the left by the more-than-tree-sized bulge in the referee's shorts and on the right by Virginie's façade-sized face. Her small teeth were visible between her lips, tightening on the hem, and her nostrils flared and narrowed irregularly as the referee worked at her. He switched hands, walking to her other side, moistening his fingertips in her sweat again and then beginning to finger her more vigorously, more brutally, sliding his fingers into her past the first and second knuckles. Virginie's nostrils flared hard and her head went back, pulling her shirt up over her *tricolore* bra. She was dribbling freely now, her pussy juice glistening as it slid down her thighs and began to drip to the pitch.

The referee switched hands again, moving back to his original position and working at her with his original hand, coating his fingers thoroughly for the fuck. His earpiece buzzed again and he slid his fingers out, stepped back, and carefully manoeuvred his cock through the slit in his trousers, trying not to rub off too much of the French girl's pussy juice. The stad-screens switched to mono-view as his cock jumped forward, and some of the Mamchester fans started up an ironic chant of 'The referee's a faggot! The referee's a faggot!' again. He nodded to the two Mamchester players holding Virginie up, the left back Teresa and the centre forward Beth, and their hands tightened beneath her thighs, locking them into place as he stepped forward, using his fingertips to guide his cock to the waiting pussy.

He lodged the blunt head between Virginie's pussy lips, then lifted his hands away, raising them to the faces of the two Mamchester players. As they began to lick and suck them, cleaning off the pussy juice, the stad-screens split again, and two-hundred thousand fans watched Virginie's face tilt back horizontal on the left, dragging her shirt fully up over her bra as, on the right, the referee's cock, huge as a bullet-train, slid smoothly into the oozing tunnel of her pussy. He paused a moment, waiting for the director's instruction, then began to fuck her. He fucked slow and deep at first, sliding his cock almost fully out before re-inserting it with a semi-circular movement of his hips. The microphone in his shorts was picking up little sound as yet and most sports editors were patching in chants from the crowd, but then, as Virginie released her first groan of pleasure, her teeth clenched hard between her writhed-back lips, and the referee began to fuck her harder, the squelching began in earnest, easily loud enough to reach the five chopper-cams hovering five metres above the scene. Teresa and Beth were still sucking on the referee's fingertips, but now his earpiece buzzed again and he pulled his fingers free and, keeping up the rhythm of his withdrawal and re-insertion, began to undo Virginie's bra. Her pussy-juice was spraying out round his cock now as it slid into her pussy, and one of the hovering chopper-cams dropped suddenly to film the drizzle of pussy-juice falling to the pitch. The lush grass glistened with it in an expanding patch, shadowed by Virginie's buttocks and thighs.

Her bra came undone with a click that was lost beneath her loudest groan yet, and the referee dragged it free and dropped it on one side before beginning work on her breasts with his hands, kneading and rolling them like stiff, firm dough. Virginie's gums were visible now, glistening in the sunlight as her lips drew back fully from her teeth, and her nostrils were flaring and narrowing in a relentless half-second rhythm. The referee was working at her nipples with his thumbs, pushing them up, down, left, right, but now his earpiece buzzed again and he dropped his hands round her, sliding them between her flanks and the flanks of the two Mamchester players holding her up, to reach and grip her buttocks as he started on the final, deepest strokes of the fuck.

It was too much for Virginie: her teeth and mouth came open in a prolonged groan of orgasm, the hem of her shirt jumping free, striking the referee on the chest as he sent his cock into her last-time-but-two, last-time-but-one, last-time, and withdrew from her with a final squelch to take a stumbling half-step backwards and begin spurting over her stomach and writhing pussy. Two chopper-cams swung downward to take close-ups, but the referee was already folding his cock into his shorts and raising his whistle to his lips to signal the restart. The chopper-cams that had hovered above and round the scene of the pink-carding now broke up, speeding back to their stations, but one that remained caught a faint moue of distaste on Virginie's face as the two Mamchester players who had held her up, thighs splayed, lowered her to the pitch and her slim buttocks, still twitching with orgasm, met the patch of mingled pussy-juice and semen lying there. The two players trotted away from her and she got unsteadily to her feet, inserting a finger between the gaping lips of her pussy as she tottered back into position for the re-start. She rolled it thoroughly in the mixture of pussy-juice and semen still oozing there, then raised the glistening finger to her opening mouth and sealed her lips round it. As the whistle blew for the re-start she pulled it slowly out.

Commentators speculated on the gesture as Mamchester launched another attack. Virginie had long been rumoured to be seeking a transfer to one of the Italian giants, Intra-Anal Milan or Flagellazio, where such gestures were commoner than in the staider English league, and cameras were now scanning the crowd with disguise-penetrating face-recognition software, searching for Italian managers and scouts. The speculation was soon dropped, however, for Mamchester were setting up another period of sustained pressure on the Slottenham goal, their wingers firing cross after cross into the Slottenham box. The referee did his best to frustrate them, awarding a series of blue cards for minor offences, and four Mamchester players were now completely stripped, their large breasts, for which the club had long been justly famous, gleaming with sweat as they bounced and jiggled in the bright sun. Two sports channels were now showing nothing but live breast action, but most still kept up some pretence of interest in the game, though slow-motion breast-action replays were becoming more and more common, particularly when Mamchester forwards chested the ball down from goal kicks and throw-ins by one of the backs with expansible-chain cuffs.

A Mamchester goal seemed inevitable, and commentators were excitedly anticipating its arrival when María, controlling a long pass out of defence neatly on her breasts, turned and sent a perfectly weighted ball through the Slottenham defence. For a moment the ball seemed too well struck, but then Virginie, long famed for her speed and given an extra burst of speed, as always, by the fuck she had received, was darting between two Slottenham defenders and steering the ball towards goal. Sofiya, Slottenham's giant Ukrainian keeper, hurriedly checked her sprint out of the box and raced backwards, beginning to crouch as Virginie bore in on goal, her still swollen pussy flashing between her thighs. The French midfielder's right boot was swinging back to chip Sofiya when Sandra took her legs from beneath her and the two players collapsed in a tangled heap on the edge of the box. The referee paused for a second, hoping to play an advantage, and his skill was rewarded when María, who had been charging in Virginie's wake, seized on the loose ball and raced into the box. Sofiya rushed to meet her but María touched the ball neatly round her and began to run past her for what seemed like a certain goal.

The Mamchester fans roared their disapproval as the giant keeper tripped their cult centre forward and one of the Slottenham midfielders kicked the ball into touch. It was an unmistakable penalty and the referee was left with no choice but to punish both Sandra and Sofiya severely. He flourished two cards, first, for Sofiya, a yellow, and then, for Sandra, who was already on a white, the game's first brown card. The physios of both teams were already sprinting on to the field with their black bags: Sandra, despite delivering the tackle, was still lying on the pitch after Virginie had limped away, and María had banged her breasts hard on the pitch as she tumbled full-length from Sofiya's trip. The referee signalled for a two-litre water bottle and one of the ball girls came sprinting on with it. María accepted it with a nod of thanks as she sat on the pitch in her knickers, the physio sponging thoroughly at her firm chocolate-coloured breasts, and drained it in one long series of swallows, offering her smooth throat to the hovering chopper-cams. When she lowered it, raising the back of her hand to her mouth to muffle a ladylike belch, the referee walked over and handed her a pair of bright yellow pills. Sofiya was already being staked to the penalty spot face-up, stripped of her shirt and her huge bra, with its famous bucket-sized cups and hawser-strength strap, ball girls kneeling at her hands and feet as they tightened the straps that had waited buried in the pitch under plugs of grass.

Maria's dark eyes narrowed as she looked across at the keeper's giant 44-B breasts, glistening with sweat and rising and falling like small hills as she recovered from her recent exertions. The Mamchester fans, watching her face on the giant stad-screens, cheered as she licked her lips and swallowed the two diuretic pills, washing them down with a final mouthful of water from the bottle and earning herself a bonus from the sponsors for the care with which she kept its yellow sunburst Urotrash logo on display for the cameras. On the edge of the box, meanwhile, Sandra was being prepared by a ball girl for her brown card. The first Slottenham player to be completely stripped, she was crouched on all fours on the pitch with the ball girl's face buried between her smooth buttocks, the girl's tongue working busily at her famously pink anus, star of a million teenage boys' bedroom walls, thoroughly moistening it to receive the referee's erect cock, which another ball girl had pulled out and was now conscientiously lubricating from head to balls, spitting on its broad dorsum and working the spittle in with her tongue and lips.

The referee watched the ball girl hungrily, obviously having to resist the temptation to mouth-fuck her, and the earpiece had to buzz twice before he gently pushed her off and advanced on Sandra, whose anus was still being tongued by the first ball girl. The referee blew his whistle and the ball girl reluctantly pulled her face back, leaving the whole cleft of Sandra's buttocks glistening with spittle. As the referee knelt behind Sandra, the two ball girls pulled her buttocks apart for him, exposing the puckered pink sunburst of her anus. He shuffled forward, holding his cock with one hand and guiding it to the anus, and when the hot cock head touched the left back a shudder ran through her whole body, seeming to linger in her firm breasts where they hung beneath her body. This referee had a reputation for brutal buggery, and in interviews Sandra had often described anal sex as one of the least attractive aspects of her job. The Mamchester fans had begun the traditional count-down chant, but the referee ignored it, taking his time, moving his cock back and veeing Sandra's anus open, sliding his middle finger up her, testing her for tightness and heat. Another shudder ran through Sandra's body as the finger entered her, and the chopper-cam assigned to her face caught her biting her lower lip.

Apparently satisfied with his exploration, the referee pulled his finger out and shuffled closer, guiding his cock to her anus again. His whistle was in his mouth and as he let go of his cock and made his first thrust, he blew on it hard, making Sandra jerk with surprise, her anus tightening against his cock. He pushed, reaching up and under her body for her breasts, kneading and rolling them hard as he struggled to enter her. Her face tightened and twitched as his cock battered at her, slowly forcing her anus open so that he could slide fully up her. The stad-screens were split again, showing Sandra's face on the left and the referee's cock, knocking for entrance, on the right. But the referee, veteran of a thousand such bouts, was merely toying with her, and when his earpiece buzzed, instructing him to begin the buggery, he easily pulled an extra couple of inches out of his locker. His huge cock, its length glistening dully now as the ball girl's spittle dried, jumped suddenly forward, its blunt head sliding firmly into Sandra's tight hot bottom. He paused a few moments, savouring her groan and continuing whimpers of protest, and then pushed again, sending the full length of his cock slowly up into her.

It sank between her buttocks with an ease belied by the way her eyes rolled back in their sockets. Then it slid out again for half of its length, paused, and began to piston slowly at her on a second-and-a-half rhythm, driving an 'Uff!' of exhaled breath out of her on the in-stroke, as though his invading cock were compressing her body, pressing on her lungs, and dragging an 'Uh!' of inhaled breath out of her on the out-stroke, as though his withdrawing cock were decompressing in her body, allowing her lungs to expand again. Large beads of sweat had sprung out on Sandra's forehead as the referee's cock entered her bottom; now they were rolling down her face, gathering on the point of her chin and dripping to the pitch. The referee was fucking her harder now, his strong hands tightening on her breasts as he sent his cock sliding into her up the root, and a day later Sandra's official website would post a new portfolio of breast-shots, showing a line of four distinct finger-bruises on the inner surface of each breast, with a broad thumb-bruise near each nipple.

The earpiece buzzed in the referee's ear again and he turned his gasping face slowly to one of the ball girls, nodding that he was ready for the ball-licking. The ball girl released Sandra's buttock-cheek and crawled quickly behind him, stopping to put her face up between his thickly haired thighs and begin licking and sucking at the sweating, leathery sack of his large balls. A chopper-cam swooped in to film a close-up in visible light and infra-red, but there was no lingering finale: the referee's Viagra was still working well and with his cock already sliding in Sandra's tight bottom the ball-girl's warm tongue and lips on his balls provoked him to an almost immediate orgasm. Sandra's face, her mouth still open and gasping to each stroke, brightened with relief as she felt the referee's semen squirting into her, each thick jet reported by the delicate walls of her rectum, then tightened again with pain as the referee began to slide his cock out of her. It came free with a thick pop, glistening with rectal mucus and ground-off rectal wall, but Sandra, like all defenders, followed a hi-NRG, lo-bulk diet for a couple of days before a match and then cleared her rectum thoroughly with an enema and douche in the dressing room, and the ball girl who now licked the referee's cock clean was thankful that it had not been a forward or midfielder who had received a brown card.

When the referee got unsteadily to his feet, thighs and knees still weak with orgasm, his cock was clean again, beginning to soften and bend as he pushed it back into his trousers and walked over to supervise the yellow card he had awarded against the Slottenham keeper. María, knickers and shorts off, her black pubic fleece pearled with beads of sweat, was now standing near the penalty spot and the staked-down Sofiya, shifting uncomfortably from foot to foot, her bladder obviously and painfully full. Normally play resumed for five minutes after a yellow card, allowing the fouled player's bladder to fill before she pissed on the player who had fouled her, but many referees liked to award them as double bills with a brown or pink card, letting the fouled player's bladder fill while another player was penetrated anally or vaginally. Sofiya's breasts were no longer rising and falling heavily, but the hot sunshine falling on their firm curves had kept them glistening with sweat and she was licking her lips thirstily as she stared, eyes slitted, at the black chopper-cams hovering impatiently above her.

The referee went down on one knee beside her, taking hold of her right breast with his right hand, the nipple under his palm, joggling at it, but the breast was so large and heavy he had to add his left hand before he could set it bouncing and wobbling satisfactorily. Sofiya's eyes closed and after a moment she released a long sigh. The referee watched the nipple of her left breast, noting how it began to swell and lengthen in time with the right nipple under his hand, then turned his head, nodding María over to him. She trotted obediently over.

'Ready?' he asked her.

'*Sí*,' María replied. The referee released his left hand from Sofiya's breast, his shoulders shaking as he compensated for the loss of power on his breast-manipulation, and ran his fingers through María's pubic hair, palpating her belly gently just above her *mons Veneris*. María pouted with discomfort as her bladder was compressed by his fingers, and the referee nodded again and lifted his fingers away as he let go of Sofiya's breast and rose to his feet, revealing the keeper's hardened right nipple. He walked round to the other side of the keeper, sucking the two women's mingled sweat off the fingertips of his left hand, then licking Sofiya's sweat off his palm, and it was apparent that the breast-manipulating and bladder-test had re-erected him: his cock was jutting firm in his trousers again. He knelt to joggle Sofiya's left breast with both hands, feeling the nipple hard and long beneath his palms. Lesbian keepers like Sofiya often required a thorough tonguing by a ball girl before they were aroused enough for the yellow card to be enacted, but Sofiya herself was famous for the speed of her response to firm manipulation of her tits even by a male referee and her pussy, capacious enough for even the referee's huge cock, was gaping stickily, its swollen pink lips and inner walls glistening in the sun.

The referee nodded with satisfaction and stood up, moving back two paces and putting his whistle in his mouth. María walked to the keeper and straddled her face with her feet well apart, glancing down to check that she was positioned right, shuffling a little further back, then looking up at the referee, nodding that she

175

was ready to respond to the whistle. Sofiya, the lower half of her face in the shadow of María's thighs and buttocks, the upper half still brightly lit by the sun, gave her cracked lips a final lick and opened her mouth, ready to receive the centre-forward's piss. The referee looked round the field, glanced up at the waiting chopper-cams, and blew his whistle. María grunted and released her aching bladder, letting a neat tail of pale yellow piss land neatly on Sofiya's forehead. The keeper's large tongue protruded from her mouth, snaking eagerly at the splatters of piss already reaching it, but now María was walking backwards and piss was falling directly into Sofiya's mouth, warm and scented but dilute.

The keeper's throat rippled as she swallowed the piss, and she raised her head, trying to follow the piss-stream as María, having paused a moment, began to walk backwards again, legs splaying even wider as she pissed over Sofiya's throat and upper chest, then reached her breasts. Here she paused again, drenching the huge, nipple-nailed globes thoroughly with piss, then walked backwards again, completing the golden shower by pissing her way down Sofiya's stomach to her mat of pubic hair, glistening with sweat, and her still gaping pussy. Her piss was coming in spurts now, not a continuous stream, but piss was lying in streaks or small pools down almost the full length of Sofiya's huge body, and was still trickling down the curves of her breasts. Drying in the sun, it would irritate the keeper's skin and delicate nipples and aureoles for the remainder of the match, but if she was caught scratching by the referee or one of the lineswomen she would receive another card, probably a white or pink. María released a final spurt of piss, then swung herself off the keeper's body, and the referee gestured towards the touchline for ball girls to come and unstake Sofiya.

Four of them sprinted on, kneeling round Sofiya again to undo the ankle and wrist straps and replace the plugs of grass, and one of them, a long-standing María fan, cheeks flushed at her daring, allowed the back of her hand to brush against the Ukrainian's keeper's piss-wet flank; when the ball girls rose from their task, sprinting off the pitch as the keeper rolled over and got back to her feet, the girl licked at the patch of María-piss, savouring its faint spiciness and flushing harder as a cheer went up in the crowd. Sofiya was on her feet again, stripped naked but for her gloves and boots, towering head and shoulders above the referee. He ordered her to turn on the spot for inspection, peeping on his whistle when her long back and firm buttocks, huge but beautifully curved, were presented to him. He peeped twice on his whistle and the keeper bent forward, drops of piss falling from her breasts to the pitch as the referee inspected her buttocks and the tight chocolate whorl of her anus. The skin of her buttocks was roughened with the grass she had lain on, and the referee ran his fingers over it before levering her buttocks apart to inspect her anus, careful to stand a little to one side so that the remaining chopper-cams could film it thoroughly.

He traced its outline with a fingertip and tweaked at the hairs that circled it, sweeping to the sphincter from the keeper's moist perineum and the well-furred lips of her giant pussy, and the Ukrainian's buttocks shivered like those of a well-trained horse as it submits reluctantly but patiently to a vet's inspection. The referee rubbed at the sweat in her arse-dell, then the sweat trickling down her buttocks, moistening his finger to the second joint, then tried to push his finger up her. She resisted, but when he peeped his whistle again she relaxed with a Slavic shrug of her broad shoulders, allowing the referee to slide his finger up her. Watching the inspection on the giant screens, the Mamchester fans cheered and by the time the referee had completed the inspection with a slap and turned to supervise the penalty he had awarded all those minutes before, some of them were chanting, 'It's tight, it's round, it's yours for fifteen pound, Sophie's bum, Sophie's bum!'

Sofiya was well known for disliking buggery even more than lesbian keepers usually did, and it was evident that the referee was now looking for an opportunity to award a brown card against her in the ten minutes of the match that remained. Sofiya trotted to her goal-line as María took the ball and dribbled it to the penalty spot where the giant keeper had lain a few moments before. The keeper's eyes narrowed fractionally and she licked her lips again as María turned and walked away from the ball, muscles rippling sleekly in her bare buttocks and thighs beneath her cuffed hands, then turned back, ready for the whistle. The referee checked for encroachment, his own eyes narrowing as he noted how many players were now stripped, then raised his whistle to his lips, paused, and blew. María bounced on the spot, making her breasts bounce under her shirt, then strode forward. Sofiya was half-crouched on the goal-line, swaying on the balls of her feet, ready to dive left or right, but María fired the ball high and straight into the top left-hand corner and the keeper's despairing dive was nearly a foot short.

María turned, grinning in triumph into the roars of the Mamchester fans, to meet the celebratory rush of her team-mates. They surrounded her in a solid mass, rubbing their breasts against hers or rasping her buttocks silkily with their pubic deltas as Sofiya retrieved the ball from the net behind them and moodily kicked it upfield. The referee tried to break up the celebrations with a blast on his whistle, but it wasn't until he'd awarded a double blue against María, stripping her of her shirt and bra too to renewed roars from her fans, that the Mamchester players broke their huddle and ran back to their own half for the re-start. 2–1, and the whole atmosphere of the game was suddenly changed.

The referee blew his whistle and Hilary touched the ball to Jemima, who set off on an immediate run, swerving past two challenges, breasts juddering, before she curved a ball out to Jocasta on the left wing. Jocasta flicked the ball neatly into her stride and accelerated past the first challenge as Hilary and Jemima raced into the box. Jocasta drew the Mamchester right back, then beat her again for pace to gain a fraction of a second in which, at full sprint, she clipped a low ball into the box, curving it expertly between the despairing lunges of the Mamchester defenders to Hilary's feet. Hilary, her back to goal, controlled it with a single touch, turned, evaded a challenge, shaped to shoot, then, sensing the position of her fellow forward almost by instinct, backheeled the ball neatly to Jemima as she raced in behind her.

The strength of Jemima's shot was legendary and Hilary's ball was perfect to the millimetre. The Slottenham fans were already erupting in celebration as the ball left her favoured left foot with a bang, arrowing for the bottom right-hand corner of the goal, but Cecilia, Mamchester's acrobatic Italian keeper, made one of her equally legendary saves, sprinting across the goal to launch herself full-length and claw the ball round the post. Corner. Jocasta received the ball from a ball girl and dribbled it quickly to the corner flag, positioned it, and took two paces back. She looked up, narrowing her eyes into the sun, and saw Sandra, legendary for her bullet headers, poised on the edge of the box, feinting first left, then right as she tried to evade the attentions of two Mamchester defenders. But just beyond her . . .

Jocasta strode forward and fired the corner in. For a moment it seemed as though it was aimed for Sandra, and Cecilia began to move across goal to cover the header, realising her mistake a fraction of a second too late as the ball passed above Sandra's salmon-like leap and dropped neatly on to the foot of Slottenham's redheaded, big-breasted Welsh midfielder, Ffion. Ffion scored perhaps three or four goals a season, but they were usually goal-of-the-season contenders, whether forty-yard thunderbolts or flashing volleys. This season she had scored two goals, and she was denied what looked like a certain third by another spectacular recovery-and-leap from Cecilia. The ball stayed in play this time, falling neatly to the feet of Rachel, who took one look upfield, saw the now naked María starting on a run with the Slottenham defence badly stretched, and played an immediate long ball. For a moment it seemed too strong, and Sofiya raced towards it from the edge of the box, but María found an extra metre of acceleration, her bare breasts bouncing furiously, droplets of sweat spraying from them in silver sparkles, and reached the ball a half-second before the giant Ukrainian, fifteen metres from the edge of the box.

It was time enough for her to chip the ball neatly over the keeper's sliding, feet-first tackle, and then leap to allow the keeper to pass beneath her. But a gloved hand caught her ankle in passing once again and she tumbled full-length on her breasts with a grunt of pain as a galloping Slottenham defender cleared the ball into the stands. The referee was already running over, blowing his whistle furiously and reaching in his pocket for the brown card he flourished above the Ukrainian keeper a moment later. She got sulkily to her feet, protesting her innocence in her thick accent as the Mamchester physio raced on to attend to María's freshly bruised breasts with his icy sponge. The referee waved the keeper's protests away and began to walk round her, unclipping his Viagra pouch as he inspected her body, lifting his inhaler out, triggering it luxuriously into both nostrils, pausing to watch the tremor of muscles in the keeper's broad firm buttocks, his cock rising again in his shorts. When he came back in front of her, raising his eyes to her heaving breasts, he blew on his whistle and she went down reluctantly on her knees, then on all fours as the referee blew again.

Now he waved on the ball girl who had been poised on the edge of the pitch and began to walk slowly back behind the keeper, squeezing at his cock, encouraging it back to full erection as the physio finished attending to Maria's breasts and trotted off the field with his black bag. The ball girl reached Sofiya and knelt behind her to lick her anus, her small head almost lost between the keeper's buttocks. The referee nodded with satisfaction as the sight of it stiffened him fully again, and he whistled the ball girl away immediately, not allowing Sofiya the usual two minutes of tongue-lubing. The ball girl lifted her head from between the keeper's buttocks and shuffled round to begin walking on her knees towards him, spitting and blowing at a dark sphincter hair clinging to her lips, but the referee waved her away. He was going up the keeper without cock-lubing either, and the chants of the Mamchester fans got louder. The ball girl turned back to Sofiya as another ball girl came running, ready to help the first swing the keeper's giant buttocks apart, and the referee lifted his cock out, still reddened and glistening from its previous insertion into Sandra's tight bottom.

As the ball girls swung the keeper's buttocks apart, strain was evident on their faces and it was equally evident that the keeper was resisting. The referee blew sharply on his whistle as he knelt behind the keeper, guiding his cock to the mouth of her anus. The Mamchester fans began the count-down to cock-up and this time the referee followed it, planting the head of his cock on the keeper's anus at 'Ten' and beginning to push hard, trying to time his entry to 'One'. But Sofiya was still resisting, and he had to blast on his whistle again before she relaxed. The referee shuffled closer to her and, with her breasts well out of reach, put his hands round and between her thighs to hook his fingers into her rug-thick pubic hair and heave in time with his renewed hip-thrusting. Sofiya grunted and swore in

Ukrainian and the hovering chopper-cams caught a look of growing discomfort on her face. It mounted as the referee pushed harder, driving his cock relentlessly at her delicate sphincter, gradually opening it, then broke into a gasp of discomfort as the referee's hips jerked suddenly forward and two inches of his thick cock sank into her.

The referee gasped too, but with pleasure, revelling in the warmth and tightness of the opening few inches of her arse-chamber, then heaved on her pubic hair again as he inserted himself deeper, thoroughly humiliating and dominating her. The ball girls released their hold now and crawled back, ready for more orders. The sense of power over a woman who could have snapped his neck with one hand tied behind her back was extraordinary, the referee would admit in post-half interviews, and when he began to bottom-fuck her in earnest, sliding in and out of her bottom in quickening rhythm, he was obviously having to struggle against responding with a premature and powerful orgasm to her almost girlish cries of protest. But now the Mamchester fans were cheering again, for one of the chopper-cams, hovering almost at pitch-level, was beaming pictures of the Ukrainian's breasts to the stad-screens. Her swollen nipples, almost as large as courgettes, testified that she was involuntarily pleasured by the buggery and another chopper-cam left the circle hovering round keeper and referee to investigate the state of her pussy on infra-red.

It was glowing with arousal and when the referee, responding to a buzz on his earpiece, released a hand from her pubic hair and put his fingers into it, he found it gaping, flooded with thick pleasure juice. 'Hetero! Hetero!' the Mamchester fans were now chanting, and the Director of Anal, watching the screens in his under-stadium control-room, decided it was time for one of the more spectacular anal tricks. The referee's earpiece buzzed again and he blew twice on his whistle, still thrusting hard at the Ukrainian's bottom as she moaned with frustration, trying to drive back the pleasure that had invaded her pussy and breasts from her violated backside. She seemed not to have heard and he blew again, motioning one of the ball girls round to her with his head, nodding as she asked him something quietly. The ball girl crawled round to the keeper and whispered in her ear and the keeper shook her head as though to clear it before responding to the order.

She would stand with the referee still inserted in her bottom, lifting his feet a clear foot or more above the ground as he gripped her waist and thrust into her for final orgasm. The chopper-cams broke and reformed in a new formation as the keeper pushed herself up on her hands and started to rise, her eyes closed and mouth working as the referee continued to thrust into her. He spat his whistle out of his mouth and grunted an improvised order to one of the ball girls, and as the Ukrainian rose to her feet, lifting his entire body with her, she ran to service the keeper's newly exposed cunt, thrusting her small fist between its splayed and swollen lips. Sofiya shrieked with pleasure, rising the last few inches that lifted the referee's feet clear of the ground, and as her anus tightened on his cock in orgasm, he could hold his sperm back no longer. Hands hooked clumsily round her huge waist, feet dangling inches above the pitch, he slid his cock fully into her for the last time and began to spurt deep inside her. As on Virginie's, the individual spurts could be read in the wondering flickers on the keeper's face.

When the referee let go of her waist and dropped free, his cock kept him nailed in place for a second or two before, with an uncorking pop-and-squelch, it slid free of her abused anus and he dropped back to the pitch, swaying on unsteady legs. The ball girls had let go of Sofiya's buttock cheeks when he entered her, but were still kneeling at her hips, and he ordered them to swing her cheeks apart again, exposing her anus to the lenses of the chopper-cams. They obeyed and sunlight flashed from the lower half of the keeper's buttock cleft, where sperm was trickling from her red-rimmed, half-gaping anus. The referee fitted his cock back into his shorts without having it licked by a ball girl, prompting speculation that he was looking to award a white card to round the half off, and blew on his whistle again, ordering the keeper back to her goal. She obeyed with whimpers and moans of pain, clenching her huge gloved hands as she began to trot back to her goal, lips writhing as she swore silently to herself. As Mamchester prepared to take the free kick for Sofiya's trip on María, commentators were speculating on how much the buggery would affect the keeper's play: statistical analysis had revealed that keepers were 9·27 per cent more likely to let a goal in within fifteen minutes of a brown card being awarded against them.

Sofiya added another fraction of a per cent to the odds, because three minutes later, shortly before the end of the first half, Mamchester scored again, Rachel capitalising on a misplaced Slottenham pass in her own half to send María scurrying through the Slottenham defence. Sofiya came rushing off her line again, but action replays revealed a gasp of pain and a momentary check as she began her run, granting María an extra metre of run-in and an extra half-second of calculation. For a forward of her calibre, it was more than enough, and even before her thirty-yard chip was in the back of the net she was bouncing her breasts in derisory celebration at the Slottenham fans who had abused her for failing to take an easier chance thirty seconds before. Sofiya clawed at empty air as the ball flew over her head, already beginning to drop into the goal. Two all. The Mamchester half of the stadium exploded again and Clitty players converged on María from all over the pitch. The Slottenham fans had reacted angrily to the tit-bouncing and the referee was running over, reaching into his back pocket with one hand while he pulled his cock out with his other. The Mamchester fans were chanting 'Clitty are back! Clitty are back!'; now they cheered ironically as the referee flourished a white card and began to whistle the cluster of players away from María.

She grinned broadly when she saw the card that had been awarded against her, and looked up theatrically to make sure the chopper-cams were gathering, ready to watch her blow the referee to his fifth orgasm of the half. The referee's cock was out and fully erect, stained with the buggery he had performed on Sofiya, and when María had knelt before him and he had blown his whistle, she spent the first minute of the blow job licking him thoroughly clean, her pink tongue curling round the swollen bulk of his cock first clockwise, then anticlockwise. Then she began the blow job proper, accepting the referee's purple cock head between her scarlet lips, sucking noisily and greedily, gradually pushing her head forward so that his cock slid between her lips. The Mamchester fans were singing their controversial María song: 'She's quick, she's slick, she'll suck the longest dick, Clitty's Spic, Clitty's Spic!', and María acknowledged their homage by beginning her mouth-thrusts, her famously firm and tremor-sensitive breasts picking up the rhythm beneath her moving chin. The Viagra-stimulated referee responded too quickly for the liking of the Director of Oral, spurting heavily and thickly into María's mouth after only two minutes of thrusting, but María saved the day by performing her celebratory fountain.

It was apparent she was still holding the referee's semen in her mouth as she slid off his cock, and when she tilted her head back, closing her eyes luxuriously, the Mamchester fans cheered again. Her lips pursed, and then she blew a shaft of sperm upwards, flashing in the sunlight, reaching the apex of its trajectory, breaking apart as it fell back into Maria's now gaping mouth. She repeated the trick twice more, not losing a drop, and then, as the referee whistled for the restart, got back to her feet with her enigmatic Blona Lisa smile, swallowing the sperm in small, ostentatious gulps as she trotted back to the Mamchester half. It was the final serious action before the referee blew for half-time and Jocasta and her Slottenham team-mates ran off the field knowing they had a mountain to climb in the second half, when Clitty, reinvigorated by their successful clawing-back of a two-goal lead, would come out all guns blazing. Jocasta, knowing that she had drifted out of the game in the later stages of the half, took a special pleasure in running atop the buttock-pavements, allowing her studs to sink into the yielding buttock-flesh, and imagining the cocks that were spurting beneath her. The two dressing rooms, both filmed and broadcast to the watching billions, were a study in contrasts: the loudest sound in Slottenham's beside the quiet voice of their manager was the pops and slurps of the blow job being performed on him by one of the ball girls, an unspoken symbol of the way his team had failed to excite him during the first half.

Meanwhile, in the Mamchester dressing room, the manageress, a tough Swedish lesbian called Caterin Lindqvist, was giving her talk above the thwacks and wails of a vigorous spanking she was handing out to bare-bottomed Virginie for refusing to keep quiet when the talk began. Because she might have picked on any one of eight or nine players for the same offence, the team rightly suspected that Virginie was also being punished for taking such obvious pleasure in the cunt-fucking given her by the referee. This was confirmed when the manageress pushed a sobbing Virginie off her lap at the end of the talk, ready to lead the team out for the second half, her trousers were stained with the mixture of pussy-juice and semen that was still leaking from Virginie's pussy. She looked down with an expression of distaste, and ordered Virginie and Sofiya to lick her trousers clean. The sight of the two players' contrasting buttocks as they knelt naked before the squat Lindqvist, lapping at her trousers, was one of the enduring images of the final. The manageress took the opportunity to deliver another brief team-talk, reminding her players that Slottenham were never more dangerous than with their backs to the wall and that they, Clitty, were now in the dangerous position of favourites.

Then she led her team out for the second half. As the two teams emerged from the tunnel, the clash of their boots cut off as they passed above a newly laid buttock-pavement. The new referee was already out on the pitch, jogging on the centre circle as he watched highlights of the first half being played on the giant stad-screens. Several players swallowed nervously as they absorbed the dimensions of the bulge in his trousers and noted that his Viagra pouch was flapping open and empty: this referee was infamous not only for his hose-like eleven-inch cock and his seemingly undrainable plum-sized testicles, but also for the number of brown cards he awarded. No fewer than eight Premiership players had been stretchered off the previous season after receiving his giant cock between their buttocks, with three of them missing the following two games. After two players from one side had been buggered off the pitch in a crucial relegation battle towards the end of the season, the Players' Union had prepared a petition asking either that he be removed temporarily from the referees' list, pending an official enquiry into his match-handling, or that artificial lubrication be introduced at matches he officiated. His appearance in the PA Cup Final was widely being interpreted as a reassertion of the power of the rival

Referees' Union, and commentators were speculating excitedly on who would be the first to receive a brown card and whether she would be able to continue the game afterwards. Many thought the answer to the first question was Celicia, the Mamchester goalie, and the answer to the second was no, she wouldn't.

They were half-right: Celicia was not the first brown card but when hers arrived, midway through the half, she was unable to continue afterwards. The referee had already handed out twelve cards when Celicia handled the ball outside the box: seven blues, stripping almost the whole of both teams naked but for their socks and boots; three whites, during one of which he had succeeded in making even María's eyes bulge in surprise as he forced his cock to the back of, and partly down, her throat; two pinks, a second for Virginie, whose pussy was well-known to be even hotter and slicker after a thorough poking, and a first for Ffion, and both players had been running with pronounced limps ever since; and a brown, for Mamchester's big-buttocked Senegalese midfielder Thérèse, who required five minutes of treatment before she could continue. Celicia, whose face had been among the most horrified of those shown on split-screen as Thérèse was buggered, appeared to faint when the brown card was flourished, and had to be revived by the Mamchester physio with smelling salts and nipple tweaks before he began to assist her on to all fours to receive a tongue-lubing from one of the ball girls.

But as he hooked a hand under her buttocks, helping her over, the referee, who had watched the revival closely, came running over, blowing hard on his whistle, and Mamchester were facing a £100,000 fine: when the contents of the tube concealed in the physio's buttock-lifting hand were analysed, they were discovered to be a combination of a high-quality anal lubricant and a skin-contact muscle relaxant. As the physio scurried off the pitch in disgrace, his ears stinging with the jeers of the Slottenham fans, a ball girl set to work between the buttocks of the now-sobbing Celicia and the referee took out his infamous cock and nodded another ball girl to blow him in preparation for the buggery. As with the previous brown card, the ball girl was unable to fit his enormous glans, large as a sliced half of apple, into her mouth, and had to lick and spit on it instead. When the referee was ready, he blew on his whistle and advanced on the trembling Cecilia, her buttock-cleft glistening with the spittle of the ball girl who had tongue-lubed her and who was now waiting with the cock-lubing ball girl to swing Cecilia's buttocks apart.

The referee knelt behind Cecilia and shuffled nearer, lifting his cock up and forward as he blew on his whistle again. The ball girls pulled her buttock cheeks apart and he placed his cock head between them, resting its glowing weight on her cringing anus. He blew on the whistle again with a dipping note and Cecilia lowered her head on to her crooked elbows, bracing herself to receive the shocks of the buggery. The referee looked up, checking that the chopper-cams were in place, then began to push slowly and relentlessly. Cecilia, whose game depended on athleticism, not bulk and strength, began to slide forward, and the referee nodded to one of the ball girls. The ball girl let go of Cecilia's buttock cheek and pushed herself to her feet, trotting round to sit on Cecilia's head and hold her in place. The referee puffed out his cheeks and began to push again, ignoring Cecilia's muffled cries of protest and pain. 'Up! Up! Up!' the Slottenham fans were chanting from behind the Mamchester goal, delighted at the prospect of the Mamchester keeper being handicapped or crippled by the referee's enormous cock. The Mamchester fans were responding with 'She can take it! She can take it!', but they were singing with little conviction.

The referee was pushing harder now, trying to force his way in, and the chopper-cam assigned to Cecilia's head and face had even spotted that she was biting the pitch as his cock head built up an irresistible pressure on her sphincter; and when, with a triumphant gasp of pleasure, the referee sent his cock sliding into her, she sank her teeth so deep into the pitch that her jaw had to be prised free when the stretcher arrived to take her off. The referee paused, savouring, as he later described, the sense of possession and power a difficult anal entry always gave him, then began to bugger her, gradually increasing the strength and depth of his thrusts until Cecilia's breasts were swinging wildly beneath her chest and the ball girl sitting on Cecilia's head was almost being rocked off. Cecilia's cries were muffled by the turf in her mouth, but it was apparent from her swelling breasts, stiffening nipples, and moistening pussy that they were gradually changing from cries of pain and protest to cries of pleasure and encouragement. The referee, staring expressionlessly into the ranks of the cheering Slottenham fans, continued to bugger her steadily till his earpiece instructed him to investigate her pussy with his fingers.

He put a hand round her thigh and delved for her pussy, discovered that a positive drizzle of pussy-juice was falling from its gaping lips to the pitch. He caught some of it up and rubbed it into her breasts with one hand as he began to squeeze and tug her stiff and aching clitoris with the other, imagining, he later revealed, that her clitoris was a nipple in her pussy and her nipples were clitorises on her breasts. The sensations of her body and juices on his swollen fingertips were increasing his own pleasure and as he felt orgasm begin to grow in his balls he blew on his whistle again, ordering the remaining ball girl round him and between his thighs to lick his balls. A hovering chopper-cam detached itself from the main formation to follow the ball girl's efforts: his balls were the largest in the pornball league, and even the fearless Maria, veteran of a thousand white cards, had had difficulty in swallowing the load they had delivered into her crammed-to-capacity mouth earlier in the game.

The ball girl later reported that licking them was like licking miniature pineapples, so stiff were the hairs that covered them and so leathery the skin, and Cecilia reported that his orgasm felt like a colonic irrigation, so warm, thick, and copious was the semen that spurted from them into her cock-stuffed bowels, triggering her own orgasm. Indeed, so well-filled were her bowels by his cock and so hard did she tighten on him as she came, the referee had almost as much difficulty in pulling out as he had in getting in, having to build a slow rhythm before he could finally wrench himself loose with another turf-muffled scream from the Mamchester keeper. When he shuffled backwards on his knees and stood up, it was apparent that even orgasm had not softened his cock, and players all over the pitch swallowed nervously as he motioned the ball girl who had licked his balls in front of him to lick his cock clean.

As the ball girl serviced him he blew his whistle for Cecilia to get back on her feet, but she didn't move and the Mamchester physio, who had been waiting on the touchline since the brown card was first flourished, came running on instantly. When the physio slid an exploratory finger into the gaping ring of her anus she gave another muffled cry, and before his digital exploration was over she had fainted. Scowling, he signalled for a stretcher as Rosalind, Mamchester's deliciously tall and slender blonde eighteen-year-old substitute keeper, kept from an Olympic gymnastics gold only by a premature height spurt in her early teens, began warming up quickly on the side of the pitch.

Play was noticeably muted on the re-start, for the bulge in the referee's shorts was an ominous reminder that he had lost little, if any, of his capacity to award pink or brown cards, and it wasn't until he awarded a blue card for the newly introduced 'wilful lack of effort' offence to Mamchester's French midfielder Charlotte that it began to pick up again. Charlotte was already fully stripped and had to submit to a close pubic shave, thighs splayed as she was held up by two team-mates. The ball girl was nervous and her blunt razor slipped several times between the Frenchwoman's splayed thighs as she harvested the blonde pubic hair clustering her *mons Veneris* and *labia majora*. It would be added to the pubic hair harvested in the general shaving that would take place when the match was over, and woven into a commemorative beer mat for sale to the highest bidder: the blonde and red hair of players like Charlotte, Ffion, and Sandra would form the letters of the match-sponsor's name, Buttvicer. After the bounced ball that re-started the game there was an almost immediate foul, an illegal breast-barge from the rear on Jemima by a Mamchester defender, but the referee played an advantage with a smile, listening to his earpiece promise him a bonus for re-invigorating the game.

The ball ran free to Hilary, who pushed it wide to Jocasta, then shouldered her way into the box. Rosalind, who had disappointed the Slottenham fans with a confident display despite the unexpectedness of her appearance, elected to punch rather than catch, and commentators preparing to diagnose her first error swallowed their words as Mamchester launched an immediate counter-attack, forcing Sofiya to make an excellent save low at the near post from the dreadlocked Mamchester forward Siân. Play was end to end for the next five minutes, interrupted only by a white card that left Ffion choking and spluttering and a further three blues, two awarded simultaneously on Mamchester's Juliette and Slottenham's Jemima, who submitted to a pubic shave side by side. With the clock ticking down to full time, play was now as frantic as at any time in the match, and commentators were confidently stating that it was only a matter of time before the referee awarded another pink or brown. But he seemed to be waiting for a foul by a particular, as-yet-unidentified, player, and penalised some blatant foul play by both sides with merely a succession of whites and blues, sucked to orgasm by Hilary and Ffion and again by María, and supervising a nearly unprecedented three-player pubic shave that prompted the game's second tri-screen.

Then it came: the dreaded third brown card. Jocasta had dribbled in fast from the wing, beaten two Mamchester defenders on the edge of the box, and clipped a short ball across to Hilary, who pushed the ball into the box past a Mamchester defender's challenge and ran on into the box after it. But she seemed to have given herself too much to do, and Rosalind was a fraction of a second quicker to the ball, gathering it at Hilary's feet as the Slottenham player tumbled theatrically in the box. Despite the dubiousness of the foul, the referee blew for an immediate penalty and produced not one but two cards: the expected brown and an unexpected pink. The Mamchester fans were howling with outrage, and the first-half referee emerged from the players' tunnel, erect cock bouncing as he ran eagerly on to the pitch. Rosalind, an anal virgin, was protesting her innocence frantically to the second-half referee, tears beginning to shine in her large blue eyes, but he waved her protests away with a blast on his whistle and the keeper, the only fully clothed player left on the pitch, began to slide her shorts down with hands that trembled in their nearly clean gloves.

Simultaneous anal/vaginal entries on a single player were rare in the English league and even rarer in PA Cup Finals, and veteran players in studios all over the world were arguing over the last to be seen in a PA Cup Final, some plumping for the third annual PA Cup Final and a taxing simul performed on Mamchester

Urino's Tania, with others disqualifying this on the ground that it had in fact been a triple entry, with the UEPA match observer sucked off at the other end of the player while the two referees serviced her bottom and pussy. The first-half referee was now in the box, listening eagerly as the second-half referee gave him his instructions. He would lie on the pitch and penetrate Rosalind *per vaginam* while the second-half referee penetrated her *per anum*. Rosalind, her eighteen-year-old face now wet with tears, was sliding her knickers off, nodding her head sadly in agreement with the chant of 'Fix! Fix! Fix!' echoing down the pitch from the Mamchester fans at the opposite end of the stadium.

The Slottenham fans behind her were gleeful, however, and cheered loudly when Rosalind removed her shirt and bra and then bent over to allow a ball girl to begin tongue-lubing her anus. Even if Rosalind managed to stay on the pitch after the double entry was complete, it was unlikely she would be in any fit state to face Jocasta's penalty. The first-half referee was now lying full-length on the centre spot, a second ball girl sucking the head of his cock as a third coated the second-half referee's cock in spittle, readying it for what would surely be a prolonged and painful insertion into Rosalind's virgin anus. The two minutes of the regulation anal tongue-lubing had barely elapsed when the second-half referee blew for Rosalind to prepare herself for entry, and the trembling keeper walked to the first-half referee and squatted above his erect cock. Another blast on the whistle and she lowered herself onto it, gulping visibly as it entered her pussy and slid deep. The second-half referee blew his whistle again and she bent forward, presenting her bottom for anal entry.

He advanced on her, cock glistening brightly in the sun, and nodded curtly to the two ball girls standing on either side of Rosalind's hips, ready to pull her bum cheeks apart. The Slottenham fans had started their anal count-down, clapping and stamping loudly after each number, but even they seemed a little subdued at the thought of the referee's huge member being inserted into Rosalind's slender bottom, to thrust there vigorously for what might be, so late in the game, with even the referee's legendarily capacious balls surely beginning to feel a little drained, fifty or sixty strokes. And indeed, when the referee closed up behind her, lifting his cock head down and forward to her tender pink bottom hole, the whole crowd went quiet and the cry of agonised ecstasy from Rosalind that announced the referee's triumph after nearly two minutes of increasingly brutal effort was heard clearly throughout the stadium. But the feared fifty or sixty cock-strokes did not materialise: the referee would later describe how the thought of taking Rosalind's anal virginity brought him to the brink of premature ejaculation even as his cock head slid into the hot, slick, and very tight vestibule of her bum-chamber.

But he held himself in check, damming his seed torrents by sheer will-power, then gradually beginning to match the first-half referee, flat on his back with his cock in Rosalind's even hotter, slicker, and tighter pussy, cock-stroke for cock-stroke. Poor Rosalind, thrown curly-blonde-head-long at only eighteen into Clitty's most important game since the formation of the Pornball League, was caught between agony and ecstasy as the huge cocks of the two referees churned away in her two lower orifices, and a mixture of tears from her still streaming eyes and spittle from her now gasping mouth was pouring down her chin and dripping into the open mouth of the first-half referee. The taste of her tears and spit and feel of her firm, eighteen-year-old breasts, which he was squeezing hard as he pummelled at her pussy, were evidently too much for him after only fifteen or twenty strokes, and as if by a kind of spermatic sympathy the second-half referee joined him in orgasm after adding only two more strokes to the dozen he had already sent sliding into Rosalind's cringing bottom.

The keeper's blue eyes widened wonderingly as sperm spurted simultaneously in her bum and pussy, and she released another long groan, half in relief that her anal ordeal was over, half in disappointment that it could not continue. The sight of her fresh young face responding to her first experience of an intra-anal sperm douching, flanked by shots of the referees' cocks still solidly sheathed in her bottom and pussy, brought the stadium back to life, and her third groan, when the second-half referee slid his softening cock out of her now gaping anus, was lost in the cheers with which even the Slottenham fans were saluting her for the display she had put on. But when both referees had withdrawn and were having their cocks licked clean by ball girls, it took the young keeper nearly a minute to get back on her feet, allowing the chopper-cams plenty of time to feast their lenses on the gaping red circle of her anus, and as she hobbled over to her goal to prepare for the penalty even the most die-hard Mamchester fans lost hope.

Jocasta was trotting on the spot, breasts bouncing as she warmed up for the penalty, and when the first-half referee had left the field after exchanging a few words with his colleague, she dribbled the ball to the centre spot and took her trademark three-and-a-half strides backward, ready for the second-half referee's whistle. The naked Rosalind was on the goal line, wincing as she crouched in readiness, a mixture of sperm and pussy-juice glistening down her inner thighs as far as her calves and droplets of sperm sparkling in the sun as they dripped from her anus. The referee, whose cock had not re-hardened even when he was licked clean by the ball girl, raised his whistle to his lips, paused a moment, and blew, and Jocasta bounced once on the spot then strode forward to put Slottenham 3–2 in the lead. Her shot was low, hard, and to the left, and the Slottenham fans behind the goal were already on their feet celebrating the goal, because Rosalind, biting her lip to control the shaft of pain that the sudden effort sent spearing into her from her abused bottom, had flung herself the wrong way.

But in the same instant their ecstasy changed to agony and it was the Mamchester fans were who were cheering wildly, then redoubling their volume as Clitty launched an immediate counter-attack: even as she flew in the wrong direction, Rosalind had flicked her heels at the speeding ball and sent it flying off the goal-line and across the box. Rachel was first to the loose ball, playing a quick one-two with Siân and then looking up to see María beginning another of her runs. Her defence-splitting through-ball was judged to the millimetre and micro-second, and María was sprinting clear for a one-on-one with the Slottenham keeper. Sofiya did very well, narrowing the angle with a rush from her goal-line even better judged than Rachel's pass, but María, breasts bouncing, belly filled with the salty semen of two referees, was in no mood for failure and curved an unstoppable shot past her into the bottom right-hand corner. The Mamchester fans, who had been on their feet since Rosalind's miraculous save, had been transported from almost certain defeat to almost certain victory in the space of fifteen seconds, and their cheers increased when a mischievous editor flashed a shot of a scowling Brian Amberson preparing a foot-cane in his dug-out.

Two minutes later, the referee blew for full time and the Final was over. Slottenham players immediately dropped to their haunches, tears already beginning to trickle down their cheeks, while their Mamchester counterparts leapt high into the air in ecstasy, breasts bouncing wildly. Rosalind, hardly even seeming to notice the pain in her violated bottom, ran from her goal to embrace María as the two players were mobbed by their team-mates. The forward and keeper, studies in both physical and psychological contrast, kissed deep and hungrily in the middle of the breast-rubbing throng, their fingers twitching eagerly in their handcuffs as though they longed to fondle each other's breasts. When the handcuffs were removed by ball girls two minutes later, it was apparent that they did want to fondle each other's breasts, and even the arrival of the wheeled Cup Presentation Podium, pushed on to the field by a squad of panting ball girls, did not distract them. The Slottenham players, still cuffed, were already lining up, heads hanging, to receive their losers' medals, evidently eager to be off the field as quickly as possible.

But the sperm-hoses had to be connected first: throughout the stadium fans were inserting themselves into the artificial vaginas or rectums that had been unlocked on the seat-backs in front of them. Lovingly manufactured of sarco-plastic and guaranteed touch-, taste-, smell-, and sight-authentic, the artificial orifices had been modelled on the real pussies and anuses of the two teams, and some of the Mamchester fans who had chosen Rosalind's anus when they booked their tickets for the final were now covering the cost of their travel to London and overnight stay by auctioning it off to the highest bidders. Slottenham fans could not match them with the orifice of any player on their defeated team, and the prices fetched for Hilary's pussy the previous year, when she had scored the winning goal in their dramatic extra-time victory over their north London rivals Arsenal, were now nothing but a memory.

The presentation podium was now in place and the lucky winners of the PA Cup Final lottery were climbing into the cells revealed when the treads of the players' up-and-down stairs were swung open. When the treads were closed, a winner's head would be sticking up through each of them, ready for the players' bare and sweaty feet to walk round and sometimes over them.

The stad-screens were showing brief shots from Jocasta's boots now as the Slottenham players were stripped finally and completely: their boots were being unlaced and pulled off, and some of the stad-screens switched to infra-red shots on which the players' feet were still sheathed in bright reds and oranges against the cool blues and whites of the pitch. Then Jocasta's feet, long expected to play a decisive role in the final, were unbooted and some of the Mamchester fans raised a derisive cheer. Jocasta, already crying hardest of the Slottenham team, began to cry even harder, her buttocks and tear-shiny breasts quivering with her emotion, and the ball girls who were unbooting her rubbed her feet sympathetically for a few moments before passing on to the next player.

The podium was nearly ready now, with a male head waiting on each tread of the stair, the sperm-plumbing hooked up to the under-pitch sperm hoses that would carry the fans' salty tribute from all corners of the ground, and match officials readying the nettles with which the breasts of the losing team would be whipped as they went up to fetch their losers' medals. The last Slottenham player was unbooted and ball girls scurried to line up with the Slottenham team: the players would be carried to the podium so that their feet would not lose any fragrance on the grass. The signal came, and the Director General of Porn switched on the artificial orifices into which most of the crowd were now fully inserted, readying tens of thousands of cocks for the mass orgasm that he would time to meet Mamchester when they climbed the stair to receive their medals and be showered in gallons of hot semen. The Slottenham players, hands still cuffed firmly, tits bouncing, were being carried on the backs of gasping ball girls, who were bent almost double under the weight of the players. Jemima was the first to the podium and slipped off her ball girl's back to begin climbing the stair.

Tread-heads, some with eyes closed hard, sniffed frantically at her bare feet as she climbed and a gout of premature ejaculation from an especially excitable foot-fetishist in the crowd splashed down on her from the sperm-fountain above the row of waiting officials, wetting her face and one of her breasts.

She licked her lips sullenly, paused for a moment, and then began to walk along the row of officials in their rubber suits and hats. A bunch of nettles whistled down on her bare and unprotected breasts as she passed the first of them, then another and another and another, and she winced and closed her eyes, biting her sperm-moistened lips with pain as her breast-skin and nipples began to redden and inflame with urtication. Another Slottenham player had reached the top of the stair, her bare feet sniffed at frantically as she climbed, and now her breasts too were being whipped as she passed along the row to receive her loser's medal. Jemima had reached the end of the row and her two large losers' medals, made of nearly pure copper and pre-heated almost to scalding, was being slipped into her pierced nipples and dropped into place by an official wearing comfortable asbestos gloves. More gouts of premature ejaculation were splattering down on the Slottenham players and the row of officials, and one caught Jemima on the back of the head as she climbed down the stair leading off the podium, her mouth oohing and aahing with the pain of the heated medals as they bounced and settled on her breasts.

One by one the Slottenham players walked along the row, their breasts and nipples thoroughly whipped with nettles, and received their pre-heated losers' medals under an irregular drizzle of premature ejaculation that strengthened almost to a shower as Jocasta, her breasts whipped most cruelly of all, walked along the row to receive her obviously extra-hot medals. Two gouts of sperm caught her on the back of the head as she descended the stair leading off the podium, trickling down her back and round her cuffed hands to slide over the tight, muscular curves of her buttocks and backs of her thighs. When the last of the Slottenham players had followed her off the podium and trotted fast for the tunnel and the further punishments that awaited them at Brian Amberson's hands in the Slottenham dressing room, ball girls were already carrying the Mamchester team over to climb the head-lined stair. The DGP had switched the stad-screens to soothing pastel anti-orgasmic abstract patterns and closed off the sperm-plumbing; now he switched the screens back to shots of the bare-breasted, bare-buttocked, bare-pussied Mamchester team and increased the suction and thrusting in the artificial orifices, which had now achieved a record 96·5 per cent cock plug-in rate among the Mamchester fans and a highly respectable 68·2 per cent among the Slottenham fans.

He watched the virtual needles that recorded sperm-flow in tens of litres, allowing the tanks to fill for the moment when María lifted the PA Cup. An uncuffed María was climbing the stairs, pausing twice with a laugh to allow a tread-head to lick her dark-skinned feet, and the row of match officials were exchanging nettle-bunches for the mink gloves with which they would stroke and fondle the Mamchester players' breasts, exciting their nipples to full stiffness to receive the winners' medals. María reached the top of the stair, crossed herself, and began to walk slowly along the row, smiling happily as her breasts were fondled and squeezed by mink-gloved hands. When she reached the final official, her famous nipples were at the stiffest any commentator could remember seeing them. The match official, his hands trembling, gently fitted her winners' medals and turned away to lift the Cup. The DGP had his finger paused over the switch that would put all orifices to orgasm mode and unblock the sperm-plumbing beneath the podium; now, as the official lifted the Cup and placed it in María's eager hands and she turned to lift it triumphantly into the explosion of ecstasy from the Mamchester fans, the finger descended. It was later estimated that the huge, fifty-litre cup was filled to overflowing in a record 1·2 seconds as a white tsunami of sperm descended on the grinning María and her Mamchester players, and sperm was still pouring down the stairs nearly a minute after the players had splashed their way down and taken the Cup on the traditional tour of the ground.

9

Spurt and Polish

She was painting her toenails when the doorbell rang, the tip of her tongue worm-pink in a corner of her mouth as she bent forward over her foot, sitting naked on the bed with a delicate *v* of concentration between the dark strokes of her eyebrows, four perfect, lightly tanned toes held apart with three little tufts of cotton-wool. She had just been laying the last even, unhurried stroke to the nail of her big toe and for a moment, such was her concentration, she was unsure that the bell had rung at all; and then it came again, pealing out through her flat with iron insistence.

She tutted, finished the stroke, slipped the brush back into the bottle of polish, screwed it shut, and slid forward on her smooth bottom to the foot of the bed, watching her feet slide ahead of her, one foot done, the other unstarted. Her feet slipped over the edge of the bed, dropping to the floor, and she stood up and walked across the room to put the bottle of polish on her make-up table, then turned for the bedroom door. As she was walking through it the doorbell sounded again, and she frowned. Someone was being a very rude and impatient little boy. She walked across the sitting room, reached the intercom on the wall beside her copy of Fraghilletto's *Youth Pursued by Bare-Foot Nymphs*, and pressed the button that allowed her to speak to whoever was waiting twenty-seven floors below.

'Yes?'

'I've got a parcel 'ere for a Mizz Callipede.'

It was a coarse, brutal, proletarian voice, full of male arrogance and will-to-power, and her frown deepened for a moment, then vanished, seeming to drain into the smile that bent her lips and lingered as she leant forward again to the intercom and said, 'Bring it up.'

She pressed the button that would open the front door of the flats, turned, and walked unhurriedly back to her bedroom. She came back eighteen seconds later loosely knotting the belt of one of her dressing gowns, looking down at her body, tugging the gown a little more open over her bare breasts. As she reached the sofa and sat down, slipping her unpainted right foot under herself, allowing her painted left foot to stick out ahead of her, the toes still separated by the tufts of cotton wool, she heard him hammer on the door, attacking it with his raw red fist, porcine face shining with sweat. Yes, she could just picture him. She leaned forward and spoke into the intercom concealed in the Japanese dried-flower arrangement on the table in front of her.

'It's open. Bring it in.'

And she touched the button that opened her front door. How dazzled he would be by the luxury of his surroundings when he entered, how full of resentment and envy, how ripe for the plucking! She heard the door swing open and the thump as he stepped forward into her flat, his cheap heavy shoes landing on the marble floor of her vestibule; and her nostrils flared delicately, as though she could already catch the uncouth tang of his working-class sweat. Thump, thump his shoes sounded as he walked forward, and there he was, walking through the door from the vestibule, blue-uniformed and with a long parcel tucked negligently under his left arm. But he was taller than she had expected. And younger. And better-looking. *Much* better-looking.

She watched him pause, blinking in the light that poured over him from the long window behind her, and suppressed the smile she knew would come when she watched his eyes widen to see what awaited him: the young and very attractive woman sitting on a yellow silk sofa in a red silk dressing gown half-open over her bare breasts. She loved to read the level of sexual experience and dominance in male eye-widening: the degree of it, the speed, even the co-ordination between left and right eye. There was the unconcealed greed of the adolescent who a few years earlier was reacting in the same way to a well-heaped birthday table; the barely perceptible flicker of the roué, his brain already and automatically busy with techniques of seduction; and the leer of the proletarian pig, undisguised not out of inexperience and surprise but out of arrogance and machismo.

His eye-widening, as she might have expected, as she *had* expected, was the leer of the proletarian pig, and already his eyes were busy on her breasts, flicking left and right as though he could fold the dressing gown wider open by gaze alone. He had barely glanced at her naked foot, his eyes flicking on and off it in half a second, uninterested, unconcerned.

'Yes?' she said coldly, noting the way his shoulders had gone back as he stood there, but he didn't even look up at her face as he replied.

'Parcel for Mizz Callipede.'

'I will take it,' she said, and he grinned easily, looking up at her now as he took a step forward, letting the parcel drop from beneath his arm, catching it in his left hand as it fell.

'No!' she barked, raising herself on the sofa, watching his reaction to the note of command in her voice. 'You will take your shoes off before you walk on my floor.'

Ah, not a flicker of surprise or guilt, only a widening of that grin for a moment, and a pause before he nodded.

'I'm sorry, Mizz.'

Sarcastic, unconcerned. He turned, paused fractionally to allow her to note the width of his shoulders, and swaggered back into the vestibule. She heard the thud as he allowed her parcel to drop to the floor, and then the grunt as he bent to unlace his heavy shoes. The heels thumped against the floor as they came off one by one, then there was another grunt as he stooped for the dropped parcel; and then he was padding back across the floor, reappearing in the door of the vestibule in dark socks, walking across the room to her.

'Thank you,' she said. His eyebrows quirked, and then he was holding the parcel out to her.

'The customer always comes first, Mizz,' he said, and she heard the way his voice had deepened even further, sex-hormones flooding into his blood, preparing him for what he had already decided was awaiting him. She raised her own eyebrows, shaking her head as he held the parcel out to her.

'No.'

'No, Mizz?'

'No. You will open it for me. I am drying my toenails.'

'Ah.'

He nodded, not even looking at her foot this time, and the half-grin was back on his face. He drew the parcel back and glanced at the end, looking for a place to begin opening it. He glanced up at her.

'And what is it, Mizz?'

'Wait and see,' she said.

'Okey-doke, Mizz.'

He began to tear at the tough paper with strong, blunt fingers.

'Careful, you oaf,' she said.

He looked up at her, still grinning, and continued to tear at the paper. He sniffed.

'It's shoes, Mizz. Or boots. I can smell the leather.'

A strip of paper came away in his hands and he dropped it carelessly to the floor, then another, and another, and he was dragging the tissue paper off and there they were in his coarse hands, her new boots, the uppers coiled tightly, like sleeping snakes.

''Ere they are, Mizz.'

'Yes. There they are. They were packed with great care, you oaf, and you have unwrapped them as though they were lumps of stone.'

'Yes, Mizz. I generally do.'

'Yes? And why is that?'

''Cos I find it excites 'em.'

'Excites who?'

'Posh tarts like you.'

'You're northern, aren't you?'

'Yes, Mizz,' he said, his accent thickening as though to mock her. 'Yorkshire born, Yorkshire bred, strong int' arm and thick –' he looked down ostentatiously at the front of his trousers, then up again '– int' 'ead.'

'How thick?'

'Very thick, Mizz. Shall I show ya?'

'No. Not yet. For now, you can put them on me.'

'Yer boots, Mizz?'

'My boots,' she said.

He took hold of the coils of upper in each hand and shook them loose, then walked towards her.

'But first, oaf, you can dry my toenails. With your breath.'

'Ma breath, Mizz?'

'Yes. Kneel before me and dry them.'

He dropped the boots on the floor (they landed upright with a clap on their soles), went down on his knees with another grin, and crawled towards the foot she was holding out to him.

'Can I touch it, Mizz?' he said.

'No. You can keep your hands off me.'

His grin faded a little.

'Until later.'

She blinked slowly as his grin strengthened again.

'For now, just blow.'

He nodded, put his head over the row of her toes, took a slow, unhurried breath, and blew, slowly turning his head so that the stream of his breath passed over each of her toes in turn, big toe to little. Then he blew the toes in reverse, little toe to big, then big toe to little again, then in reverse, little toe to big, then big to little, little to big, big to little, little to big, big to little. And stopped, looking up at her.

'Is that OK, Mizz?' he said easily, not out of breath.

'My,' she said, 'what big lungs you must have.'

'All the better to blow you with, Mizz.'

She leaned forward, swinging her foot to meet her stretching fingers, and lightly touched each toe with the tip of her little finger, big toe to little. She nodded, and swung the foot back again, lifting her right foot out from under her to join it.

'Yes. It's OK. Now put my boots on.'

She watched him swallow with excitement as he twisted his upper body and reached behind himself for the two boots, setting them to either side of his body.

'Which one first, Mizz?'

'Right foot,' she said. His warm hand took hold of her right foot and she read a faint tremor in them as he pushed the opening of her right boot over it and began to tug it upwards, the bulge in the front of his trousers steadily growing. He'd seen now that she was wearing nothing under her dressing gown.

'My,' she said, 'what a big cock you have.'

He looked up at her, his face slightly flushed with the effort of pulling the boot up her leg, and his lip curled with contempt.

'All the better to fuck you with, Mizz.'

She nodded silently, drawing the hem of her dressing gown back to allow him to pull the boot up over her thigh. His hands were brutal on her flesh, handling her like a piece of meat, and she wondered for a moment whether she'd made a mistake. He looked up at her again, jerking his head to swing a comma of sweat-moistened hair out of one eye, and she met his heated eyes coolly, levelly.

'Enough,' she said. 'Do my left boot now.'

'Bitch,' he said. But he let go of her right leg, picked up her left boot, and started to slide it up over her left foot.

'If you damage the polish, oaf, you will be punished.'

He grunted, his face truly shining with sweat now, and tugged harder at the boot, squeezing her leg hard. She counted off three, leaned forward, and slapped him. Only his eyes swung up to acknowledge the blow and he continued to tug and squeeze hard. When he had finished she said, 'Move back. No, keep kneeling.'

Now she stood up, tugging the right boot up her thigh the final couple of inches, adjusting the lie of the left boot, her dressing gown open and flapping. When she was satisfied, she shrugged the gown off and let it fall on the sofa behind her.

'Well?' she said, looking down at him as he knelt in front of her. His eyes lifted to hers for a moment, then dropped, lingering on her breasts, then dropped again, to her dark pubic triangle and the light silver chain hanging in a curve from the gold studs in her pussy lips. He pursed his lips and blew and she felt the chain jump and swing against her pussy. She reached down and took hold of one of his ears, twisting it hard, adjusting his face to meet her gaze.

'You've been a nasty, uncouth little boy, and teacher is very unhappy with you. So you must come with her to her Chamber of Corrections.'

He blinked sullenly and she twisted harder at the warm, moist flesh of his ear.

'Well?'

'Yes,' he said.

'Yes, *please*.'

'Yes, please.'

'Yes, please, *Miss*.'

'Yes, please, Miss.'

She let go of his ear and turned, bending in front of him, pushing her buttocks into his face, knowing that his eyes would be burning on her buttocks and crotch-gap as she pulled the collar and lead from its hiding-place. She turned back to him and dropped the collar neatly into place over his head, tightened it hard, fastened it, and set off for her Chamber with the lead in her hand, the high heels of her thigh-boots stabbing at the polished wood of the floor. For a moment, as the lead tautened and the collar jerked on his neck, she thought he wasn't going to play, and then the lead slackened a little and she heard him crawling after her. She walked to the door of her Chamber and punched that day's code into the keypad sitting beside it, then laid her thumb over the tiny glass square of the scanner. There was a hiss of hydraulics and the door slid open. She jerked on the lead.

'After you, oaf,' she said, and he crawled past her on his hands and knees into the Chamber. She released the lead as he went and heard it dragging across the floor, then go silent as it crossed the threshold. She turned and walked back to her stereo, opened the Inkspots compilation CD, slipped it in, turned up the volume, and found track seven. The strumming of the guitar vamp followed her across the room as she walked back to the door of the Chamber and walked inside. He was waiting for her, turned to face the door, still on his hands and knees, the lead hanging from the collar round his neck.

'Yeah, yeah . . .'

Bill Kenny's soulful tenor followed her into the Chamber and she had to raise her voice as she said, nodding round her, 'You like it?'

He turned on his hands and knees, looking round the Chamber, the lead trailing on the floor.

'What is there to like?' he said.

She walked past him to the shelf where her black gloves were waiting.

'Yes,' she said, turning back to him as she pulled them on. 'It is a little minimalistic, isn't it?'

'It's like the inside of a witch's hat.'

'So I've been told.'

'Your feet's too big,' the Inkspots informed them as she tugged her left glove up into place, pointed her index finger, and counted off the row of small black buttons down one side of it with her thumb. The Chamber was conical, with a single circular black wall sloping inwards to a point high overhead.

'Or like that fucking scene in *Spinal Tap*. "None more black."'

'I've been told that too,' she said.

'But what the fuck is that?'

She didn't like the tone he was adopting now. Not at all appropriate to an oaf on his hands and knees with a dog-collar round his neck.

'It's for you,' she said. She walked over to the Discipline Post, the two-metre-high, three-metre-thick black stump rising in the exact centre of the Chamber.

'What does it do?'

She reached up for the top of the Post, going on the toes of her boots, knowing he was watching her bare thighs and buttocks stretch, and pulled the wristlets and anklets down.

'Why not see for yourself?' she said, turning back and tossing them to him. They landed on the polished black marble floor with heavy little thumps and stopped sliding almost at once.

'What are they?' he said, picking a wristlet up.

'They go round your ankles and wrists.'

He tugged it open with a spurt of Velcro and looped it round his wrist.

211

'What's inside it?' he said, fastening it.

'Ball-bearings.'

'Oh. Like this?'

He held his wrist up.

'Yes. You put them on and then you go and hug the Post. It's a test of strength. But you have to take your clothes off first.'

She walked back to him, clack, clack, clack, and unfastened his dog-collar.

'So get them off,' she said, pulling it loose and tossing it away. He started to push himself up and she said, 'No. You stay on your knees. Get undressed and get your anklets and wristlets on.'

He took the wristlet off and started to get undressed. She walked over to her shelf and turned round to slip her buttocks up onto it, sitting there and watching him.

'You need a shave, you ape,' she told him as he tugged his shirt up over his head, not bothering to undo all the buttons, revealing a tanned torso covered in black hair. Even his back. He looked sideways at her, undoing his trousers.

'Some posh tarts like it,' he said. 'Turns them on. Sleeping with an ape. Like.'

He pulled his trousers down and cycled his way out of them.

'This posh tart would rather sleep with a real ape.'

He grunted with amusement and slid his boxer shorts off, having to hold his stiff cock up against his belly as he did so, then began to put the anklets and wristlets on. When he was finished he went down on his hands again and looked up at her.

'I'm ready now. Mistress.'

'Then crawl to the Post, ape,' she said. 'And await your next order.'

She watched him crawl to the Post.

'Now, tell me, ape. Have you got any metal in your body?'

He grunted.

'What d'you mean?'

'Steel plates in your head. Pace-maker. Bullets. Anything like that.'

He shook his head.

'No.'

'What about that ring?'

'Gold,' he said. 'And the earring's silver.'

'Good. Then stand and hug the Post. Hard.'

He stood and hugged the post, lifting his arms round its bulk, hugging it hard.

'Now, tell me, ape,' she said, 'are you strong?'

His head was turned away from her, pressed to the shining black surface of the Post; now he turned it to face her.

'Strong enough,' he said.

'Yes?'

She lifted her left hand, pointing the forefinger of the glove at the Post, and thumbing one of the buttons along the forefinger. She heard him give a little grunt of surprise.

'Then if you're strong enough, ape,' she said, 'walk over here. And fuck me.'

He grunted again and she saw the muscles stand out in his back and shoulders.

'Walk over here, ape,' she repeated. 'And fuck me.'

She opened her legs and dropped her left hand to her pubic hair, tugging at it, running her fingers through it with a silken rustle. His eyes dropped to her moving hand, widening, and he grunted again.

'Come on,' she said. 'Walk over here. *And fuck me.*'

His face was reddening, veins swelling in his neck as he strained to push himself away from the Post. She slipped off the shelf and began to walk towards him, the high heels of her thigh-boots clacking on the polished floor through the dying notes of 'Your Feet's Too Big'. She reached him in the silence between tracks and said, 'What's wrong, ape?'

213

'I . . . I can't move my fucking hands and feet.'

The piano vamp of the next track came pouring into the Chamber.

'Yes?' she said. 'A big, strong ape like you, and you can't move your hands and feet?'

'No,' he said sullenly.

Bill Kenny's voice swelled over them.

'I'll never smile again . . .'

She pointed at the door with her gloved left hand, thumbing another button on the forefinger, and the door slid shut, cutting off the sound completely.

'My witch's hat is soundproofed, you know. A Mars rocket could take off outside that door and you'd not hear a thing. So any time you feel like screaming, be my guest.'

'Witch's twat,' he said.

She stepped behind him and put the fingers of her gloved hand to the opening of his buttock-cleft.

'Do you want to know why you can't move?' she asked him.

'I already know why.'

'Why?'

'It's fucking magnetic, isn't it?'

'It's fucking magnetic,' she agreed, sliding her fingers through the dense hair paving the buttock-cleft, down over his arsehole, over his perineum, down and over his scrotum to seize and control his balls.

'Are they full?' she asked.

'Find out for yourself.'

She squeezed harder and yanked, hearing him hiss with pain.

'Less insolence, ape,' she said. 'They'd better be, because you're not leaving here until both of them are polished *thoroughly*.'

She released his balls and turned away to stroll back to her shelf, knowing that he was listening to her sharp heels on the floor. Clack. Clack. Clack. She picked up the chains and strolled back.

214

'Aren't you going to ask me what are going to be polished?' she said.

'I already know,' he said. She reached up and slipped the eyelet of the right-hand chain into its hook, then stretched it down and across his back to his right hand, snapping the bracelet into place.

'What?' she said. She slipped the eyelet of the left-hand chain into its hook and stretched it down and across his back to his left hand.

'Your boots,' he said.

'How quick on the uptake you are, ape.'

She chained his ankles, then walked back and pointed at the Post with her left hand, pressing the button that turned the magnetism off. She heard him grunt with relief.

'Turn round,' she said. The X of chains crossed on his back swung apart as he obeyed, his thick cock swinging to face her, still erect. She pointed with her left glove and pressed a button and the chains rattled as the hooks slid back into the Post, dragging his hands and feet apart, spread-eagling him. She stepped back to him and unfastened the wristlets and anklets, tossing them aside one by one. She sniffed, feeling her nipples peak at the musk of his sweat.

'You stink, ape,' she told him, tall enough in her boots to look him directly in the eye.

'Some posh tarts like it,' he told her as she walked back to her shelf and picked up the nipple-clamps and artificial vagina.

'This posh tart doesn't,' she said, turning back. 'This post tart thinks you should be shaved and disinfected. Before you're put into a zoo.'

She laid the artificial vagina on the floor and straightened to take hold of the skin on either side of his right nipple. She squeezed, forcing the nipple out so that she could attach the first nipple-clamp.

'A women's zoo,' she said, holding the clamp poised

over the nipple, serrated jaws open. 'Where women can stroll and throw filth at male apes in their cages.'

She released the clamp and he sucked in breath for a moment before mastering the pain. She stepped to the right and took hold of his left nipple in the same way, glancing down at his cock.

'Would you like that, ape? To be in a cage and be pelted with filth by laughing women?'

She squeezed, forcing the nipple out, and poised the clamp over it, serrated jaws open. He didn't answer and she released the clamp, smiling as he stiffened with pain. She bent and picked up the artificial vagina, then straightened and took hold of his cock with her other hand.

'From the state of this,' she told him, staring into his eyes, 'you do like the idea of it. Don't you?'

She masturbated him slowly, one stroke, two, three, then stopped.

'Well?'

She lifted the mouth of the vagina to the head of his cock.

'In a cage. Pelted with filth. Women laughing at you gleefully.'

She pushed the vagina over his cock, watching his face as he slid deep into it.

'I can arrange it for you, if you like. I have all the contacts. Lots of women who would love to get their hands on a hairy ape like you, and treat you as you deserve to be treated. Like shit.'

She thrust the vagina finally into place and stepped back, clack, clack.

'Like fuck,' he said.

'Don't deny it. Don't deny your true desires. You're as stiff as a post. Just at the thought of it.'

'Apes are excitable. Polymorphous perversity.'

'Careful,' she said.

She pointed her forefinger at the harvey and thumbed the code that switched it on. He gasped as the ridged plastic walls tightened on his cock and began to ripple and vibrate. She switched it off.

'Pleasure,' she said. She pointed her forefinger at his chest and thumbed the code that electrified the nipple-clamps. The chains attached to his wrists suddenly clattered against the Post and he grunted, his whole body stiffening and jerking. She switched the clamps off.

'Pain,' she said. 'Light . . . and dark. Sweet . . . and sour. Up . . . and down. All that I need to train you and teach you your true place in the scheme of things. Which is on your knees before me.'

She looked away from him, pointing at the wall of the Chamber, thumbing another code, and the door of the Throne alcove slid aside. She looked back at him, still pointing at the alcove.

'On your knees, worshipping my feet.'

She thumbed the Throne-code, not having to look, and the Throne purred forward into the Chamber. He laughed when he saw it: a black, motorised throne on four small wheels, rolling up to her and nudging her legs like a dog. Expressionless, she stepped in front of it and lowered her buttocks to it, her gloved right hand poised above the joystick set into one of its arms. Then, her face still expressionless, she reversed, turned, and began to ride round the Post, slowly at first, gradually getting faster. He laughed, watching her, and she allowed a widening smile onto her face. She circled the Post ten times, then swung the Throne abruptly in a half-circle and began to circle it in the opposite direction. When she'd finished ten circuits, she swung to a halt, facing him as before.

'You find my Throne amusing, ape?' she said. He nodded, his eyes shining with amusement, and she slipped her left forefinger into the hole that awaited it on the arm of the Throne. She thumbed the code and, after a moment of surprise, his laughter burst out again. The Throne was rising on its four wheels, telescoping

217

steel rods lifting it towards the ceiling of the Chamber. Soon the pointed toes of her boots were two foot high, three foot, four, five, six. The Throne stopped rising. She leaned forwards slightly and looked down on him, lifting her forefinger from the control hole. He looked up at her, face creased with laughter, and she pushed the joystick forward. The Throne rolled towards him and stopped with her boots in his face. She rested her left hand on the arm of the Throne, forefinger pointing down, angled at his invisible body.

'Kiss my boots, ape,' she said.

'Fuck off.'

She thumbed the code that electrified the nipple-clamps and counted aloud, 'One . . . two . . . three.'

She thumbed the clamps off.

'Kiss my boots, ape.'

She heard him gasping, trying to control his breath.

'F . . . fuck off.'

She waited two seconds, then thumbed the clamps on again and counted off, having to raise her voice through his gasps this time.

'One . . . two . . . three.'

She thumbed the clamps off.

'Kiss my boots, ape.'

He didn't reply this time.

'We're going up 5 per cent of full power at a time, ape,' she told him. 'This is 20 per cent.'

She thumbed the clamps on and counted off into his gasps and a short scream.

'One . . . two . . . three.'

She thumbed the clamps off.

'Kiss my boots, ape.'

He groaned.

'Kiss them, ape. You have five seconds and then you experience 25 per cent. One . . . two . . . three . . . four . . . five.'

She thumbed the clamps on and he screamed fully

this time, so she counted off silently, then thumbed the clamps off and waited for him to control his breathing.

'Kiss my boots, ape.'

He muttered something through his gasps.

'Kiss them. You have five seconds and then you experience 30 per cent. One . . . two . . . three . . .'

He groaned.

'Four . . . f –'

Something pressed against the toe of her left boot and she leaned forward and looked down to see his head bent to place his lips there. He kissed it and put his head back, still gasping, tears of pain and humiliation running freely from his eyes. She reversed the Throne and lowered it, then pointed at his cock and switched the harvey on. He jerked with surprise and the texture of his breathing softened as the ridged walls tightened on him again and began to ripple and vibrate.

'You are being rewarded for your obedience, ape,' she told him. His skin was glistening with sweat, darkening and plastering down his chest-hair as his gasps of after-pain turned into gasps of pleasure. She adjusted the temperature of the harvey, setting it slightly above blood-heat, and grunted with surprise as he responded almost at once, groaning as he began to ejaculate, his sperm spurting against the transparent bulge on the harvey's head.

'Good ape,' she told him, moving the Throne forward and lifting the harvey to inspect the reading on the spermometer. He lifted his head from his chest, gasping.

'Bitch,' he said.

'Twenty-eight point three cc,' she said. 'Very good, ape. That's enough for a whole boot.'

She reversed the Throne a couple of inches, held the harvey over her raised right boot, and pushed the sperm-release. Sperm fell over the toe of the boot in a thin stream, dividing in two and falling to the floor of the Chamber in two thinner streams. She moved the boot forward and back and twisted it side to side, soaking the toe thoroughly with the falling sperm. It was falling from the harvey less strongly now and she took her finger off the sperm-release.

'You can lick it off the floor when we're finished,' she said. 'For now, you only have to lick it off my boot.'

She slipped her forefinger into the hole and the Throne began to rise again on its telescoping steel legs, sperm still dripping from her boot to the floor. When it was six feet above the floor, she drove the Throne forward, presenting the boot to his face.

'Lick it, ape,' she said, slipping her forefinger out of the hole and pointing it down at him.

He was ready for her, his breathing almost back to normal.

'Fuck off.'

'Starting again at 5 per cent,' she said, and thumbed the clamps on. He gasped, sucking in air as though it were ice-cold and his lungs were red-hot, searing inside his chest, and when she thumbed the clamps off she heard him breathing fast.

'Lick it, ape,' she repeated. She heard him swallow and try to say 'Fuck off', and she sighed.

'Ten per cent, ape,' she said, and thumbed the clamps on. He barked with pain this time, and her ears rang with the sound as she thumbed the clamps off and waited for his gasps to subside.

'It's getting worse,' she told him. 'I'm sensitising you. Tenderising your flesh. Can't you feel it? Yes? So lick it.'

He groaned.

'Lick it.'

Another groan.

'Fifteen per cent, ape.'

She thumbed the clamps on, letting the electricity sing into him half a second longer than before, knowing that her words would have worked on him and that he would be feeling it more intensely, his nipples shrieking with electro-anguish. She thumbed the clamps off.

'L –' she started to say through his sobbing gasps for breath, but she was interrupted by the sound of his lips and tongue on the toe of her boot, as he greedily sucked and lapped his own sperm off the leather.

'Good ape,' she said. When he had finished she lowered the Throne again and inspected the harvey. It was still firmly in place over his cock, and through the windows in its sides she could see how his cock-veins had swollen even more, pressed flat against the glass. She thumbed the harvey on, setting the suck-and-vibrate low to begin with.

'I need some more,' she told him. 'More for my left boot. Are you ready to supply some? Some more for your Mistress?'

She looked up at his face. It was red, congested with blood, and the lower half of it was shining with spittle and tears that had dripped to his chest too, flashing as his chest rose and fell fast, the clamps on his nipples shaking. She pushed the temperature of the harvey up, watching his face for a reaction, and his head shook slowly from side to side, his lips working, coming together, opening.

'Yes,' she said. 'I am a bitch. A bitch on heat. You can feel that. I'm a bitch on heat.'

The harvey was well above blood-heat now and must have been starting to get painful. She pushed the suck-and-vibrate higher, pleasuring him as she punished him. His chest swelled and quivered, and she pushed the temperature higher.

'Bitch on heat. A boiling bitch. So it's unfortunate that you've got your dick deep in the hottest part of me. So would you like to pull it out?'

The harvey was shuddering on his cock now, sucking at him hard as it pulsed back and forward, and she almost expected to see steam hissing from it at the end of each stroke.

'Well, would you? Just nod your head and you can pull it. Pull it out of me, and not have your dick boiled. Just nod your head, ape-man. Nod it.'

She watched him, pushing the temperature higher, knowing that she was approaching the limit of safety, that another few degrees and another thirty seconds would burn his cock, burn it for sure. But it was up to him.

'Nod, ape! Nod your head if you want to get out!'

Then she laughed with glee. Tears and spittle were flashing left and right from his eyes, mouth, and chin as he shook his head. He didn't want to come out of her. He wanted orgasm even at the expense of a scalded cock. She thumbed the harvey to orgasmo-throb and dropped the temperature fast, knowing that the sudden change, from near-boiling to near-freezing, would bring him off even faster. And there, yes, he was coming, his sperm spurting like thick cream inside the transparent bulb at the end of the harvey.

She drove the Throne forward and lifted the harvey to read off the quantity he had provided for her, feeling residuary heat glowing in its plastic even as his tormented cock was soothed with cold.

'Good ape,' she said. '*Very* good ape. Thirteen point seven cc. That was excellent for a second orgasm. Exceptional. In fact, unprecedented.'

She held the end of the harvey over the toe of her left boot and triggered the sperm-release, letting his essence stream on to the leather. When she was finished she raised the Throne again and drove it forward, presenting her left boot to his face.

'And now we begin again,' she said. 'Elicktricity.'

222

10

Paws for Thought

He watched the Land Rover bump towards him over the sun-baked earth, leaving a cloud of dust that caught up with it and swirled over him when it braked a couple of metres away. He had to close his eyes and turn his head down and away, hearing the driver's door swing open, the double thump of a pair of sturdy boots, and the slam of the driver's door as the dust tickled over the skin of his face. The boots thudded towards him, then stopped in front of him.

'Good morning, sir. I'll be your guide for the day's hunting.'

He opened his eyes, still looking down, then reached out for the short-nailed hand that was offered to him through the last traces of dust, watching the faint glitter of blonde hair along the slim tanned forearm for a moment, then looking up over the large breasts beneath the tight shikari's uniform to see the spark of amusement in the clear blue eyes beneath the wide-brimmed hat. Her grip was very strong and his eyes must have widened with surprise for a moment, he realised. The contact seemed to arrow straight to his groin and he felt his cock jerk half upright, ready to swing into full erection if her hand stayed in his a moment longer.

It didn't: she squeezed harder, then released him, but as she turned away back to the Land Rover he thought her eyes had dropped to his groin for a moment, measuring the outlines of the bulge she had provoked. But the bulge got bigger now as he watched her walk away from him back to the Land Rover, her backside firm and rounded in the tight khaki shorts with the polished leather holster on one hip, her legs flowing smooth and golden to her rolled white socks and boots, and when she reached the Land Rover and leaned through the open window, one leg lifting off the ground, her backside straining even harder at her shorts, he couldn't restrain a groan.

She turned back to him, holding what she had lifted out of the Land Rover: the rifles, one in each hand. She walked back to him and he noticed her expression had changed again: no longer amused, flirtatious, but fixed, professional, and when she started speaking he noticed that her South African accent had got stronger. Or Rhodesian.

'You've done some hunting before, so they tell me, so I'm letting you out with one of the higher-powered guns. Good for a running shot at thirty metres, forty even, if the wind's right. Here.'

He took the rifle from her, putting his hand to the stock where her hand had just rested, his cock quivering at the faint trace of warmth and moisture, then blinked and tried to focus his attention as she began to describe how the rifle worked. He was paying a lot for this and he wanted to get his money's worth. She broke her own rifle in two, demonstrating how to load, explaining what she was doing crisply, efficiently, not wasting words or effort, then handing him one of the darts when she'd finished, watching him silently as he broke his own rifle and loaded it, then snapped the rifle shut and raised it to his eye in one smooth movement. When he lowered it and looked at her she stared at him for a moment, then nodded and smiled.

'They told me right,' she said. 'You have done some hunting. Come on. I'll get the binocs, then we'll be on our way.'

This time when she leaned through the open door of the Land Rover both legs came off the ground and her thighs splayed for a moment, revealing the shadowed gaps between her shorts and her inner thighs before she pushed herself out and turned back to him, a pair of binoculars dangling from her left hand. She was rewarding him for his quick learning, he thought, knowing that his eyes would be fixed on her, that his cock would be bulging even harder in his shorts when she turned back to him.

'Come on,' she said, looping the strap of the binoculars over her neck, allowing them to drop to her breasts, and set off under the trees without another word. He paused for a moment, savouring the image of the bounce of the binoculars on her breasts, his cock straining in his shorts, then followed her, his loaded rifle suddenly much solider in his right hand. As he trotted to catch up with her, watching her firm round backside roll in her shorts, a sudden fantasy flashed in on him. Why not shoot her now, at point-blank range, right in the arse? He could see the white feathers of the dart quivering as it phutted home into the swell of her left buttock, and just had time to read the quiver of movement there and raise his eyes to meet hers as she turned to look back at him, still striding along the trail.

'Fifteen seconds,' she said, then turned her head back and strode on. His steps faltered for a moment, then he caught up with her.

'What?' he said. 'You mean for the anaesthetic to take effect?'

'Yeah. On average.'

She stepped ahead of him, bending to pass under a branch, backside protruding at him, the cloth of her shorts straining over her buttocks, then carried on walking as he bent under the branch himself and trotted back to her.

'It goes by bodyweight,' she said. He was already starting to feel a little out of breath from the pace she

225

was setting, but her voice was even and unhurried. 'Most of the game in the park's round fifty kilos, and you can add on an extra second for every ten kilos above that.'

'Doesn't it make a difference wh –'

He broke off. She'd stopped dead, turning to step in front of him, her free hand swinging up over his mouth, then dropping to lift the binoculars resting on the firm swell of her breasts. She raised them and he strained his eyes along her line of sight. He licked his lips.

'What is it?' he whispered.

'Leopardess,' she said. 'That tree dead ahead there. 'Bout twenty metres up, on the first big branch to the right. See for yourself.'

She held the binoculars out for him, but the neck-strap was short and he had to bend and press himself against her body to see through them. Christ, she was muscular, and he could feel her body glowing with warmth through the cloth of her uniform where it was pressed to his shoulder and flank.

'See?' she said. He blinked and tried to concentrate, settling his eyes properly into the eyepieces, putting a hand that shook faintly for a moment over hers to move the binoculars. There was the tree, but where . . . Then he saw, and groaned with lust for the second time that day. The leopardess was basking full-length in the sun, her slim patterned body splayed belly-down along the branch, sleeping face turned towards them, one long leg dangling, her heavy breasts pressed to the rough bark. He felt as though he could almost reach out and touch her, run his fingers over the warm, smooth swell of the breast nearest him, then down her flank to her buttocks, fingers sliding on smooth, rosette-spangled skin, down the cleft of the buttocks to . . .

'Well?' she said.

He came back to himself almost with a physical shock, realising that the leopardess was a good hundred

226

metres away. He pulled his head back from the binoculars and she swung them away from him, dropping them back on her breasts.

'Can we stalk her?' he asked.

The guide shook her head.

'Nah,' she said. 'Not that one. She's far too fucking cunning. No one's had her for at least three months, and that was a lucky shot from the hip. Here, watch.'

She stepped forward from the shadow of the trees and clapped her hands sharply, facing across the grass towards the isolated tree in which the leopardess, so tiny at this distance, was sleeping. For a second nothing happened, and then, as the head of the leopardess lifted from the branch and he saw the eyes open in the striped face, he realised that the sound had taken a second to reach her ears. He watched as she pushed herself up on all fours and shot up the branch into the cover of the foliage. Leaves shook for a few moments longer and then there was nothing: no trace that she had ever lain there, basking in the sun.

The guide grunted and strode off along the trail again. He paused a moment again, still staring at the tree, preserving the memory of the smooth, spotted body in his cock, then trotted after her again.

'No cover,' the guide said as he caught up with her. 'She's got ears like you wouldn't believe and we wouldn't have got within twenty metres of her. Nah, we'll try the water hole. There's a good chance of a menstruer today, maybe two even. One of the cheetahs is due on, 'n'so's one of the lionesses, I reckon.'

'Mens . . .?' he started to say, then realised what she'd meant.

'Yeah. Menstruer. Slows 'em up real good, if they get cramps, and this cheetah does, I happen to know.'

He opened his mouth and started to speak again, but she raised a finger to her lips.

'Best to keep quiet when we're getting close,' she whispered. 'There's always a chance of a late arrival.'

He nodded without speaking and followed her as she led the way to the water hole. Soon they were moving at a crouch, communicating by hand-signals as she guided him to a clump of tall grasses.

'On the other side of this,' she mouthed, and carefully began to part the stems a fraction of an inch at a time, her body tense with anticipation. But then the tension went out of her and she shook her head.

'Nah,' she said aloud, and led him round the clump to the water hole that lay in a hollow on the other side. As they approached the water she suddenly swore.

'Shit.'

'What?' he asked.

'Look. Water's still muddy just there. You can still see it swirling. We musta missed one by a couple of minutes, maybe.'

She led him to the wide fringe of mud that surrounded the hole. It was patterned with hundreds of footprints, bare women's footprints, toes well-separated. He felt his cock jerk upright in his trousers at the sight of it, then jerk again as she bent over the mud, the cloth of her shorts tightening over her backside, and began to examine the footprints carefully.

'Plenny of cheetahs,' she said. 'They usually approach from this side. Leopardess here. Here. And here. An' this is a lioness.'

He followed her pointing finger, wondering how she could tell the footprints apart, and was about to ask when she whistled with pleasure.

'Ah!' she said. 'Found ya.'

Now she was pointing at a small splot of red in the heel of one footprint.

'Menstruer, see? The cheetah, I reckon. We'll be able to track her by the blood and there's a good chance . . .'

She found the next drop of blood and moved off, head bent. He followed, taking a curious pleasure in

walking over the mud behind her, crushing the footprints flat with his boots.

'Good chance of what?' he asked, catching up with
her.

'That she's not too far away,' she said, stopping and
scanning the mud ahead of her for the third drop. He
was absurdly pleased with himself when he spotted it
first, though later he wondered whether she had let him.
Soon they were on the grass, tracking the menstruating
cheetah by the drops of blood she had let fall as she
returned from the water hole. They were getting thicker
and the guide dropped on one knee and touched her
finger to one lying along a blade of grass.

'She's started leaking like a tap,' she said. 'Musta
been the effort of getting down to the hole. And I
reckon . . .'

She lifted her finger and licked the smear of blood on
the tip.

'Yeah. It's fresh. She's . . .'

Then she broke off, and raised the binoculars suddenly, staring through them at a clump of thistles about
twenty metres away.

'What?' he asked.

'She's there, lying in the shade. Musta caught the
cramps bad after she took a drink.'

She dropped the binoculars and motioned him forward. He followed her, narrowing his eyes as he looked
hard at the clump of thistles, but it wasn't until the
cheetah moved that he saw her. She sprang to her feet
and he gaped after her, his cock saluting the speed and
grace with which she was running.

'Fire, you fuckwit!' the guide yelled beside him and he
raised his rifle and fired almost by instinct as soon as the
spotted buttocks were in his sights. There was a *thuck*
of compressed air being released and after a moment a
cry of pain broke the morning air. The guide thumped
his shoulder and ran forward.

'Good fuckin' shot!'

He followed her, hardly able to believe that he'd hit the fleeing cheetah, so fast was she still moving. But then the flashing legs faltered, then faltered again, and she suddenly staggered and fell, tried to get up, fell again, and lay motionless. The guide reached her first, standing over her with rifle cocked, but when he ran up panting he saw that there was no need for a second shot: the cheetah was out cold, sprawled against the grass, her bleeding cunt peeping from between her slender, spotted thighs. Only it wasn't a cheetah. The guide bent and plucked the dart from the buttocks into which it was stuck.

'It's a fuckin' leopardess,' she said. 'And I don't recognise her. You wanna keep this for a souvenir?'

'Yeah,' he said, taking the dart from her. He was still breathing fast from the excitement of the sudden sighting and equally sudden shot, and from the thought of what he was now going to do. He moistened his lips.

'Uh . . .' he began. The guide smiled.

'Don't worry. Most of you are nervous after the first success. Wonderin' how to open the batting, as it were. But it's up to you: that's what you pay for. You wanna a b.j. to warm up on?'

'Uh, please,' he said.

'Right-oh. And you decided how you want to take her?'

He hesitated.

'I think . . . anal,' he said.

'Good choice.'

She took his rifle from him and laid it crisscross on the grass with her own beside the sprawled leopardess, then knelt in front of him. As she began to unzip him and take his cock out, she continued conversationally: 'Anal's usually best with a menstruer, particularly a leopardess. And if she's cramping up when you get going, you can get some wonderful rectal squeezing, so they tell me.'

He was about to reply but his cock was out now and she'd closed her mouth over it and begun sucking. A tremor ran through the leopardess's body and he realised she was beginning to wake. The guide must have read the sudden knowledge in his cock, because she reached out and put her hand down to the leopardess's thigh and squeezed. She let go and her mouth came off his cock with a pop.

'Two minutes yet,' she said, and her mouth went back over his cock. She was right: when her mouth came off his cock for the second time a minute and a half later, tremors were running through the leopardess's body almost continually. His fingers slid on her smooth warm skin and he pinched a fold of it loose, tugging at it as he examined the pattern of rosettes tattooed over her whole body.

'Is it permanent?'

'Nah,' the guide replied as she helped him position the leopardess to be buggered. 'It's a full-body tattoo, but the ink's steam-delible. When one of 'em decides she's had enough of the open-air life, she's just pops into a sauna for half-an-hour and comes out good as new.'

The leopardess growled, shook her head, and woke up. Her first action was to try and twist out of his grip, reaching behind her and swiping at him with a razor-nailed hand, but the guide intercepted the hand in mid-air, seizing it by the wrist and dragging it up the leopardess's back as she put a knee there and forced her down, holding her steady for him.

'Lube her with blood,' she said, and he took the advice, putting his hand into the blood-slimy cunt between the spotted thighs and working blood into the pink disc of her anus. She was snarling and spitting now, trying to break free, and when he positioned himself between her and brought his cock forward, ready to begin, the guide was sweating with the effort of holding her in place.

'Fuck me, she's a spirited one. I'll have to have a look-see in her locket and see who she's paired off with.'

He put his cock to the mouth of the leopardess's anus and began to push slowly, not understanding what the guide had meant. But she was reaching round the neck of the leopardess now and lifting something forward. Ah, locket. As he slid into her with a gasp of pleasure she snarled so loudly that he felt the sound of it quiver along the walls of her rectum, exciting his cock still further. The guide had flicked the locket open; now she whistled.

'Wh – ah what ah is it?' he asked, beginning to arse-fuck her.

'Our little friend up the tree,' the guide said, lifting the locket on its stainless steel chain and letting it dangle in front of him. He blinked, trying to focus on the spotted face staring back at him.

'I don't ah I don't ah under ah stand ah.'

'They pair off,' said the guide. 'Usually same species with same species, like here. And from the look of this we've gone and caught ourselves Sylvia's new girlfriend, which means, with any luck, that we can go and catch ourselves Sylvia next.'

He nodded, feeling orgasm building up in his balls. He was too excited to hold himself back, too excited by the hunt, the early success, the guide's expertly provocative blow job, and by the way the snarls of the buggered leopardess had turned to whimpers as he penetrated her deep and brutally. He almost began to snarl himself as he ejaculated inside her, firing eight or nine shafts of thick sperm into her tight bowels.

As he pulled out, hearing his cock come free with a moist pop, his voice was still trembling with orgasm.

'Sylvia's the tree-leopardess, you mean?'

'Yeah,' said the guide, still holding the leopardess down under her knee. 'You want that licking clean before the photo?'

His cock was streaked with sperm, menstrual blood, and leopardess shit, he realised.

'Thanks,' he said.

'The pleasure's all mine,' said the guide, and seemed, from her greedy licking and sucking, to mean it. When she had finished, leaving his cock fully erect again, she said: 'Plant your boot on her and turn this way. Careful: she's going to struggle.'

He obeyed, planting a boot on the leopardess's back, as the guide produced a small black camera from a pocket of her shorts. She backed away three steps and raised the camera to her eye, licking at a last trace of cock-junk on her lips.

'OK, turn a little to the left. I need your cock in better profile. OK, great. And smile . . . Right, hold it.'

A tiny red eye blinked open on the camera and closed.

'And back this way. Get a hold of your cock this time. And smile . . .'

The tiny eye blinked open again, closed.

'And let's have one with you pointing at her arse-hole . . .'

When the session was over the guide put the camera back into her pocket and joined him again, helping him to hold the leopardess down.

'Normally we'd shoot her up the arse again at this stage, leave her out cold while we continued the hunt, so as we could pick her up in the 'Rover at the end of the day. But we want this one awake, as a bait for Sylvia. Here, hold her while I get her hog-tied.'

This time it was a coil of twine and a knife that she drew from one of her pockets, and he watched in admiration as she swiftly and expertly tied the leopardess helpless, looping lengths of the twine round her wrists and ankles, tightening them hard to growls of anger. His cock, which had begun to soften, twitched again and stopped as he watched the leopardess's buttocks writhing as she struggled vainly to free herself, the cleft glistening with his sperm.

'There,' the guide said. 'Now, carry her over to this tree. I'll bring the rifles.'

He knelt beside the vainly struggling leopardess and tested her weight with one hand under her belly and one under her firm breasts, then hoisted her on to his shoulder with a grunt. He could feel the power in her body as she continued to struggle against her bonds, but she was surprisingly light, easy to carry the ten metres to the tree the guide had pointed out to him.

'This side,' the guide said, propping the two rifles against the trunk, and he carried his jerking burden beneath a branch over which the guide now threw a length of twine.

'Put her down. No need to be gentle.'

He laid the leopardess on the ground as the guide looped one end of the twine round the tree, then stood back, wiping at a patch of sperm that had dripped from her arsehole on to his shoulder.

'Here, hold it.'

He stopped wiping and took the end of twine the guide had handed to him as she walked over to the leopardess and tied the other end securely to her ankles.

'Right, haul 'er up.'

A minute later the leopardess was hanging upside down from the branch, growling with fury as she jerked from side to side. The guide watched her, smiling for a moment, then looked at him as she reached into a pocket of her shorts again.

'We're gonna torture her now,' she said. 'So guess what comes out next.'

'Whip,' he said at once.

'Nah. Try again.'

'Uh . . . clothes-pegs.'

'What?'

'Clothes-pegs. For her nipples.'

'Oh. Yeah, I see. Nice idea. I'll have to remember it. But no, wrong this time. Last try.'

He thought hard, frowning.

'Feather.'

'Nah.'

Her hand came out of the pocket, closed on something. She lifted the hand and shook it and he heard a rattle.

'Matches?' he said wonderingly.

'Yep.'

She opened the hand and a box of matches lay on her palm. The label said *Belcon Safari Park* above the head of a snarling leopardess, her artificial cat's teeth shining beneath her plastic whiskers.

'You can get 'em in the souvenir shop,' she said as she turned from him and walked to the dangling leopardess. 'Everyday stuff, which is just the kind I like to use for torture.'

He followed her, watching curiously as she stooped and shook the box again under the leopardess's nose, trying to attract her attention. Then she straightened, opened the box, and took a match out.

'Can you guess what I'm going to do?'

The leopardess had stopped struggling and was watching the guide's hands with narrowed eyes, twisting her head to keep them in view.

'Nothing too drastic, I hope,' he said.

''Course not. Think I want to lose my licence? Just this.'

She reached up and slipped the match between the leopardess's little and fourth toes, adjusting it so the red splot of flammable chemical stood well clear of them.

'Here,' she said, tipping more matches on to the palm of her other hand and holding them out to him. 'You do her other foot.'

He took the matches from her and began to slip them between the toes of the other foot. When they had finished and both feet were prepared the guide stepped back.

'I'll tell her what she's got to do now. Though she's already guessed, I'd reckon.'

She stooped and began to growl and purr to the leopardess, who was struggling again, trying to work her toes and shake the matches free. The leopardess growled in reply, and the guide grunted, growled and purred again for a few moments, paused as though waiting for a reply, then straightened when the leopardess stayed silent, glaring at them as she swung by her feet from the branch.

'What did you tell her?'

'That she'd better start calling for her girlfriend or we'll start lighting the matches, one by one.'

'She can't understand English?'

'She *is* English. Cheltenham Ladies' College and Cambridge, but their linguistic centres are hypno-blocked before they start work here and she won't be able to ask you to scratch her arse till she signs off. They've all got to use Felingua.'

'What?'

'Felingua. It's a language they've devised for use on the park. Initial vocab of about 300 words, but the cats have added mebbe half a thou more since then, s'far as we can tell. And dialects have started to evolve. Leopardish, Cheetese, Leonic.'

'And that was what you were speaking to her then? Leopardish?'

'Yeah. She was telling me my accent was fuckin' awful, cheeky bitch.'

'And she's not going to do it?'

'She's not. But she will. You want to light the first?'

'No. I'll watch.'

'Fine by me. I'm going to enjoy this.'

She produced the box of matches again, growled and purred at the leopardess briefly, waited, then took a match out and struck it. She growled again, paused, and then stepped forward and put the burning match to the head of the match sticking between the leopardess's little and fourth toes.

'That was her last chance.'

She lifted her match away, shaking it out, and they watched as the match between the leopardess's toes burnt quickly down. When the flame began to near her toes she let out a yowl and jackknifed her body, trying to dislodge the match, but it burnt inexorably down and her yowl increased in pitch, ringing out over the park. Then the match was out and she was twisting hard on the twine, growling and purring furiously. The guide listened, pursing her lips, then snorted.

'She's telling me what she'd like to do to the two of us. Very inventive, but I'm not sure they're physically . . .'

She listened again, and shook her head with a laugh.

'*That* one for sure isn't. Your turn?'

She held the match box out and he took it, removing and striking a match. He stepped forward to the hanging leopardess, feeling his cock re-stiffening in his shorts as he caught the musk of her pain-and-exhaustion sweat. He plucked the spent match out from between her toes and touched the burning tip of his match to the next in line, then stepped back. The leopardess tried to stay silent this time, but when the little flame reached her skin the yowl that had been trapped in her throat burst out again, echoing over the park.

The guide laughed, turning and looking away from the tree.

'That'll do it, I reckon. Her girlfriend should have heard that clear enough. Light the next one?'

'No, you do it.'

'Better get the rifles. If her girlfriend's making her way over here to mount a gallant rescue bid, we'll want them ready.'

He walked round the tree to fetch them, hearing the spurt of a match being lit, then the scrape of the guide's boots on the dry earth beneath the tree as she stepped forward to the leopardess's feet for the second time. Then he stopped, mouth opening in surprise. The rifles were gone. He turned, beginning to shout out for the guide, and ducked by sheer instinct a moment before he heard the *thuck* of the rifle being fired behind him. A dart buried itself in the tree at neck height, and he was on his hands and knees, scrambling to put the trunk between him and the rifle as it *thuck*ed again and a dart sprouted suddenly from the earth next to his left hand.

Then he was round the tree. The guide was standing watching the third match burn down, and gaped at him in surprise as he pushed himself back to his feet.

'What the . . .?'

'They've got the fucking rifles. Run. Run!'

He seized her by the hand as he ran past her, dragging her with him for the first few steps before she recovered from her surprise and ran with him. Again instinct made him look back, and he saw three spotted shapes running round the tree, faces snarling with anger. Two of them were carrying rifles, and he shoved urgently at the guide as one was raised and pointed at them.

'Swerve!'

Thuck.

He'd knocked the guide over with a shove and had to drag her back to her feet, losing precious seconds as two of the mutinying cats came after them, one remaining to release the hanging leopardess. The guide seemed to have recovered from her shock now and led the way as they ran. He looked back over his shoulder and shouted 'Swerve!' again, throwing himself to one side as he did so, but the *thuck* and the sprouting of a white dart on the guide's left buttock were simultaneous. Like the leopardess, she managed to keep on her feet for five, six, seven more strides, and then her left knee buckled and she went over. He paused, reaching for her, but she looked up at him with eyes that were already glazing.

'No. No. Get to the fucking *zareba* an' . . .'

Her head lolled on her neck and she was out cold. He flung a glance behind him and ran, swerving from side to side, his back and buttocks and thighs and calves tingling with the anticipation of a dart. *Thuck*. He was still running, still running, he hadn't been hit, he hadn't been hit, but suddenly, strangely, his knees weren't working any more and he was going over and he hadn't felt a thing, he hadn't felt a fucking . . .

He woke to a cry of female pain, his head throbbing with congested blood, and couldn't see for a moment when he opened his eyes. Then the cry of pain rang out again, just to his left, and he was blinking, clearing his eyesight, and seeing the circle of spotted bodies that surrounded him as he hung naked by his feet from the branch. There was an odd sensation between his toes, as though something was sticking between them, and he tried to look upwards, feeling sick with dizziness. One of the circle of watching cats, a lioness, growled suddenly and another, a cheetah, stepped forward to him, her thighs at just the height of his head. After a moment he felt a sharp-clawed hand taking hold of his limp cock, lifting it where it hung on his belly and beginning to squeeze and pump at it.

He grunted with reluctant pleasure, feeling his cock beginning to rise and stiffen. Another cry of female pain from his left, very near, and he realised the guide must be hanging on the branch a metre or so from him, being tortured as he was about to be tortured. The lioness growled again and the cheetah's hand released his cock, and she stepped back.

'Hey!' he shouted, realising suddenly that he didn't even know her name. 'Is that you?'

He tried to twist his body so that he could look to the left, but his feet were bound too securely and the guide's voice was replying anyway, thick with fury.

'Who the fuck do you think it is? No, no, no, you fucking bitches.'

He heard a match flare, and then the guide's voice was suddenly muffled, as though something had been thrust into her mouth. Her knickers, he thought. The lioness growled for the third time and then caught something thrown from the left. The matchbox, and he knew what was sticking between his toes now. The lioness lit the match and growled another instruction to the cheetah, who came forward and took hold of his erect cock, beginning to work at it with her warm hand as the lioness set fire to the first match. He began to struggle, trying to work his toes and shake the burning match free as the pleasure of the moving hand on his cock mixed with the dizziness in his head, but it was useless. He felt the first breath of heat on the skin of his toes, growing steadily, mounting towards the first direct kiss of flame, but when it came it was worse than he could have imagined, a vicious little searing of flame that seemed to go on far longer than it had for the leopardess.

Then the match was out and through the dizziness in his head and the sting of the burn between his little and fourth toes the hand of the cheetah worked relentlessly on at his cock, ushering him towards his first orgasm. The lioness lit a second match and stepped forward to encouraging growls from the watching circle of lionesses, leopardesses, and cheetahs, and he began to struggle again, feeling his balls start to tighten even as the match was touched home and the second of the matches between his toes began to burn down towards his flesh.

NEXUS BACKLIST

This information is correct at time of printing. For up-to-date information, please visit our website at www.nexus-books.co.uk

All books are priced at £6.99 unless another price is given.

------ ✂ --------------------------------

Please send me the books I have ticked above.

Name   ....

Address   ....

              ....

              ....

              .... Post code ....

Send to: **Virgin Books Cash Sales, Thames Wharf Studios, Rainville Road, London W6 9HA**

US customers: for prices and details of how to order books for delivery by mail, call 1-800-343-4499.

Please enclose a cheque or postal order, made payable to **Nexus Books Ltd**, to the value of the books you have ordered plus postage and packing costs as follows:
    UK and BFPO – £1.00 for the first book, 50p for each subsequent book.
    Overseas (including Republic of Ireland) – £2.00 for the first book, £1.00 for each subsequent book.

If you would prefer to pay by VISA, ACCESS/MASTERCARD, AMEX, DINERS CLUB or SWITCH, please write your card number and expiry date here:

....

Please allow up to 28 days for delivery.

Signature ....

Our privacy policy

We will not disclose information you supply us to any other parties. We will not disclose any information which identifies you personally to any person without your express consent.

From time to time we may send out information about Nexus books and special offers. Please tick here if you do *not* wish to receive Nexus information.   ☐

------ ✂ --------------------------------